TANGLED IN
TIME

ALSO BY BARBARA LONGLEY

Heart of the Druid Laird

Love from the Heartland Series, Set in Perfect, Indiana

Far from Perfect
The Difference a Day Makes
A Change of Heart
The Twisted Road to You

The Novels of Loch Moigh

True to the Highlander
The Highlander's Bargain
The Highlander's Folly
The Highlander's Vow

The Haneys Series

What You Do to Me
Whatever You Need

TANGLED IN
TIME

BARBARA LONGLEY

 Montlake
Romance

Published by Montlake Romance, Seattle

www.apub.com

Amazon, the Amazon logo, and Montlake Romance are trademarks of Amazon.com, Inc., or its affiliates.

ISBN-13: 9781542048231
ISBN-10: 1542048230

Cover design by Erin Dameron Hill

Printed in the United States of America

Physicists and other scientists push the boundaries of our understanding of time, space and everything in between. This book is dedicated to those modern-day wizards who continue to forge new paths of understanding.

Chapter One

Regan couldn't see the passage tomb in the predawn darkness, yet every single internal here-be-spirits antenna within her stood on end. And the closer she got, the more those antennae boogied. Newgrange, aka Brú Na Bóinne, was like Mecca to beings not of this world, not to mention a central hub for magic.

She'd sensed the powerful vibrations the day before, while visiting the ancient tourist attraction. What she'd sensed had compelled her to come back to take a closer, more private look. If she could tap into the energy here, perhaps she'd figure out how to harness a portion. Maybe then she'd be able to use the magic to shut out the ghosts once and for all. That was her hope anyway, and the driving force behind her trip to Ireland.

Legend had it her family's giftedness sprang from the fae, a boon bestowed upon an Irish ancestor in their distant past. She wished she could give the gift of sight back to that ancestor, or at least learn how to close herself off from it. "If you want to shut off the flow, you have to find the source," she muttered to herself. So here she was in County Meath, schlepping through dew-covered pastures, about to trespass on a national historic site.

The rolled yoga mat hanging from the strap over her shoulder swayed to the rhythm of her strides. Her shoes and the bottoms of her leggings were sopping wet. Regan trekked on, her blood humming in concert to Brú Na Bóinne's pulse.

She paused as the dim outline of the wooden shack she'd been looking for took shape in her flashlight's beam. The kiosklike structure stood at the base of the large hill. This was where visitors purchased postcard photos of the interior of Newgrange while waiting for the park shuttles to take them back to the visitor center. Focusing on getting through a patch of brambles without tearing her clothes, Regan aimed for the low wooden fence she needed to climb to get onto the grounds. What would happen if someone caught her trespassing? She went a little breathless at the thought. Would the Irish police, the Garda, come take her away?

Just as the first blush of dawn crested the eastern horizon, Regan made it to the top of the hill. The large, flat stone guarding the entrance to the tomb came into view. The spiral glyphs etched into the surface were only dimly visible. She reached out and traced one of the coils, and a tingle ran up her arm, coursed along her nerves throughout her entire body and raised goose bumps in its wake.

The view from the top of the hill was incredible. Miles and miles of green, rolling hills in every direction, with the River Boyne meandering in a winding path through the lush landscape. The verdant surroundings carried the sweet scent of growing things and spring blossoms. Birds had begun to stir, singing their own trilled version of the sun salutation.

Regan took a few steps back and dropped her things. She tucked the flashlight into her day pack before unrolling her mat on a relatively flat stretch of grass. After toeing off her shoes, she settled on the mat in a half-lotus seated position and closed her eyes, adjusting her position until she found her center of gravity. Hands on her thighs, palms up, thumbs and pointer fingers touching, she stilled.

Immediately all kinds of ghostly whispers and pleas intruded, distracting her. Some were unintelligible, ancient languages she didn't recognize; others came through clear as day with the same old familiar refrain. *Help me! Where am I?* And of course . . . *I want to go home.* She mentally brushed them aside like so many cobwebs in the corners of her mind. "I'm ignoring all of you," she called out. "So you may as well quiet down."

Regan narrowed her throat for *ujjayi pranayama*, the breath of victory. The inner sound of her breathing, like ocean waves, helped her focus. Concentrating, she opened her mind to the magic surrounding her.

According to everything she'd read, practitioners could use magic to repel unwanted energies. Some were able to mask their presence with a spell. Hiding from dead people and their bereaved families would work. If she couldn't divest herself of her abilities, at least she'd have a shield.

Thoughts flitted around for a few minutes, but at least they were hers and no longer ghostly. She simply observed them until her inner self quieted. Reaching for the powerful vibrations, she waited—and waited some more. Regan meditated as hard as she could, inviting the magic in.

The minutes ticked by, at least forty of them, and nothing happened. No flow, not even a trickle or a drip seeped into her. Magic all around, and she couldn't touch it. So, this was not the way magic worked, or she lacked what it took to call that kind of power to her. Disappointed, she heaved a sigh and rose to standing.

Despite her failure in this first attempt, she couldn't help but appreciate the glory of the rising sun. She'd greet the day here, so slogging through dewy fields wouldn't have been a total waste of time. Besides, holding on to disappointment wouldn't do her any good. Better to embrace the newly born day with gratitude.

Facing the east, she brought her hands together over her heart and began her salutation. "With hands folded in prayer, I face the sun, feeling love and joy in my heart." She moved into the first asana. Flowing into the second pose, she continued her prayer. "I reach out and let the sun fill me with warmth. I bow before the sun's radiance, and place my face to the ground in humility and respect."

By the time Regan had completed four sets of the sun salutation, the burning orb had risen in a blaze of orange and pink against an azure background. She switched to Ashtanga Yoga, and moved through the more challenging poses. *Inhale. Move into the posture. Exhale, and . . . hold.*

"What is the daft lassie doin' then?" a very male voice said from behind her.

A burst of adrenaline wrecked her meditative state. She drew in a long cleansing breath, letting it out slowly through her nose. He had to be a ghost, because she would've heard a fellow trespasser's approach.

"Until you interrupted her, the daft lassie was doing Ashtanga Yoga," she said, coming out of her pose. So much for ending her practice with another brief meditative effort to grasp hold of the magic here. So much for shutting out the dead.

Since birth, it had been deeply ingrained in her by her family that her gifts were meant to be shared. She'd been born to guide confused spirits to the light, offer the bereaved some closure and chase away beings who had no business messing with humans.

Whether she wanted to or not, interacting with the spirit world was her lot in life. Doing so took a lot out of her and left her empty. It wasn't always the dead who stole her energy, though their proximity chilled and exhausted her; sometimes it was their needy, grieving relatives who drained her the most. The living didn't always want to let go, and they were persistent with their demands for her help. The worst part, though, was the effect her abilities had on her social life. Communing with the dead and otherworldly often repulsed potential love interests among the living.

"You hear me?"

"Apparently."

"Grand. Do the thing where ye balance on one foot, arch your back like a bow and touch your toes to the back of your head again, if you please. Only . . . face me this time. Liked that one, I did," he said. "'Twas quite . . . provocative."

Ghosts remembered lust and sex, though they no longer experienced the physical sensations. Annoyed, she turned to scowl at him, only to gape instead. As far as ghosts went, this man was one fine-looking apparition. Lean and fit, he stood maybe five foot ten. He wore his long, auburn hair in numerous braids, held back in a knot bound with strips of leather. *The original man bun?*

His features were strong and angular—broad forehead, long, straight nose, flaring slightly at the nostrils, high cheekbones and a wide, expressive mouth over a tapered chin. Though he was fair and freckled, his eyes were a deep, rich brown, and they were filled with keen intelligence. He must have been quite strong in life to be this vivid in death. He was the most colorful spirit she'd ever encountered. He looked almost corporeal.

She eyed his coarse linen shirt, worn under a vest made of some kind of sleek fur. *Seal?* A green woolen cloak rested over his shoulders, held in place with a gold brooch of Celtic knots with a crouched wolf effigy in the center. Suede leggings fit him snugly, and the soft leather shoes he wore resembled moccasins. He reminded her of the ancient Roman descriptions she'd read of Celtic warriors, and the pictures of equally ancient rock and wood carvings she'd studied in books.

Standing a bit straighter under her perusal, he cocked his head slightly. "What might ye be called, *Álainn?*"

Aww, he'd just called her a beauty, and he'd said it with such an enticing Irish lilt too. "Regan MacCarthy. And you?"

"Fáelán of Clan Baiscne at your service," he said with a bow. "Fáelán means wolf."

"I believe it's the diminutive form of the word, isn't it? That would make you Little Wolf."

"Ah, well, even the mightiest bear starts out as a cub, aye?" He winked at her. *"An bhfuil Gaeilge agat? An dtuigeann tú?"*

"I don't speak Irish well, but I do have some Gaeilge, and yes, I did understand what you just said."

"Hmm." His gaze bored intently into hers. "And ye see me."

"I do. Just so you know, I've helped many like you, and—"

"Many like me?" He crossed his arms in front of him, widened his stance and lowered his brow. "Meanin' what, exactly?"

"Ghosts."

He stomped around in front of the tomb's entrance and let loose a string of expletives, all in his native Irish. "I'm no *scáil*; I'm cursed. Woman, do ye have any idea who or what I am?"

Huh. She'd been demoted from *beauty* to *woman.* "Little Wolf, better known as *Fay*-lon of Clan Bask-nuh?" Regan hid her grin and checked the horizon. The visitor center would open at nine. She slipped into her shoes and gathered her things.

"I am one of Fionn MacCumhaill's elite, one of the Fianna who served the high king, Cormac MacArt himself. Do ye have any idea how difficult it was to become one of the few skilled enough, clever enough to be ordained into the Fianna? Do ye have any idea how prestigious it was to be counted amongst their ranks? Why, I defeated nine warriors at once, I did."

"After walking barefoot through snow up to your waist and climbing over a mountain, no doubt," she muttered. His ego certainly hadn't diminished with death.

"Nay." He flashed her a look of confusion. "'Twas midsummer. I passed many such tests to become one of Fionn's warriors, not the least of which was proving my skill with sword, bow and lance."

"Good for you." Out of all the deceased she'd encountered, this boasty ghosty took the prize for being the most entertaining. Regan couldn't wait to call her sisters to tell them about today's encounter. Was she supposed to help him? Was that what drew her back to Newgrange and not the magic after all? *No.* Fáelán was but one of many ghosts hanging out on this hill. And she had no interest in working with dead people anymore. Honestly, she never had. All she'd ever wanted was to be ordinary and to have all the ordinary things life had to offer, like a job she loved, a husband, children and a nice house in the burbs.

She started down the hill, heading for the fields she needed to cross to get to her rental car. "I believe you, but the Fianna existed in what . . . the second and third centuries? This is the twenty-first century, so—"

"Ye know our history." His gaze lit with approval. "I'm cursed, I tell ye, by the Tuatha Dé Danann princess Morrigan. Tricked me, she did. Came to me in the guise of a mortal and seduced me into her bed. Had I known her true identity, I never would have lain with her, and—"

"And you'd be long dead regardless. Nobody lives into their thousands."

"*And*"—he scowled—"not knowin' the brief tryst meant aught to her, I took another lover soon after. Morrigan caught me and my lover between the furs once upon a winter's eve, and that is when the fae princess cursed me."

"Killed you more like." No point in mincing words. If he was to cross over, he had to first accept his state of deadness.

"Nay. I told ye, I'm no ghost."

Fáelán strode ahead, turned and faced her, forcing her to stop in her tracks or walk right through him. She hated the walk-throughs, hated the creepy chill and the overwhelming fight-or-flight instinct that shot through her every time it happened. Even thinking about it caused a shudder.

"Do ye want to hear the curse, lassie?"

His expression was so earnest, so hopeful, how could she resist? "I'm guessing you wish to share it with me."

"I do," he said, his gaze roaming over her face, coming to rest upon her lips.

She turned away. Too strange, this feeling of attraction to a dead man. "Go ahead, but we need to keep walking. I'm trespassing here and don't want to get caught."

"If we must, but I won't be able to do justice to the recitation."

"Oh?" He was funny, charming and somehow vulnerable. Add to that his breathtaking good looks, and she could see why a fae princess might want to crawl between the furs with him. "I know how difficult it can be to walk and talk at the same time, but I trust you'll do the best you can," she teased, earning her another disgruntled look from her ghostly companion. "You remember the curse word for word after all this time?"

"Of course." His shoulders squared. "I had to commit to memory all the verses of poetry about our people's history, and I recited every last word to Fionn without error afore I could be ordained into the Fianna. I also proved myself a poet in my own right."

"Boasty ghosty," she muttered.

"Cursed," he snapped back, just as they reached the wooden fence separating the heritage land from the fields beyond. "I'd lend ye a hand, lassie, but I fear I cannot. I exist in the void, whilst ye reside in the earthly realm. We cannot touch."

More likely, if he tried, her hand would go right through his. "It's all right. I can manage." She climbed over the fence, only to find him already on the other side by the time both her feet hit the ground. "So, the curse?" She set off across the field.

Fáelán cleared his throat, shook out his arms and huffed out a breath. He began, in a rich baritone, projecting his voice from his ghostly diaphragm . . . in Irish.

She hated to admit it, but her curiosity had been piqued. "Wait. My Irish isn't good enough to get much out of what you just said. Can you translate the curse into modern-day English for me?"

"Of course. I've had centuries aplenty to learn all forms of English, French and German. I suspect ye might be from the Americas, but your accent is none too familiar. Where are ye from, *Álainn*?"

"Tennessee. The curse? Please continue."

He cleared his throat again and seemed to ponder for a few moments. Finally, he began.

> "Foolish, fickle human,
> 'tis a royal covenant ye have broken.
> Harken well to my edict,
> for 'tis your penance now spoken.
> By wind, water, earth and fire I vow,
> 'til blood of sidhe in a mortal will tell,
> 'twixt here and shadow shall ye dwell.
> Not without mercy, a daughter of Danu be,
> I grant ye one path by which ye might be free.
> During the interludes when the realms collide,
> in the earthly world may ye bide.
> Seek she who sees ye, and woo her well.
> For once your heart is fully given,
> when your life for hers ye'd gladly give,
> in the earthly realm may ye once again live."

"Impressive." He truly was a poet if he could spew out something like that at a moment's notice. "What does the curse refer to when it mentions realms colliding?"

"During solstices and equinoxes, the veil between the worlds lifts, and the realms merge. I know of only three: the shadow realm where the dead go to be judged afore rebirth, the void realm where the fae make their home and the earthly realm where we humans are meant to dwell."

She'd read the Celts believed there were different realms, and building his fantasy upon what was culturally relevant to him made sense. Besides, ghosts had to go somewhere when they stepped into the light, and she'd often wondered where that might be. Who was she to say there weren't other dimensions? "When did this happen, Fáelán?"

"Mid-third century."

Getting a ghost to think about time's passage was the first step in a multistep process for helping them accept they were dead. She should write a manual for ghost whisperers, a twelve-step program for helping spirits depart. Once she found a way to rid herself of her gift, she could pass the manual along to some other unfortunate soul who'd been born with the sight. Perhaps she *would* write that book. Now that she'd sold her chain of yoga studios, she had the time. Step two: confront the ghost with empirical evidence of their demise—or at least the implausibility of their continued existence. Regan glanced at her ghostly companion. "How do you explain not aging or dying after all this time?"

"I cannot, for I do not understand the reasons myself. 'Tis said the Tuatha Dé Danann, the children of the goddess Danu, partake of the Elixir of Life, which is the source of their immortality. Morrigan may have slipped a drop or two of the elixir into the food I am provided with in my captivity."

"Hmm." *Poor guy.* Clearly, he was a ghost with a rich imagination, unwilling to accept his own mortality. And why would he? He'd died so young. No wonder he'd stuck around. Acceptance would be difficult for such a strong personality. She'd encountered the same denial many times with accident victims, especially young men. What was it about young males that led them to believe they were immortal?

"Ye see me," he said, sweeping his arm in a wide arc and turning in a circle. "Seek she who sees ye, and woo her well." He lowered his chin and winked at her again. "Perhaps you're the lassie I'm fated to love with all my heart, aye?"

Speaking of hearts, hers broke a tiny bit for him. He was so deep in denial, he'd created an entire fantasy for a way to return to the land of the living. Despite her wish to be done with ghost busting, she was tempted to help this spirit come to grips with his reality.

"'Tis a wonder. Might you be *mo a míorúilt lómhar*, my precious miracle? I do hope so, for a lovelier miracle I could not have imagined."

His over-the-top flirty tone didn't match the desperate hope she glimpsed deep in his eyes. "For a ghost, you certainly are a shameless flirt." She couldn't keep from grinning. The notion that she could be anyone's precious miracle tickled her. "It's highly doubtful I'm the one destined to win your heart after all these years, but I'll help you in any way I can."

Meaning she'd come back to Newgrange a few more times and lead him as gently as possible to the realization that he was no longer of this world. Once he accepted his death, she'd guide him toward the light, and he'd cross over.

A sense of rightness settled over her. For this boasty ghosty, she'd put aside her search for a way to cut herself off from the spirit world. Temporarily. Once he'd departed, she'd take up the search right where she'd left off.

Regan MacCarthy saw him! Thank the gods, both old and new, for it had been centuries since he'd been seen by any but his blood kin. As elated as he was, Fáelán's strength had begun to wane, and soon he'd be forced to leave his wee miracle. He uttered a few choice curse words under his breath.

Being away from his island prison depleted him, which was one of the reasons he continued to train as hard as he did. If ever he was to gain his freedom, he needed to maintain his strength and his skills. For truth, he could not court a lassie if he couldn't spend time in her proximity, and being away took all his energy and his strength.

He gazed at the beauty walking beside him. Her shoulder-length hair was the color of nutmeg, and he longed to run his fingers through the lustrous tresses, to feel its softness against his skin. Her eyes were wide set, an enticing bluish-gray fringed with thick dark lashes, and her full lips . . . ah, her full lips were meant for his kisses, 'twas certain. For the first time in more centuries than he cared to count, hope ignited within him, warming him through and through.

He had maybe an hour, two at most, afore he'd be forced to return to his gaol. Best make the most of whatever time he had with the lovely Regan MacCarthy. They marched on through the fields in silence, and he could almost see her mind working through everything he'd told her.

She didn't believe him, that much was clear, but she would in time. He'd see to it, and the summer solstice would soon be upon them. He'd have five full days of freedom in which to fall in love. Woo her well he would. Why, he'd charm her right into his arms. After all, he was one of the Fianna. How could she not succumb?

Ah, but she didn't have to love him back for the curse to be broken, did she. Though 'twould be most pleasing if she gave her heart as well. Regardless, once free of his curse, he'd work most diligently to win her heart. After all these long centuries alone, he was more than willing to take a chance and pledge his troth. God willing, she would prove herself worthy of a Fiann such as himself. The thought of touching Regan, of holding her sweet, womanly curves against him, sinking into her welcoming heat—

"So, let me get this straight," she said, stepping from the field through a narrow gap in the hedgerow and onto the lane where a single car had been parked. "To be free of the curse, you must first find a woman who can see you while you're . . . 'twixt here and there, and then you must give her your heart. You have to fall desperately in love to the point where you'd lay down your life for hers, but the object of your affection doesn't have to return the favor?"

He'd grown hard as wood thinking about making love with Regan, and she believed he was a ghost. He did naught to hide the effect she had on him. Ghosts didn't stiffen with want of a woman, did they? Proof he was no *scáil*.

"'Tis true. The object of my affection does not need to return the favor, as ye say, but 'tis my deepest longing that she will. Like most young men, I had hoped to marry one day, sire a passel of children and grow old with my beloved." He cast her a sideways look. Had she noticed the proof of his desire for her?

"Doesn't that strike you as odd?" She used a button on a key fob to unlock the doors and walked toward her car, keeping her eyes on the vehicle and away from his crotch.

Either she'd noticed and was pretending not to, or she really hadn't. At any rate, without encouragement, his proof of life deflated. He blamed it on his weakening state.

"In most faerie tales, isn't it true love between *both* parties that breaks a curse or a spell?" she continued.

"I've not made a study of such things, lassie, and I doubt the Tuatha have either. Morrigan fancied herself in love with me, whilst I felt naught but a fleeting attraction in return. I'm guessing she intended me to suffer the same unrequited misery she imagined she suffered."

Regan opened the back door of the car and tossed her belongings onto the seat. "You use words like *fancied* and *imagined* when you speak of Morrigan's feelings. Why is that? Isn't it possible she really had fallen for you?"

She'd drive away soon, and he'd not be able to find her again if she did. He couldn't lose her, yet how might he convince her to spend more time with him? "Morrigan is fae, immortal and magical in the very worst sense of the word. For her own gratification, she came to me pretending to be an ordinary mortal woman. We spent a se'nnight together, no more, and our brief union had naught to do with love. We did very little talking, if ye catch my meanin'."

He shook his head. "Nay, *Álainn*. Morrigan did not fall for me. She's a demigoddess with a reputation. Morrigan has a knack for stirrin' trouble. She's known well for starting wars, she is, and for creatin' drama where there's no need for such. I'm but a mouse, and she the cat, and naught else."

He let loose a weary sigh and rubbed his temples. The pull from the void grew stronger by the minute. "'Tis truth, I fear she's forgotten all about me over the centuries, though time to the fae is not the same as it is for us. I haven't seen her since the first weeks of my captivity, when she tried to persuade me to become her consort."

"You refused?"

"I did, and I'd refuse her again today if given the choice."

"And then she killed you." Regan nodded to herself, as if she'd worked it all out for herself.

"Nay. She *cursed* me." Clearly, his fated one had a stubborn streak. "Where might ye be off to, lassie?"

"I have a town house in Howth. I'm going there to have breakfast and change my clothes, and then I'm off to explore Dublin. I think I'll visit the National Museum of Ireland today, the archaeology branch."

"Hmph." He shifted his stance, bracing himself against the growing tug from his island prison. "I lived much of the history on exhibit there. In fact, the museum has an armband of gold belonging to me. I'd very much like to have it back, truth be told."

"I'm sure." Regan's expression turned to one of pity.

"I could tell ye all ye wish to know about such things. Might I join ye for a bit longer? I've not spoken to a soul other than my kin for so long, and—"

"Your kin see you? They talk to you?"

Regan's lovely eyes lit with interest, and he grasped at that wee bit of straw with both greedy hands—anything to entice her into willingly spending time with him. "Aye. Some of them can see me whilst I'm in the void, but not all."

His chest tightened at the memory of his poor mam's tears the day he'd returned that first equinox, and the way his da had scolded him for a fool after Fáelán explained how he'd been tricked and cursed. His da always scolded when he wished to cover strong feelings. Fáelán had learned to see through the bluster when he was still a wee laddie, and he never doubted his parents' love and pride for their only surviving son.

His four sisters had also grieved that day, their husbands, his nieces and nephews, cousins, uncles and aunts as well. Hell's fire, his entire clan had lamented his loss, for he likely would have become their chieftain once he'd left the Fianna. By then, his da would have been ready to retire the position. Fáelán would have done his best by his clan too. He'd let everyone down, disappointed his da and broken his mam's heart, and all for lust.

"I came home to my clan during the spring equinox, when I was free to bide in the earthly realm. I explained what had happened. My kin swore to help me in any way possible, and they aid me still to this day."

For centuries, his relatives had led a string of women known to be gifted afore him while he dwelt in the void, hoping one might prove to be his fated love. Only a few were able to see him, and those few who had . . . fled. They too believed him to be a ghost from the ancient past. Regan hadn't run away, and she was willing to talk with him. His spirits soared at such an auspicious beginning. Why, he'd already fallen half in love with her for that alone. "Would ye like to meet my kin?"

"I would."

"Grand. Take me with ye to your dwelling in Howth, so that I might see where ye dwell. That way, I'll be able to find ye again. I'll arrange a meeting with my kin ere long."

"I don't think so." Her eyes narrowed as she scrutinized him. "How about I come back and visit you at the passage tomb now and then? We can stay in touch that way, talk some more about your situation, and then maybe we can make plans to visit your family." She opened the driver's side of her car and slid in.

Fáelán willed himself into the seat beside hers, and she gave a tiny gasp at finding him there before she'd even settled behind the wheel.

"What do you think you're doing?" She frowned.

"I think I'm coming with ye to Howth, so that I might be able to find ye again."

She shook her head but didn't order him away, and he took that as another good sign. Regan pulled her car away from the hedgerow and started down the lane.

"If you aren't a ghost, then how do you do that? How do you just . . . pop up wherever it is you want to be?"

Pondering such matters over the centuries always made his temples throb, and thinking about all that fruitless mental effort had him shaking his head. "I cannot explain how I manage to move about. 'Tis another fae aspect of this accursed void realm, I think, and I don't know the whys and wherefores myself. I can tell ye it took months to figure out how to leave my gaol and elude my fae gaoler. I've oft wondered if Morrigan didn't intend that I learn how to wander about, or she would have put a stop to it, aye? How else was I to seek she who could see me whilst in the void?" He slanted her a wry look.

"See, I focus all my will upon where I wish to be, and there I am, at the very edge of the boundary betwixt the realms, leastways. Leaving my island takes a great deal of strength." He met her gaze, unrelenting in his attempt to impress her. "I'm quite strong of mind and body, well able to protect and provide for a wife and children."

"Said the man who couldn't lend me a hand to get over a fence." One side of her mouth quirked up.

He grunted, faced the road and concentrated all his will upon remaining right where he was, at least until he saw where Regan lived. He had to have the location of her dwelling firmly planted in his mind, and he needed to convince her to spend more time with him. Once he'd accomplished those tasks, he'd take his leave with some dignity, afore being dragged back unwilling to his island in the swirling mists. He contented himself with taking note of his surroundings as she drove.

Soon enough, she pulled her car in to a parking spot in front of a nondescript white two-story cottage sharing a wall with an identical dwelling next door, and another beside that one. At least her door boasted a bright and cheery red.

"Here we are," she told him.

Fáelán peered out of the window. "Ye own this cottage?"

"No. I'm leasing the town house for the year I'll be in Ireland."

"A whole year, ye say? Grand." A spark lit within him. He'd have two equinoxes and two solstices with her, should it take him that long to lose his heart. Twenty days in full in which to touch her. Surely physical intimacy would aid him in falling in love, aye?

Regan nodded. "I want to get to know the land of my ancestors, maybe trace my family tree, see what I can dig up about the Mac-Carthy branch. I intend to visit every corner of the island, do all the touristy stuff and some of the less touristy things as well."

"Let me be your guide, *Álainn*. If 'tis history ye be wantin', who better than I to teach ye?"

"Sure, why not," she, murmured, glancing at him for an instant.

He couldn't identify the expression flickering across her features just then. Sadness? Resignation? No matter. She'd agreed, and 'twas enough for now. "'Tis settled then. When shall we begin your tour?"

"Well, today is Wednesday, and I want to spend this day and tomorrow exploring Dublin. How about Friday, and we can get out of the city?"

"Right. I'll be here Friday morn, at half eight."

"You have clocks in the void realm?" she asked, her eyes wide.

"Nay." Unable to fight the pull any longer, he broke out in a cold sweat and dread knotted his gut. "Trust me, lassie, and be ready. I must leave ye now."

An instant later, he found himself flat on his back in the sand on his island's only beach. He didn't attempt to sit up, but turned his head to gaze out over the clear lake to the thick swirling mist beyond. His jaw tightened, and his hands curled into fists. By the gods, how he loathed this place. The desperation to be free had nearly driven him mad in the beginning. At one point, he'd even considered taking his own life just to spite Morrigan. Would she have allowed him that end? Not bloody likely.

The unfairness of it all, the self-recrimination he suffered for his own foolishness—'twas the worst. To this day, he still couldn't fathom why one fae princess would trouble herself over a mere mortal like him.

Surely Morrigan had forgotten him by now. And if she'd forgotten him, her anger had to be a thing of the distant past. After all, she would've had leagues of lovers since their brief tryst. How many times since the two of them had dallied had she fancied herself in love? For that matter, how many more poor mortals had she cursed?

Even after all these centuries, his longing for freedom was as sharp today as it ever had been. More so, for he'd found the woman he'd prayed for every single day of his miserable existence. He yearned to live his life to the fullest. All he had to do was fall in love and give his heart fully. "Easy, aye?" Doubt edged its way into his thoughts.

He'd had plenty of opportunities to lose his heart afore Morrigan's curse, yet he never had. He'd come close a few times, but some indefinable reluctance always barred the way, and he'd held back. He'd always believed 'twas because he had ambition, hopes of rising within the ranks of the Fianna. Now he wasn't so certain. No matter. This time would be different, because this time he willed it so. How difficult could it be? He'd see the deed done, and that was all there was to it. Like any other challenge set afore him, he'd rise and conquer.

How long had it been since he'd conquered anything, anything at all? His pulse raced at the thought of a new challenge. He'd always loved pitting himself against any and all obstacles in his path, which was another reason his confinement chafed so.

"Ah, well. Tomorrow is another day." Yawning, Fáelán wrapped his cloak around himself and drifted into sleep. For the first time in more than a thousand years, he closed his eyes with a broad smile upon his face, already dreaming of the day he'd hold lovely Regan MacCarthy in his arms.

Chapter Two

Regan stood on Dublin's Kildare Street, staring at the impressive columned entrance of the archaeology branch of the National Museum of Ireland. She climbed the marble stairs, entered the rotunda and gawked at the opulent, dimly lit interior. A gift shop on one side and a café on the other lined the outer rim of the rotunda, and an intricate circular marble mosaic of the astrological signs took up the entire center.

A tall glass case holding museum reproduction jewelry in the gift shop caught her eye, and she drifted over to get a closer look. She wandered through the shop, finally buying a book filled with the histories and pictures of the museum's permanent exhibits, along with a great foldout map of the interior.

Here I am. I know you can see me. Why won't you listen? I want back what was taken from me. Unhappy spirits clamored for her attention. She set off for the *Ireland's Gold* exhibit, pretending she couldn't hear them.

Fáelán had piqued her curiosity with the mention of his armband. Would she sense which one belonged to him? Why did it matter? Though he'd made plans with her, he might never pop into her life again. He was, after all, a ghost. Who made dates with ghosts? *Damn.* She needed to meet a nice man—someone who breathed and had a pulse. There had to be several Irish online dating sites. Irish men might be more accepting of her interactions with the dead. A ghost whisperer could hope, couldn't she?

Her reaction to Fáelán surprised her. She'd never obsessed about the nonliving before, but here she was . . . obsessing. One minute she'd been talking with him, and the next he was gone. Almost midsentence, he'd disappeared. How much energy had it taken him to manifest himself to her for as long as he had?

His sudden disappearance shouldn't have left her feeling let down, but it had. He'd been good company, funny and larger-than-life, which was amazing for a dead guy. He must've been impossible to resist when alive. Cocky, self-assured and proud though he was, for some reason he didn't come across as vain. He carried himself like a man sure of his place in the world. After all, he'd earned his way into the Fianna. She'd have to read more about the legendary army once she returned to her town house.

Regan went down a short flight of steps, entering a large, two-storied branch of the museum. The bottom floor held glass cases full of ancient artifacts of gold. Ghostly complaints bounced around the long gallery, and though she didn't recognize all the words being spoken, she got the gist. *Mine. Want it back. Stolen from me . . .* She'd heard it all before.

Too many souls failed to pass from this world because of an attachment to an item that meant a great deal to them in life. As she walked along, she passed through a few chilled pockets of air, signaling the presence of spirits. She refused to acknowledge them in the hopes they wouldn't notice her.

The dead had taken up enough of her life. Guilt pinged through her. It wasn't that she didn't empathize, but the dead who lingered were often small, petty souls with incessant demands. Some were angry, but the majority were consumed with sadness and confusion. While dealing with the dead and grieving, she lost track of the living and neglected her own life.

When she'd first begun helping spirits cross, the process had all but consumed her. Yoga had saved her. She'd learned how to become centered and turn her focus inward for a change. But as her business grew, she'd once again lost track of herself. She'd worked far too many hours in an effort to avoid what her family insisted was her true calling. And working all the time, she didn't think about her loneliness. What would it be like to find a healthy balance in her life?

Regan walked behind a guided tour group, listening in as the guide talked about the artifacts and the history of Ireland. She studied each exhibit. There were torques of solid gold, bracelets, earrings and rings, along with a few armbands of Nordic design. She saw buttonlike fasteners, brooches with tiny swords to pierce through wool or leather, and gold balls resembling jingle bells, but none of the pieces drew her.

The group took the stairs leading to the second floor, and the exhibit hall emptied. Regan moved around a corner, and approached a large rectangular glass case holding a treasure trove of golden bracelets and armlets. Her attention caught on one unique piece, and her heart leaped. This piece had been cast in the shape of an animal's body. The band had been designed to wrap around a man's upper arm. Fáelán's upper arm.

A bit of space separated the animal's head from its tail. Small garnets had been set for the beast's eyes. She leaned closer to get a better look. A wolf. Of course it would be a wolf. Come to think of it, this piece matched the brooch fastening Fáelán's cloak. The wolf effigy carried Fáelán's energy and radiated waves of his essence to her. Her boasty ghosty had been a wealthy man to have owned something like this. How much would an artifact like this be worth today?

Why did Fáelán's energy resonate so strongly with her? She'd worked with lots of spirits over the years, but she'd never reacted like this with any other ghost, or felt their presence so powerfully. Fáelán's bold personality surpassed any she'd ever encountered—living or dead.

A chill drifted over her, and the fine hairs on the back of her neck and on her forearms stood up. *Great. Company.*

A ghostly voice whispered into her ear in a language she couldn't understand. Latin? Norse? Regan risked a glance over her shoulder. The faint outline of a woman wearing a long, flowing gown and a mantle of fur hovered behind her. She was beautiful and very young, and Regan ached for the lost soul. Though she spoke a different language, after so many years of ghost-whispering, Regan understood the message. *Help me. I'm lost. I want to go home.*

The woman wore amber beads around her neck, gold bracelets on each wrist and rings on several of her fingers. Her blond hair was braided and wound around the crown of her head.

The spirit's confusion and sadness settled upon Regan's shoulders like a sandbag. "They await your homecoming, my lady," she whispered, hoping the apparition would understand. "You only have to let go." Regan scanned the hall, making sure she was still alone. Then she returned her gaze to the case before her. "Stop clinging to whatever it is that holds you here, and look for the light."

"I just want to go home! I miss my husband. I miss my children." The apparition spoke in English this time. Covering her face, she wept into her hands. "I cannot find my way. I do not know where I am."

"Don't try to find your way. Be open. Think about the light, and it will appear. Let the light guide you to your family."

Two of the bracelets in the case in front of her looked exactly like the ghostly bracelets on the apparition's wrists. The poor thing had probably attached herself to the ornaments and was brought to the museum with the artifacts. "Turn away from your worldly possessions, my lady. Set aside your attachment, and walk into the warmth of the golden glow."

Regan's phone rang, the cascading tones echoing through the hall. The spirit disappeared, and the air returned to its normal temperature. Regan sighed with relief that she was once again alone. The woman had been too fixed upon her confusion, fear and grief to hear what Regan had said. It took a concerted, uninterrupted effort to get through to ghosts like her. Probably better if Regan didn't return to the museum.

She fished her phone out of her purse, checked caller ID and hit "Accept." "Meredith," she whispered to her sister. She glanced at the watch with multiple time zones she'd bought for her trip. "Shouldn't you be in class?"

"I have a final late this afternoon, but that's it, and then I'm officially finished," her sister whispered back. "Why are we whispering?"

"I'm in a museum, and I don't want to disturb anyone." Regan watched as a young couple strolled in, hand in hand. "Can I call you back once I find a quiet place where we can talk?"

"Sure."

"Give me five minutes." The museum closed at five, which left her with only another three-quarters of an hour anyway. Tucking the phone into her purse, she hurried toward the exit, through the doors and across the street to the car park. She settled herself behind the wheel of her rental and called her sister.

"Hey, is everything OK at home? Mom and Dad are good? You and Grayce?" Regan was four years older than her twin sisters, and they'd been like her own personal doll babies when her parents had brought them home from the hospital.

"Everyone's fine, Rae. I sensed something momentous happening to you earlier, something exciting. And since my life is utterly boring, I called to live vicariously through your adventures. I'm putting you on speakerphone. You can tell me what happened while I fix myself a sandwich."

The mention of food made Regan's stomach rumble. "I became a lawbreaking trespasser this morning. I sneaked into the Newgrange heritage park at dawn."

"No, I don't think that's what I sensed."

"I met a ghost while there. He claims he's not dead, but cursed, which if true, would make him around eighteen hundred years old." Hearing the number out loud made his story all the more ridiculous. "He's strong, Mere. Extremely, and he's . . . colorful."

Something else that hardly ever happened with ghosts. Generally, spirits had a washed-out appearance, closer to a blurry black-and-white photo than real life. Some were transparent, other stronger spirits were not, and sometimes spirits appeared as nothing more than orbs of light. "He has brown eyes," she said, as if that had anything to do with anything. "And he wore a green cloak."

Everything about Fáelán had been dynamic. What must he have been like in life? Her heart skipped a beat. She'd never know the boasty ghosty in life, and that made her sad. Which was absurd, since she'd known him for all of a day and might not ever see him again.

"That feels right. Your meeting him is what I sensed. Could he be telling the truth?"

"About being cursed and not dead?" She huffed out a breath. "After eighteen hundred years? I doubt it. He's had all kinds of time to create a story in his head to make sense of what has happened to him, something he can cling to rather than accept death."

"Is he attached to Newgrange? You could get through to him with that reality if he is."

"No." Which made her wonder why he'd been at Newgrange at all. "He joined me when I drove to Howth." Ghosts were often trapped in an area significant to them, like a house where they'd lived and raised a family, or the place where they'd died. Using that type of evidence to convince a confused soul that time had passed often helped them to cross. "So, what can you tell me?" Regan asked. Her sister's gifts included precognition, and she too saw and could communicate with spirits.

"Your meeting him wouldn't have registered with me if he weren't important. Keep an open mind."

"I always keep an open mind."

"No, you don't," Meredith said with a snort. "Fasten your seat belt, because I predict your mind is about to be blown in ways you couldn't possibly imagine. Ireland is the land of magic after all."

Regan frowned, remembering her failed effort to capture some of that Irish magic. "So, have you and Grayce figured out when you're coming to visit?" She'd leased the furnished townhome in the hopes she'd have visitors. Her rental had two bedrooms and a loft area with a couple of futons.

"No specifics, but it'll be soon." Meredith sighed. "Have I mentioned how wonderful my life will be once I graduate? No more writing my thesis, studying and taking tests. Ever."

"More than once. Just think, in a few weeks you'll have your master's degree. All that studying was worth it, Mere."

"I hope so. I'd really like to be gainfully employed, so I don't have to keep leeching off Mom and Dad. Speaking of our parents, Mom and Dad send their love and said to tell you to call them on Sunday."

"I will."

"So, are you homesick yet?" Meredith asked.

Regan grinned. "I've only been here four days. Ask me again in a few months."

"All right. I'm jealous, you know."

"You're welcome to stay with me rent-free whenever you want. I'll buy airline tickets as graduation gifts for you and Grayce. You can both stay as long as you like. Wouldn't that be a nice break before you begin the grind of looking for a job? You could work on your résumé while sitting on the bluffs overlooking the ocean and breathing in the Irish air."

"I'd love it. I'll talk to Grayce and let you know. Any idea what you want to do with your life once you come home?"

The past five years had been intense. Too intense. After her painful breakup with the man she'd thought was her one and only, she'd thrown herself into growing her business, working around the clock, managing three yoga studios, while also ghost-whispering. She'd burned out, hit the proverbial wall. She'd been well on her way to a breakdown by the time the offer for her business had come to her.

Her chest tightened, and she forced herself to breathe. The emptiness of her life had led her to take this trip. She just wanted to be . . . idle, recharge and explore the island as well as her own inner self. She knew the odds of turning off her gift were slim, but that too was always at the back of her mind.

"No, but I gave myself a year to figure things out. I'm in no rush. I do have the option of teaching classes at the yoga studio in Knoxville if I want, but who knows. Maybe I'll do something completely different, start something entirely new."

"Hmm. Something completely different feels right. You might be surprised by what your future holds," Meredith mused. "I'm getting the strong impression that you're supposed to help your new ghost friend. That much is certain."

She'd been afraid that was the case. No problem. One more ghost, and then she'd be done for good. One of the reasons she'd crossed the ocean to Ireland was to distance herself from pressure to use her gift of sight. It came not only from her family but from the word-of-mouth recommendations spread by people she'd helped. Here, no one knew, and that was a relief. "You'll tell me if anything else comes to you?"

"Only if you need to know. Sometimes it's better to wing it, Rae, and I'm not like Grayce. I don't have visions of things to come; I only get impressions, gut feelings."

"Right." She'd ask Grayce if she'd had a vision, but both sisters insisted that unless someone's life was at risk, it was better not to interfere with fate. What was wrong with knowing or being in control? Maybe that was part of her problem. She needed to be in control, and she'd never been able to control the voices of the dead.

"Gotta go eat my lunch, Rae. Love you."

"Love you too. Bye for now." Regan stowed her phone in her purse and started the car. Tomorrow morning she'd visit Grafton Square, a touristy outdoor shopping mall where street performers gathered, not a likely place to attract ghosts. By lunchtime she might brave the archaeology museum again, ghosts and all. Or not. She could also go see the Book of Kells exhibit at Trinity College, or she could tour Christ Church Cathedral, except those two ancient sites would also have ghostly residents. If she pretended not to hear them, would the spirits leave her alone?

She turned toward Howth, planning to stop for takeout somewhere along the way. Curling up on the couch with her books on Irish history and mythology sounded good. She'd learn as much as she could about the Tuatha Dé Danann, Fionn MacCumhaill and his Fianna. Couldn't hurt, and it might help in leading her boastful ghost to the light—if she ever saw him again.

Crouched upon a patch of grass, Fáelán peered at his reflection in the onyx bowl of clear water and pulled the triple-blade, plastic-handled razor down his cheek. Next time he was free to walk the earthly realm, he'd find a wee mirror to bring back to his island. Unless the coming solstice brought an end to his curse, in which case he'd have no need. He'd smashed his last mirror against a tree whilst in a fit of gut-wrenching loneliness . . . and frustration.

Regan. Mo a míorúilt, his miracle. He grinned . . . and nicked himself with the modern razor. "Feck."

Dabbing at the cut with a bit of rag, he glanced at the sun to judge the hour. The sun, moon and stars were the same in the void as they were in the earthly realm. He'd spent hours puzzling over that fact. If the sun, moon and constellations were the same, it must mean the realms existed side by side. He was home, yet separated by . . . what?

He'd heard the border referred to as a veil oft enough. If 'twas a veil, he ought to be able to move it aside. The opposing forces between the realms felt nothing like a veil to him, so what was the force dividing one place from the next?

And here his pondering faltered. If he could figure out how the realms remained separate, or how they merged during a solstice or an equinox, he should be able to discover how to cross through whenever he chose. The fae did, so there had to be a way.

He finished shaving and bathed quickly in the lake. Swiping water from his skin, he walked to the clearing where he kept his few possessions, including his clothing. A wooden tray holding his breakfast sat upon the flat top of a boulder in the center of his camp. All his meals appeared in that same spot.

Occasionally, he caught a glimpse of the servant bringing his food to him, but he or she never tarried and never spoke. The servant sometimes glanced curiously his way but always disappeared the moment Fáelán tried to talk to him or her, which left him feeling like some kind of curiosity kept in a cage. *Damned fae.*

The warm air dried his skin while he ate the bread, cheese and fruit. As always, the tray held two goblets. One filled with fae wine and the other pure water. He chose the water. Fae wine was far stronger than that of mortals. "I'll be wantin' a clear head," he murmured to himself. "I've a—" He shut his mouth before the words *a woman to fall madly in love with* slipped out. After being alone for so very long, he'd gotten into the habit of talking to himself. 'Twould not serve him well to do so now.

If Morrigan still spied on him, he didn't want to give her the merest hint Regan existed. Besides, best not call the fae princess's attention to him in any way, lest her interest in him rekindle.

His nerves overwrought, Fáelán dressed and glanced at the sun for the fiftieth time. Would Regan welcome his presence, or would she turn him away? Aye, she'd been friendly enough the morning they'd met, but she'd also believed him naught but a fecking *scáil*. She'd had two days to think things over, and he couldn't imagine anyone wanting to have aught to do with a ghost himself. *I've helped many like you*, she'd said. He grunted. She helped ghosts? To do what? Haunt?

"I'm no *scáil*." Ah, but he was trapped like a fly under a bowl. His gut tightened, and the familiar mix of rage and frustration within him fomented into a nasty brew. He couldn't take Regan's hand in his, treat her to a fine meal or take her dancing like the men of today did when courting a woman. What would others think when they caught a glimpse of her talking to empty air? *Damn you, Morrigan.*

Years of training rose to the fore, and he set aside his rage. Focusing upon Regan's dwelling, he willed himself there. She had to know he couldn't knock on her door, and she'd be watching for him. The familiar whoosh and the odd sensation of everything rushing past propelled him to the very edge of the void, where the realms bumped against each other. Here the borders held firm, barring him from crossing.

Drawing a breath for courage, he pretended to lean—casually, mind—against Regan's car, cushioned by the opposing forces between the dimensions. He hoped like hell she'd grace him with her lovely presence once again.

Her front door opened. Regan appeared, and his knees nearly buckled with relief at her welcoming smile. He had one chance, one woman who saw him, and so much hinged upon her willingness to spend time with him. How could he not be a wreck? All the air in his lungs deserted him, and his heart leaped like a startled hind. Straightening, he did his best to smile back.

"*Tá an aimsir go hálainn,*" she called, her tone filled with pride.

He laughed. "Someone's been practicin' their Irish. Aye, 'tis a beautiful day indeed. Even more so now that I've caught sight of ye, *Álainn.*"

"Smooth," she said, coming to stand before him.

Wild roses could not compare to the bloom of color upon her cheeks at his praise. Had any woman's eyes ever sparkled thus? The morning sun brought a sheen to her hair, and her smile filled him as if she'd poured warmth and light into the darkest recesses of his deepest loneliness. Transfixed, he stared . . . barely breathing, lest she prove naught but a vision he'd conjured for himself. If he breathed, she might vanish like a wisp of wood smoke caught in a sea breeze.

"You OK, Fáelán?" A crease formed between her delicate brows.

"Aye, I'm fine." Heat rose to his face. He'd been staring at her like a green laddie who'd just experienced the first stirrings of desire for a woman. "Why would I not be?"

She studied him. "No reason."

"Where do ye wish to go today?"

"Kilkenny," she said, opening her car door and climbing in. "I want to tour the castle, and there are buildings across the street that have been turned to shops and studios for local crafters. I'd love to see weavers, potters and jewelers at work." She climbed into her car.

He settled into the seat beside hers. "Hmm."

"What?" She slid a sideways glance at him, her brow raised in question.

"Shopping," he grumbled. Regan's burst of musical laughter brought forth an answering smile he could no more control than he could the cycles of the moon. "'Tis interesting, is it not? In all the centuries I've lived, the one thing women today have in common with women of the distant past is a love of shopping. How is it that a female can spend hours poring over goods she does not need? A man will go directly to the source for what he needs, buy it and be done." He shook his head. "Not so with a woman."

"That is such a stereotype, but I'll let it go this time." She fiddled with the GPS attached to the windshield until it spoke directions. "While I shop, you can hang out in the castle where they keep the weapons and armor."

"Thank the gods, both old and new, armor didn't exist until long after the Fianna were no more," he muttered. "Give me boiled leather over steel armor anytime. Damned uncomfortable, heavy, hot and restrictive, I'd imagine."

"Speaking of the Fianna, I've been doing research." She flashed him a probing look before pulling her car away from the curb. "Did you really have to run barefoot, and remove a thorn from your foot without breaking stride?"

"Aye, whilst runnin' full out, I might add."

"I also read that to be ordained into the Fianna, a man had to bind his hair and run miles through a forest. Afterward, if any of his hair had come loose, he was disqualified. Is that true?"

"'Tis true. Did I not tell you I had to pass many feats of skill, strength and cunning to be found worthy?" His chest puffed up with pride, hoping to bask in her admiration.

"What's the big deal with hair?" Regan glanced at him for a second. "If I were a man who wanted to join the Fianna, and I'd heard about that test, I'd shave my head. Done. Problem solved."

Not even a hint of admiration shone in her eyes, and disappointment galled him. What would it take to impress his fated one? "The test had naught to with hair, Regan." Ah, well, despite her lack of proper appreciation, he couldn't help but be pleased that she'd gone to the trouble of learning about the Fianna. Did that mean she was interested in him? His heart tumbled over itself. What would he give to be able to reach out and touch her cheek right now? He curled his hands into loose fists and turned his attention to the passing landscape.

"The hair binding had to do with attention to detail, to performing an assigned task with great care. Carelessness in battle leads to death, yours and your brother's."

"I see." She nodded. "The Fianna were like the special forces of today."

"Nay." He huffed out a derisive snort. "We were far better, tougher and more canny. I'm assuming you read all of the trials a man had to pass to be counted among the elite, aye?"

"Yes, and I have more questions, but they can wait." She frowned and shifted in her seat. "I found your armband at the museum, Fáelán."

His chest tightened, and regret stole his breath. "My da had the set made for me when I gained acceptance into Fionn's army. The armband and this piece as well," he said, touching the brooch fastening his cloak. "He said if ever I found myself in desperate straits, I'd have something to barter for what I might need. Or if I found someone else in difficulty, I could cut off a portion of the gold to offer in charity."

His da had been both proud and grieved by Fáelán's acceptance into Fionn's army. He had but one living son, having lost the other two to childhood fevers. His da hadn't wanted to lose Fáelán to war.

"I read that the Fianna were recruited from those in the upper echelon of society—princes, young men related to royalty, sons of chieftains, that sort of thing." She cast him a shy look. "Which were you?"

"Were?" He grunted and fixed her with a scolding look. "Ye mean *are*, lassie. I am not dead, but cursed. I am the son of the chieftain of our entire clan, who was once a Fiann himself."

"Fáelán, it's been how many years now?" she asked, her tone chiding. "In all that time, haven't you ever caught a glimpse of a glowing light that seemed to beckon to you? As much as you want to believe you're cursed and not—"

"Soon enough ye'll learn the truth." Damn, but Regan possessed a most vexing stubborn streak. In his day, women had fawned over him, hung on every word he spoke and *never* accused him of lying. The Fianna never spoke falsehoods. "The summer solstice approaches, aye?"

"June twenty-first, a few weeks away."

"On nineteen June, I will once again bide in the earthly realm." He held up one hand and counted off the days. "For five entire days and nights, I shall be back where I belong. Then ye shall eat your words, oh doubting one."

"Shall I?" She laughed.

"Ye shall." Uncertainty rose like an ocean wave, swamping his hopes. His mouth went dry, and he tensed. What if Regan quit him afore then? "Will ye spend those five days with me, *Álainn*?" *And the nights? Especially the nights.*

She slanted him a pointed look. "So you can fall desperately in love with me and end the curse?"

"Exactly."

"Sure." Smugness suffused her features. "Why not?"

"Stubborn as stone, ye are, and don't think I'm not knowin' ye think me cracked." It might not be as easy to fall in love with her as he'd hoped. He growled low in his throat for good measure, and crossed his arms in front of his chest. But then her laughter spilled over him again, and despite how much she vexed him, his mood brightened.

"Tell me about yourself, lassie. How do ye earn your keep? What of your family?"

"I have a mother, father, two sets of grandparents, an extended family and two younger sisters who happen to be identical twins." She entered a roundabout and turned onto the ramp for the freeway leading south.

"As for how I earn my keep, the year I graduated from college, the owner of the yoga studio where I'd been working part time decided to retire. I offered to take over managing the place, and I made a deal to buy her out within twenty-four months. Once I owned that studio, and it was doing well, I opened another about forty miles away."

She glanced at him. "The second was located in a touristy area in the Smoky Mountains of Tennessee. I opened the third a year later in a popular vacation spot, also in the mountains."

"Ye've accomplished much for one so young." He barely knew her, and yet pride in her swelled his chest. That must be a good sign. Fionn would be pleased one of his warriors had found such an industrious woman. Every indication proved her to be virtuous and kindhearted as well. After all, she'd helped many *like him*, had she not? "And the teaching of this yoga does well for you?"

"It did, but managing three studios got to be too much. I was looking for an assistant manager to hire, and I had plans to open more, but then I was approached by a corporation wanting to buy me out. The offer was good, so I accepted. Selling has given me a little breathing room, and it's made this trip possible."

Though she smiled, her eyes hinted at an uncertainty lurking beneath the surface. "And the purpose of this trip?" His fated one's expression closed at the question, sharpening his curiosity. Clearly, Regan intended to share only a wee bit of truth regarding her motives.

She shrugged. "I told you, this is the land of my forebears, and I want to do a little genealogy search. My great-grandparents on my father's side were both MacCarthys, though not related, other than being married." Another quick glance his way. "Do you see ghosts?"

Change the subject, would she? Regan was easy to read. He bit the inside of his cheek to keep from grinning. Eventually he'd get to the bottom of what troubled her. "Nay, and 'tis glad I am that I do not. Only those who have a touch of fae blood have the sight."

"That's what my grandmother says too." Regan's grip on the steering wheel tightened. "If you can't see ghosts, why were you at Newgrange? What drew you there?"

'Til blood of sidhe in a mortal will tell. Aye, his lassie carried a trace of fae blood, and 'twas the gift of sight that troubled her. 'Twould vex him as well to carry such a burden. "If I tell ye why I'm drawn to Brú

Na Bóinne, ye'll think me even more cracked than ye already do." He stared ahead and held his breath, awaiting her response.

"I don't think that's possible," Regan said, her tone gently teasing.

He barked out a laugh. "Nay? Well then . . ." Gathering his thoughts, he closed his eyes for a moment, gaining mastery over his grief and the ensuing helpless frustration. "I was already cursed when Fionn MacCumhaill, the leader of the Fianna, is said to have fallen in battle," he began. "Many say he did not die that day, but that he lives yet and is hiding in a cave somewhere along the River Boyne. 'Tis said there are others with him in that cave." Fáelán stole a glance at Regan before continuing. "I oft visit that hill in the hopes I might encounter one of my brethren there, or Fionn himself."

"Oh, Fáelán. That must be painful for you."

"Hmm." He crossed his arms in front of him again. "Ye think me cracked."

"No. I think you're grieving for what has been lost to you, and I'm sorry for that loss, but—"

"If you realized I'm not dead, but cursed, ye'd see things differently. 'Tis only logical that if I exist in the void realm, then there must be others like me who also dwell there. Fionn is part fae himself. Wouldn't his fae kin have intervened on his behalf when he was mortally wounded?" He waved a hand in the air. "Wouldn't they whisk him away from the battlefield then? The Tuatha have the means to heal mortal wounds, they do. They possess this magical bit of hide that—"

"It's all a myth, Fáelán. I mean, I know faeries existed once upon a time, long, long ago, but couldn't they have always lived here? Maybe they were the ancient indigenous people of Ireland, and they just happened to have special abilities. All the stuff about how the Tuatha Dé Danann came to Ireland in a ship sailing in the clouds could be nothing more than a tale they concocted to set themselves apart."

She shrugged a shoulder. "It's not dissimilar from the Dakota mythology. They claim to have come to earth from the Pleiades constellation. The cauldron of Dagda, the spear of Lugh, the singing stone and the magic swords . . . and finally, the piece of hide that heals all mortal wounds . . . it's all make-believe. You know, don't you, the Celts were not the only culture to come up with the idea of a healing hide. The Greeks had their golden fleece with the same miraculous powers."

She flashed him a pitying look. "You've been around for centuries, and you have to have been exposed to *some* science and history. All ancient cultures created mystical, aggrandized stories about who they were and where they came from, but that doesn't mean the stories are true. Isn't it possible that, somewhere along the way, you bought into the mythology, using it to weave a tale to explain—"

"Enough." Her dismissive assumptions nearly choked him. Fall in love with Regan MacCarthy? Impossible. She'd insulted him in the worst possible way, accusing him of deluding himself with faerie tales as if he were a laddie of but a handful of winters. Cursing his fate, he was sorely tempted to return to his island to wait a hundred years or so afore seeking out another woman who might see him. "Ye are the one who clings to illusion. Not I."

Feck. That had come out all wrong, making him sound like a petulant child—proving her right. His jaw clamped shut. He refused to utter another word, but he didn't take his leave of her either.

Chapter Three

Regan had done it this time. Her words had wounded her boasty ghosty, and judging by the way he'd snapped at her, the hurt ran deep. She'd been too blunt, too honest and not the least bit compassionate. "I'm sorry, Fáelán. You're right. I know nothing of the past but what I've read, while you lived it. Who am I to say what is fact and what is faerie tale? If I promise to let go of the academic version of Ireland's history, and to be a better listener, will you forgive me?"

He flashed her a hurt-filled look, distrust clear across his handsome features. "Will ye cease your doubting and quit your persistent nagging?"

Nagging? Was that what she'd been doing? That stung, mostly because he was right. She'd been pushing him to accept her version of his truth. Hadn't Meredith admonished her to keep an open mind, while at the same time accusing her of the opposite? Her eyes prickled, and she got that tingly feeling at the back of her throat. Why was she so sensitive when it came to this spirit?

She drew in a long breath, letting it out slowly. Her sensitivity to the situation probably had more to do with all the changes she'd gone through lately, coupled with frustration with her life. She was used to being busy, so busy she never allowed herself a second to think about what her life lacked. She hadn't adjusted yet, or found a compass for whatever was to come next. That was all. Well, that and the fact that no ghost had ever asked to spend time with her before. Of course she was off balance.

She'd sworn to help Fáelán, and she would. Only she needed to dial it back a bit, ease him into reality more on his terms than hers. This was about what he needed, and not about her at all. "I will quit my persistent nagging."

"And . . . ?" He lowered his chin and glared at her from beneath his very fine brow.

"And what?" she snapped. "You can be plenty annoying yourself, you know. You're every bit as stubborn as I am, probably more so." He threw his head back and laughed, and all the tension filling her car disappeared. The tightness she'd been holding between her shoulder blades eased, and she smiled. "Am I forgiven, Little Wolf?"

"Can ye put aside your doubt for a few weeks, *Álainn*?"

"I'll do my best." It wasn't doubt, dammit. Clearly, he was not of this world.

"That's all a man can ask, aye?" He flashed her a crooked grin and winked.

His winks did things to her insides, sexy, erotic things. Too bad he wasn't corporeal, because he tempted her beyond reason. The GPS alerted her to yet another roundabout. The Irish Department of Transport certainly were big on roundabouts, and she found them extremely confusing, much more so than driving on the left side of the road.

She steered the car onto what she believed was the correct ramp. "So, back to Newgrange. I take it you haven't encountered any of the Fianna there, or Fionn MacCumhaill. How would they know to gather there? Are there caves nearby somewhere along the River Boyne?"

"Aye, well . . ." He uncrossed his arms and rested his hands on his thighs. "In this instance, I believe the word *cave* is a metaphor." He cocked his head, and his expression turned pensive. "Like the word *underground* is to the fae."

"Oh? Explain."

"Ye've read the myths and legends, aye?"

She nodded.

"Then ye'll know when the Milesian wizard Amergin defeated the Tuatha Dé Danann, he banished the fae to dwell underground. Since I live in the fae realm, I can tell ye for a fact 'tis not underground, beneath mounds or in deep hollows. The fae exist in the void realm, which, as close as I can tell, is another dimension or plane right here— right beside the earthly realm, in fact."

"Interesting." More interesting still were the reason and intellect that went into creating his own mythology. He certainly presented a challenge to her skills as a ghost whisperer.

"Aye, and it stands to reason the word *cave* as it pertains to Fionn and his band of remaining Fianna also refers to an alternative dimension. 'Tis my belief Fionn MacCumhaill and his men live in the void realm." He turned to her, his mien a dropped gauntlet if ever she'd seen one. "As do I." One of his eyebrows rose, indicating he was waiting to see if she'd refute what he'd said.

"OK," she said with a nod. "That still doesn't explain why you'd expect to find any of them at Newgrange."

"We Fenians oft gathered there to camp. The hill provided an excellent vantage point in all directions," he told her. "To maintain our strength and to keep our wits sharp, during all but the worst months of winter, we Fianna lived out of doors. We wandered about, foraging, hunting and sleeping beneath the stars. In exchange for keeping the peace, defending our island against foreign invaders and settling disputes throughout the land, the clans were obliged to take us in during the winters."

"Ohhh. When you told me about being cursed, you said 'once upon a winter's eve,'" Regan murmured. "The night you were cursed, you were shacking up," she said with a snort. "Some buxom bimbo took you in for the winter. Am I right?"

"I'm not familiar with the word *bimbo*, but I was taken in by my lover's family, aye." One of his knees began to bounce.

"What was her name?"

"What has her name to do with aught?"

"I'm just curious." The sign for Kilkenny appeared, and Regan turned onto the road that led into the village surrounding the castle. It was still early in the tourist season. Hopefully they wouldn't encounter a huge crowd. "What happened to her? Did Morrigan curse her as well?"

"There was naught I could do," Fáelán rasped, his tone bleak, defensive. "I was banished to the void that very night."

Regan frowned. "She died?"

"On the eve I was cursed, I knew Morrigan meant to kill Nóra. I did the best I could to protect her." He shifted in his seat and blew out a breath. "I begged and pleaded with Morrigan to spare Nóra's life. My pleas fell upon deaf ears."

He stared out the window, his hands fisted in his lap. The knee bouncing had stopped. "Nóra was innocent of any wrongdoing. As was I. None of what happened that night makes any sense at all, but the fae need not worry over making sense to mortals. As a Fiann, 'twas my duty to protect those unable to defend themselves. I failed."

Pain pulsed off him in waves, and she hurt for him. "I'm sorry, Fáelán. Did you love Nóra?"

"I was quite fond of her, but nay. She did not hold my heart."

"Yet you did your best to protect her and at your own peril." To his last breath, he'd been Fiann to the core. How could she not swoon a bit over that? Morrigan had killed him and his girlfriend, and that devastating, unresolved injustice could be the reason he still lingered here on earth. Warmth surged for her boasty ghosty, warmth tinged with deep sadness.

"Here we are," she said, pulling into a parking spot. The day had started out sunny, but clouds had moved in, and with the clouds came a chill. Regan twisted around and grabbed her flannel-lined rain jacket from the back seat.

Fáelán sucked in an audible breath.

"What?" Her gaze flew to his.

"Naught is amiss," he croaked. "I wish I could catch a hint of your scent, or touch your lovely"—his gaze dropped to her breasts—"hair, is all."

Heat flooded her cheeks. Twisting and reaching as she had, she'd thrust her breasts practically in his face. Worse, her V-neck T-shirt did show a bit of cleavage. She groaned inwardly. No doubt he'd been a lustier-than-the-average-bear kind of man in life. She'd have to be more careful, considerate. No need to torture the poor ghost with what he could no longer experience. "Sorry," she muttered, climbing out of the car. "Let's go."

Fáelán followed her through a town square lined with businesses on either side. A broad walkway called The Parade took up the center of the square and led up a gradual hill to the castle, which was situated on the River Nore. They walked together in silence all the way to the stairs leading to the castle's entrance. Following the signs, Regan headed toward the admissions booth. "Let's see the castle first, and after that we can tour the grounds. I promise not to shop until late afternoon."

"Hmm."

Did that mean he agreed? She fished inside her day pack for her wallet and approached the woman selling tickets. "T—uh, one, please," she said, handing over ten euros. She'd almost asked for two admissions. Fáelán was becoming more real to her with each passing moment.

"Would you like a book about the castle's history?" The woman handed her the change and pointed to the books.

"Not now, thanks." Regan took one of the folded maps of the castle and grounds and moved on. Fáelán had gone quiet. She studied the map and whispered, "You're awfully quiet. Everything OK?"

"Aye, but we cannot have people thinkin' ye talk to yourself, now can we?"

"Good point." Her heart ached for him. What must it be like to be invisible to the world, to want life so badly you'd create an entire fantasy in order to fool yourself into believing you hadn't died? "Fáelán . . . do you believe in reincarnation?"

Fáelán stomped in a circle around the irritating female. "Ye make me want to tear out my hair, ye do, Regan MacCarthy, and that's a fact!"

She turned her wide eyes his way. "What'd I do now?" She blinked, false, owl-eyed innocence suffusing her features.

He wanted to give her a good shake. Instead, he threw his hands in the air. "If I believe in reincarnation, then I should accept my death, because if I'd only accept my death, I'd cross over to be reborn. The sooner I make myself available for rebirth, the sooner I can rejoin the living. Aye? Admit it, ye wee termagant. 'Tis what ye were plannin' to say, and after swearin' not even an hour past ye'd cease with your dogged wheedlin'." At least she had the good sense to blush . . . and to avert her gaze.

"I . . . oh." She bit her lip. "Maybe, but I didn't mean to—"

"Nag?"

"It just kind of—"

"Popped into your head, and ye couldn't spare it a thought afore it flew out of your mouth?"

"Hey." She glared.

"Go on your tour, Regan. I need to go for a run."

Her glare was replaced by a look of puzzlement. "Go for a run?"

"Aye. 'Tis like walking, only faster."

"I'm sorry. Making suggestions . . . it's a hard habit to break. I've dealt with so many ghosts, you see, and—"

He growled, gave her his back and ran for the exit, taking note of the alarmed stares turned toward Regan. To them, it would appear she was holding a conversation with herself. Once outside, he circled around to the side of the castle and took the path leading past the long, rectangular castle wing to the extensive parkland beyond. Fáelán ran full out along a well-groomed trail until his irritation, his utter frustration at the most vexing female he'd ever encountered in nearly eighteen hundred years—excepting Morrigan of course—leached out of him bit by bit.

Still he forged on at a good clip. Sweat trickled down his back, chest and face. He turned onto a path leading toward the river. After half an hour or so, he slowed his pace to a steady jog to cool down.

He'd been at it for some time before his lungs began to burn. Finally, he slowed to a walk, much calmer now, steadier. He'd always been quick to anger, one of his many faults, to be sure. Placing his hands on his hips, he gazed out at the River Nore, a familiar sight.

He'd oft been here with his family, attending fairs and markets. Where the castle now stood had always been a strategic location for defense. Boats could be easily unloaded here, and the bank of the river at the bend was the best place for people to disembark, including enemies.

There had been no castle back then, only a fort of stone, wattle and daub, built upon a knoll with a ditch moat, and defended by a territorial chieftain sworn to the King of Leinster. He could be sharing his memories with Regan right now, pointing out places of interest to her. After all, he'd been born and raised not so very far from Kilkenny.

His thoughts centered upon Regan, unsure whether she was his miracle or yet another curse. Chuckling, he rubbed the back of his neck. She was a trial, to be sure. Once again she'd provoked him into behaving like a petulant child, and they'd been together for only a single morn. He should return to the castle and look for her afore she took it into her mind to leave him.

There must be a way for them to come to some accord. Of course, the way would require he take the high ground, control his temper and behave as a Fiann ought. He barked out a wry laugh. Who amongst his brethren would be able to maintain their composure with Regan poking and prodding at them, doing her best to herd them in the direction of her choosing?

He fixed in his mind the image of the castle entrance, and, unbidden, images of Regan with her slender back bowed, one leg raised, her foot in her hands, touching her toes to the back of her head interfered. He shook it off, and the whoosh and rush enveloped him. He stood in front of the entrance once again. His gazed drifted toward the terraced garden overlooking the man-made pond of the castle gardens.

He found Regan outside, sitting upon a stone bench, her shoulders slumped and her head bowed. By the gods, seeing her so dejected twisted him into a knot of remorse. He should not have snapped at her as he had. Even though she was completely wrong, her heart was in the right place. 'Twas generous and kind of her to give of her time to a man she saw as naught but a *scáil*, and he'd best keep that in mind.

Resigned, Fáelán strode toward her, ready to form a truce at any cost. After all, wasn't she the woman destined to steal his heart? "Not bloody likely," he muttered under his breath. As if she'd heard him, Regan lifted her head and turned his way. Her face fell at the sight of him, and his heart dropped like a stone through water. He took a seat beside her, at a loss as to how to proceed. "What are ye doing out here, lassie? Have ye seen all there is to see inside the castle?"

"No, but . . ." She sighed heavily. "The castle ghosts started to pester me, and I wasn't in the mood, so I came outside," she said, gazing out over the pond. "I've been thinking."

"As have I."

"I'm not doing you any good, Fáelán. In fact, I'm probably making things more difficult for you." She studied her clasped hands where they rested upon her lap. "It seems like all I do is upset you."

"My thoughts exactly." He extended his tired legs, crossing them at the ankles.

"Well, at least we agree on one thing." She shot a disgruntled look his way. "Anyway, I think it would be best if we part ways. I didn't really come to Ireland to—"

"On *that* I beg to disagree."

"Really. Because of the *curse*?" She grunted. "Because I have to be honest—"

"Are ye willin' to hear my thoughts on the subject, Regan?"

"I have a feeling you're going to share your thoughts with me regardless, so go ahead."

"What if ye stop tryin' so damned hard to do me good? What if we just be ourselves, spend some time together and see what happens?"

Regan opened her mouth as if to say something, closed it and studied him intently. "You look flushed. You're . . . sweaty."

"I do my best thinkin' whilst I run."

Her brow creased. "Ghosts don't sweat."

"Nay, ghosts *don't* sweat," he agreed. "But I do. What do ye say, lassie? No more good deed doin' where I'm concerned. Leave it be for now. If I'd wanted help finding this light ye claim will beckon, I'd have asked for it. Relax. Can we not enjoy a bit of time spent together for no other reason than 'tis good to have each other's company?"

She studied him, hoisting the strap of her day pack higher on her shoulder. Did she mean to leave? "I was born and raised not too far from this land, and right here is where I began my journey with the Fianna. Fionn oft recruited for his army at fairs and markets, and this was a popular area for both."

"Really?" Her expression brightened.

"Aye. I'll tell ye all about it while we shop."

"You're going to shop with me?" She laughed and rose from the bench. "This should be interesting."

"If I'm not mistaken, this is the second day of June. Seems an auspicious day for us to begin anew."

"Why's that?" She blinked. "What's special about the second of June?"

He stood up and shrugged. "'Tis as auspicious as any other day, aye? Are we in agreement? I vow I'll quit harping about the curse."

"All right, and I vow to stop trying to be the voice of reason and a do-gooder where you're concerned. And . . ." Regan fished her phone out of her jacket pocket. "I also came up with a way we can talk without raising eyebrows," she said, holding the phone to her ear and grinning at him. "What do you think? When anyone looks at us, all they'll see is me talking to someone on my phone."

"Brilliant." Gladness replaced his earlier irritation, and he longed to place his hand at the small of her back, or better yet, draw her into his arms and kiss her breathless. Soon. Less than three weeks separated him from the earthly realm—and from touching Regan.

"We should choose a safe word for when either of us slips up," Regan said, still talking into her phone. "When you bring up the curse, and how you're going to fall madly in love with me, or when I start nudging you toward the light, we say the word and it will remind us of our promise."

He chuckled. "All right. Although, all I need do is exert my considerable self-control."

"Is that what happened when you turned tail and ran out of the castle? Was that you exerting your considerable self-control?" she said, mimicking his arrogant tone.

"Aye." He winked at her. "For what I truly wanted was to throttle ye."

"Ha!" Her eyes filled with amusement. "How about *Newgrange* as our reminder word?"

Barbara Longley

"Newgrange will do well enough. I've a place in mind to show ye, but 'tis a fair distance from Howth, more than a day trip. Would ye be interested in taking a tour around the Ring of Kerry? 'Tis popular with the tourists, and the view is breathtaking."

"The Ring of Kerry is on my list of places to see," she said, her tone excited. "I'll make a reservation at a B&B nearby." She glanced at him through her thick lashes. "Um, do you know of any places that might be . . . magical?"

"Why do ye ask?"

"Just curious." She bit her lip.

"I imagine many places in Eire hold magic, but I'd not know of them." He peered at her, pointedly. "I don't see ghosts, and I don't sense magic, Regan. Other than being a Fiann, I am unremarkable in any way."

"OK." She sighed. "When would you like to go to the Ring of Kerry?"

"Tomorrow. I'll come for ye at daybreak. 'Twill give us most of the day and the next to explore."

"It's a . . ." Regan's mouth shut and turned down for an instant. "Sounds like fun."

His breath caught. She'd been about to say *it's a date*, the modern term for courting, but who dated a *scáil*? Less than three weeks until the solstice, and then he could place his hand at the small of her back. He'd take her out for a fine meal, music and dancing. After which, he'd hold her close and kiss her delectable lips. And if he had any luck at all, his kisses would lead to more intimacies, and he'd taste other enticing, sensitive places. Blood rushed to his groin thinking about tasting the tender spot behind her ear, the swell of her breasts, the softness of her inner thighs. Heat sluiced through him, and his breathing grew ragged. A few more weeks, and she'd see how real he was, and virile. He hadn't even reached his prime yet.

48

"We've a plan, *Álainn*. 'Tis grateful I am to ye, for it has been a long while since I've enjoyed the company of such a lovely, good-hearted woman."

Regan made a sound deep in her throat, that sound only women made. The one that said she doubted her man's sincerity. Fáelán grinned. How could he not? 'Twas such an ordinary reaction between an ordinary couple engaged in a dance as old as time itself—the dance of growing close, of becoming familiar with each other's faults alongside their good qualities. Thank the gods, both old and new, his good qualities far outnumbered his faults.

Chapter Four

"I've lost my mind," Regan said, her computer open to Google Hangout. "I'm making dates with a *ghost*! What's worse is that he . . ." She'd been about to say Fáelán turned her on, but that was not the sort of thing she'd admit to her sisters. She couldn't admit that to anyone. "He's not like any ghost I've ever encountered. Today, he and I argued, and—"

"You argued with a ghost?" Grayce asked, looking bemused.

"Yes, because he's stubborn and won't accept he's dead." She waved a hand in the air. "Anyway, he got angry and took off . . . on foot." Why hadn't he simply disappeared? Any other ghost would have. "He said he needed to go for a run, and when he came back, he was all flushed and sweaty."

"A ghost who exercises and sweats?" Grayce said. "That's a new one. Does anyone other than you see him?"

"Does anyone we know—not counting immediate family—see ghosts? You don't, Grayce." Regan raked her fingers through her hair. "He's not my imaginary *friend*, if that's what you're implying."

"I'm asking because I'm not convinced he *is* a ghost. Hey, maybe your guy is telling the truth about being cursed and not dead. I've read stuff, you know, like quantum physics. Could be your new friend really is stuck between dimensions."

"I don't know about that, but . . . we can't possibly know about all the types of spirits and supernatural beings there are in this world," Meredith added, her tone thoughtful. "Think about some of the beings we've encountered and what they were able to accomplish in the physical world."

"I agree that he might be a type of spirit we haven't encountered before, but cursed, not dead? Like I said before, it's been nearly eighteen hundred years! Even twelve-foot-thick castle walls crumble after that long. He'd be dust by now. It's impossible." Regan flat-out refused to consider Fáelán's outlandish claims. Elixir of Life? She hadn't encountered a single mention of anything like that in all the research she'd done about the Tuatha Dé Danann. Fáelán had probably picked that up from hearing stories about other cultures, and he'd incorporated it into his fantasy.

"Oh, oh . . . he might not be human at all, but some kind of creature who shape-shifts to make you think he's a human ghost," Grayce said. "Be careful, Rae. Maybe it's not such a good idea for you to hang out with this thing."

Regan bristled. Whatever he turned out to be, Fáelán was not a *thing*, not to her anyway. "I don't have your empathic abilities, Grayce, but I'd still sense malevolence. I haven't caught even a whiff of evil or the slightest hint he intends to cause me any harm." She shivered. "Remember the awful demon creature we drove out of that old house for the young couple in Nashville, Mere?"

"God, yes," Meredith said. "That being moved furniture around and turned electric appliances on and off."

"The thing even stole the wife's jewelry and hid it," Regan added. "She found her engagement ring in one of her shoes! And the creature threw things at the couple all the time."

Meredith nodded. "That poor couple was traumatized, and it took both of us, armed with crystals, and cleansing the house with burning sage to herd the thing into a corner before we could chase it away. I agree. Evil is easy to sense when it comes to otherworldly creatures. Even for people without any extrasensory perceptiveness, evil makes their insides squirm, their hackles rise, and it triggers an overwhelming need to get away."

"OK," Grayce interjected. "Maybe Fáelán is a Celtic pixie or a brownie, some kind of mischief maker you two haven't encountered here in the States. Could he be fae himself?"

"That's possible." It hadn't occurred to her that he might be fae, but it was worth considering. Faeries liked to mess with mortals for their own amusement, but did faeries still exist? Regan had her doubts.

"I think Grayce and I should come sooner rather than later. No matter what, you need our support."

"I'm not in any danger." Her insides melted at her sisters' protectiveness. "He can't touch me. Wait until after your commencement, and then we'll choose a date and book the flight." Regan yawned. "Anyway, it's late, and I'm beat. I'm going to let the two of you go. I'll call back tomorrow."

"All right, but I'm standing by my original perceptions," Meredith told her. "This being, whatever he may be, is somehow significant to you."

"Like you've never been wrong before," Grayce quipped. "Until I get a read on this thing, I want you to be careful, Rae."

Meredith snorted. "Because you're infallible, and I'm error prone?"

"All right, you two, time to end this conversation." Regan rolled her eyes. She'd been mediating their squabbles for as long as they'd been able to snatch toys from each other. "Good night."

"It's afternoon," Meredith chimed.

"Not here it isn't. We'll talk tomorrow." After goodbyes and ending the call, Regan headed upstairs with her laptop in hand. She'd do a little yoga to relax; then she'd crawl into bed and open her computer.

Once she was settled, Regan did an Internet search on ghosts and supernatural Celtic creatures. Fáelán didn't fit neatly into any of the categories. Could leprechauns change their appearance? Could elves? Sighing, she put her laptop aside and set her alarm clock for an ungodly early hour. Her boasty ghosty filling her thoughts, Regan was just drifting into an erotic dream involving herself and one touchy Irish warrior when her phone rang.

She snatched it from the nightstand and peered at the screen. Pushing "Accept," she sat up. "Hi, Mom."

"Regan, I hope I'm not calling too late. How are you? Are you settled in yet?"

She smiled. "I am, and I'm beginning to learn my way around. How are you and Dad?"

"Your dad is right here."

"Hi, sweetheart," her dad called in the background.

"Hi, Dad. Are we on speaker?"

"Yes, and we're fine, but we miss you. This is the first time you've been so far from home," her mom said.

"It's only for a year."

"We know, but it's still . . . strange. We've gotten a lot of requests for your help, and we were wondering if you've connected with our community there in Dublin."

"Our community?" Dread knotted her stomach.

"It must be so exciting to be in Ireland, the birthplace of our gifts," her mother gushed. "Have you found others like our family?"

"They'll help you plug in and connect with new clients needing your help," her dad offered.

"Oh no, I haven't looked. I don't—"

"Regan, honey," her mom interrupted. "You don't want to waste the time you have there, do you? Think of the good you can do."

Regan braced herself for the spiel she'd heard since her gifts had become apparent. Yep. She'd been hearing what she was supposed to do with her abilities since she was old enough to let her parents know she had friends none of the other kids could see. Her mind wandered while her mother wound down.

"Meredith mentioned you've been approached by a ghost you met at a tourist site," her dad said. "That's good. Already on the job."

Great. Thanks, Meredith. She would have to have a few words with her sister. Grayce knew better than to share Regan's business with their parents, while Meredith had always been the one to fully buy into the our-gifts-are-meant-to-be-shared parental propaganda.

"Uh-huh. I'm helping him, and only him, and then I'm taking a break. Even those of us who are *gifted* deserve a vacation now and then."

"A vacation?" her mother asked. "How does one take a vacation from who they are?"

Exactly what Regan hoped to find out. "So, what's new? What have you two been up to?" She managed to steer the conversation into mundane territory, and she kept it light for the next few minutes.

"I'm glad you two called, but it's getting late, and I'm beat."

"Oh. Of course. We'll let you go, sweetheart. Call and let us know how you are now and then."

"I will, Mom. Love you."

"We love you too," her dad said. "Good night."

She ended the call and snuggled down under the covers. How *did* one take a vacation from who they were? By hanging out with a hot ghost, or a cursed Fiann? Sighing, she closed her eyes and drifted off, already anticipating her day with Fáelán.

Regan yawned and shuffled to the bathroom, only half-awake. What time was daybreak exactly? Did *daybreak* refer to when the sun first peeked over the horizon, or did it have to be fully risen to qualify? Because according to what she'd found, the former would occur at 5:03 a.m., which didn't give her much time to get ready for her date with the ghost of her dreams.

What was wrong with her?

An hour later, dressed and fed, Regan peered out the front window, anticipation thrumming through her veins. She hadn't been this excited about a man since her disastrous relationship with her ex. Even though she'd known he was a things-are-black-and-white kind of guy, she'd fallen hard for him. Keeping her psychic gifts a secret had worn her out, though, and eventually, she'd begun to slip. He'd caught her talking to ghosts more than once, and she'd been forced to tell him the truth.

At first, he hadn't believed her, and he'd urged her to see a psychiatrist, fearing she might be schizophrenic. Later, once she'd convinced him she was telling the truth, he'd called her a freak and broken up with her. After that, she hadn't wanted to risk dating again.

At least she didn't have to worry about revealing her true self with Fáelán. They had a lot in common when it came to the supernatural, like . . . she saw ghosts and he was one. *Damn.*

And there he was, appearing out of thin air to stand by her car. Grinning like a fool, she grabbed her things and headed out the door. "Hey, good morning," she said, ripples of pleasure spreading through her at the sight of him. She really needed to get a handle on her attraction to this ghost, or whatever he turned out to be.

"Dia dhuit, mo a míorúilt lómhar," he said with a slight bow. *"Cén chaoi a bhfuil tú?"* he asked. "Tell me what I said. Ye need to practice your Irish."

"You said, 'Hello, my precious miracle,' and then, 'How are you?'" She thought for a moment. *"Tá me go han-mhaith."*

Fáelán chuckled. "*Very* well, eh? I'll take that to mean seeing me gladdens your heart."

"You can take it however you wish," she said, unlocking her car doors. "I'm excited to tour the Ring of Kerry, and I also want to visit Valentia Island and maybe the Skellig Islands, where the monks once lived. I'll have lunch in Valentia, and you can watch me eat," she teased.

"Ah, well"—he patted a sack hanging from his shoulder—"I brought food, so ye can watch me eat as well."

Taken aback, she bit her tongue before the words *ghosts don't eat* flew out of her mouth. What the hell was he if not a ghost? Could he be so powerful he had the ability to manifest ghostly images of a meal, so he could pretend to eat? "Shall we?" She gestured toward her car.

"We shall."

They hadn't been on the road for long before her curiosity got the better of her. "I've been reading about Celtic mythological creatures." That elicited a grunt from her passenger, and she glanced at him for a second. "Are leprechauns real? What about pixies and brownies?"

"Other than the fae, I've not seen any mythical creatures. No leprechauns, brownies, pixies . . . or banshees for that matter. I believe leprechauns might have been remnants of a people who lived here in ancient times. They may be what is left of the Fomorians." He looked askance at her and folded his arms across his chest. "Are ye thinkin' I might be some mythical being, set upon a bit of mischief where you're concerned?"

Man, he was quick—and perceptive. "Just curious. According to what I've read—"

"Which was written by men who were not likely Irish, nor were they here at the time those ancients lived. They were puffed-up men, I might add, academics who could only speculate as far as the limits of their own narrow mind-sets, ye see."

"Granted." She so enjoyed talking to Fáelán, even when they were disagreeing, especially then. He always seemed to be a few steps ahead of her, spurring her to think faster, reason better. She could see why he'd been ordained into the Fianna. "Anyway, in the books written by the men of limited mind-sets, the Fomorians were the dark gods representing destruction, while the Tuatha Dé Danann were the gods of growth, light and civilization to the Irish people."

"Ha. Shows what they knew, which was naught. I've a question of my own, *Álainn*."

"Oh? What?"

"Is there no man in your life?"

"Nope. No man in my life." The familiar sting of rejection she'd suffered over the years welled, and loneliness swamped her. "This might surprise you, but a lot of men have a problem with the fact that I see and commune with ghosts and other things not of this world." *Beings like you.*

"Well, the men of this era are bloody fools, is all. In my time, those with the sight were highly regarded, and a laddie counted himself rich indeed if he had such a wife."

"Thank you for that," she said, flashing him a grateful look. "My sisters and I have been taught that our giftedness was meant to be shared. Ghost-whispering, working with the dead, takes a toll, even if you limit the hours you're willing to be available to them."

"I imagine having the sight must be a heavy burden to carry. Can ye close your mind to it?"

"No, but I'm looking for a way, which is why I asked if you knew of any places where you might have sensed magic. I can ignore the ghosts, but I can't escape the sensations caused by their presence."

Her heart pounded with sudden realization—ghosts brought an unnatural cold with them. Being near the dead always chilled her to the bone, yet no coldness emanated from Fáelán. She didn't feel warmth either for that matter, but . . . what did it mean?

"Aye?" He cocked a brow and waited. "What sort of sensations?"

"I always experience a prickling at the back of my neck, goose bumps on my arms, and when a ghost is near, the temperature drops."

"Mmm." He nodded slowly, his expression smug. "And now you're puzzling over why ye feel none of that whilst you're with me, aye?"

"Newgrange," she muttered.

Fáelán laughed. "Fair enough. I made my point."

"Mind if I turn on some music?" She'd already plugged in her phone before they'd started out.

"A bit of music would be a fine thing."

She tapped the music icon, and they continued on their way. Occasionally she commented on something she saw, or her passenger from the past would share a history lesson about the area they happened to be passing through. And no matter where she looked, the gorgeous Irish countryside offered spectacular views.

Clouds were gathering. Would they be forced to take their tour in the rain? Maybe not. "You know what I've noticed?" she asked, breaking a long span of nothing but music filling the interior of her car.

"Tell me, lassie."

They were close to the peninsula now, and she drove slowly through a village. It began to sprinkle outside, and she flipped the wipers on. "The weather in Ireland is extremely changeable. I find I put on and carry clothing for any and all possibilities, and in the span of one day, I'll use every single combination possible."

"'Tis true." He pointed. "See the wee white sign across the street?"

"The one with the arrow pointing to a castle?"

"Aye. Turn there."

She did, following a narrow lane not wide enough for two cars. They were nearly to the ferry crossing to Valentia. "You want to show me a castle?"

"Nay, a fort. I'll direct ye from here."

By the time she parked and they climbed out of the car, a steady rain had begun to fall. Blue sky peeked through the clouds to the west, though. The precipitation wouldn't last long. Regan pulled up the hood of her rain jacket and huddled into the warmth of the flannel lining. "OK. Lead on."

"This fort is ancient. Perhaps ye'll find a bit of magic within." Fáelán gestured toward the gravel road across from the lot. "This way."

They walked down the lane side by side, and she wished like hell they could hold hands, or even better, that he could put his arm around her. And his cloak. She shivered, glanced at him and frowned. Leaving off the *if you're not a ghost* part, she asked, "How is it you're not getting wet in this rain?"

"'Tis not raining in the void, Regan."

"I don't like constantly being confronted with these things I don't understand," she groused, unconvinced. Seemed like further proof of his ghostliness to her.

"And I don't like not being able to shelter ye from the wet and cold, *mo a míorúilt.*"

Her pulse leaped. "If you could, you would?"

"Of course." He sent her a smoldering look. "Nothing would please me more than to hold ye in my arms and share with ye the warmth and protection of my body."

Gulp. Heat coiled low in her belly, and his sinful wink stole her breath. "Double entendre much, oh flirty one?"

"Resist much, oh doubting one?" he said with a laugh. He jutted his chin forward. "Look ye there, lassie."

A massive circular wall of stones rose from the crest of the hill to their right. "It looks a lot like the outside wall of Newgrange," she said, in awe of the structure. They climbed the hill and came to a mounted plaque with information written in both Irish and English. "Cahergall Stone Fort. No mortar, and the walls are thirteen feet thick in some places," she read. "Says here this ring fort was built for defense sometime between the fourth and fifth centuries."

"Nay. 'Twas here when I was but a wee laddie, and the old folk told stories about the ring being here long afore they and generations of their predecessors were born. Come, let us go inside. From the top of the wall, we can see Ballycarbery Castle ruins across the way, and I've a story to tell ye about the site."

They were the only two visiting the fort. Probably because of the chill and the drizzle, but the precipitation had stopped for the moment. "All right." She had to crouch to get through the small arched entrance. Fáelán already stood on the inside, waiting for her.

"Must you do that?"

"Do what?"

"Pop in and out like you do," she grumbled. "It's disconcerting."

"My apologies. 'Tis easier for me to will myself into places that might be difficult to navigate whilst I'm in the void." He swung his arm in an arc. "What do ye think?"

She wanted to ask what that meant, but he'd already moved on. "Impressive. Whoever built this knew what they were doing." Round stones, like those found in the surrounding fields, had been fit snugly together to form a thick wall. No mortar held the wall together, yet the structure remained intact against the elements after countless centuries. Regan studied the area within. The wall was about twenty feet tall, and the interior yard measured maybe a hundred feet across. Steps leading to the top had been built all along the inside of the ring.

A smaller circle of stones stood in the middle of the grounds, and Regan went over to investigate. A large slab of gray rock, slightly hollowed out in the center, took up most of the interior of the smaller ring. "What do you suppose this was for?" She'd seen similar slabs of stone in the three chambers of Newgrange. Those too had been a flat gray and slightly hollowed out in the center. Faint ghostly orbs hovered above the center stone, none strong enough to manifest their presence. Old, very old, spirits were trapped within the smaller circle, their sentience fading with the passage of time.

"Perhaps humans were sacrificed to the old gods here," he said, waggling his eyebrows.

"Is that what you've heard?" She sucked in a breath. "That would explain what I'm picking up here."

"What is it ye sense?"

"Traces of spirits too weak to make much of an appearance, and for that I'm relieved." She shivered.

"'Tis likely the stories I heard whispered in the dark of night about this place were true then. Who can say? The Fomorians were sometimes referred to as the stone people. Perhaps forts like this are remnants of their ancient kingdoms." He surveyed the interior yard. "'Tis a good place for defense, to be sure, and to perform sacrifices to appease the old gods, I imagine." He gestured toward the wall. "Would ye care to climb to the top?"

"If you'll climb with me instead of just popping up once I'm there." She strode toward the outer wall.

"If you insist," he said, trailing behind her.

Regan took the stairs that spiraled around the interior to the top. Fáelán climbed along behind her, even reaching out a hand as if he wanted to ensure she didn't slip and fall. Her heart skipped a beat, and *if onlies* danced around in her head. Like . . . if only he were real and not a ghost, one of the fae or a shape-changing whatever. If only she could feel his heat and his lean hardness pressing against her. A kiss would be nice, in a torturous way, because honestly, she wanted more than kisses with her Fiann.

By the time she reached the top step and scanned their surroundings, she'd gone breathless, and it had nothing to do with the climb. She pointed. "That's Ballycarbery Castle?"

"Aye, what's left of it." Fáelán came to stand beside her. "Do ye know the story of Donal of the Feathers?"

"No." She flashed him a questioning look. "Should I know his story?"

"Mmm. Perhaps. Could be he's a distant relative. He was a Mac-Carthy and grew up in Ballycarbery Castle during the sixteenth century. 'Tis said he haunts the area still. He was the bastard son of the last king of Desmond. Donal is famous for the way he fought against the English at the Gap of Plumes. That's how he got the nickname *of the Feathers*. He had the reputation of being something of a Robin Hood. He and his lads harried and harassed the English. Worse than biting flies, they were, darting in to sting and out again too fast to slap. They would disappear into the surrounding bogs before the English could retaliate. Donal took back what the English had stolen from his clan and returned the land to its rightful owners, one hectare at a time."

"Wow." Regan gazed toward the site with greater appreciation. "I need to start doing a genealogical search on my family. My MacCarthy ancestors are from the Munster area." She leaned against the wall of stones and gazed at the castle ruins and the river moving past in its sluggish pace toward the sea. "Wouldn't it be amazing if my family was related to the Ballycarbery MacCarthy clan?"

"Aye. Would ye like to go take a look? Perhaps Donal awaits ye there."

"I would." Regan started back down the steps. If Donal's ghost was there, and they were related, he might be able to tell her something about her ancestor, the first in their line to have the gift of sight.

"I am thoroughly enjoying today, and you are an excellent tour guide, Fáelán." And he was sexy as hell. Confusion reigned where Fáelán was concerned. Insane as it was, she was developing a mighty big crush. *Not good.* He wasn't real, or at least not part of this world, and this world was where she lived. *Damn giftedness.*

Fáelán gloried in Regan's praise. He'd pleased her, and that pleased him. Regan's smiles were like patches of warm sunshine after a long, dismal winter, warming him and brightening his horizons. As they walked toward the car park, he studied her out the corner of his eye. Her face had gone pink from the chill and exertion, and a soft smile played about her mouth. The delicate curve of her cheek had him enthralled.

Her beauty took his breath. The urge to wrap his cloak around her, to draw her close and warm her with his kisses, grew stronger with each passing moment. His need to protect and provide for her . . . 'twas a good sign.

"We get on well when not trying to convince each other of this or that, aye?" he asked, longing to tuck her hair behind her ear, or run his knuckles down her soft-as-petals skin.

She grinned and looked sideways at him. "We do."

"I thought tomorrow we could tour the Dingle Peninsula, and there's another stone fort to see on our way around the Ring of Kerry. Staigue Fort, 'tis called."

"I'd like that. So, the castle, the ferry to Valentia Island for lunch, drive around the Kerry Peninsula, see the other fort, and by then it'll be time for me to check in at the B&B." They'd reached the car. Regan unlocked the door and climbed in.

He took his place in the passenger side. "By then I'll need to return to my island."

Her brow furrowed as she drove the car around to the exit. "The other day, you just kind of disappeared. What happened?" she asked, leaving the gravel lot and turning onto the road to Ballycarbery ruins. "What's your island like?"

"My island is naught but an illusion," he said, his tone bitter. "And it exerts a hold on me at all times. I am wrenched back once my energy is spent." A shudder racked him as memories flooded his mind of the misery Morrigan had put him through in those first weeks of his imprisonment. "Naught but swirling mist exists within the void realm. The fae have powerful magic, and they project whatever they want to exist into that otherwise bleak hell. 'Tis where they make their homes."

"If you're confined to an island, how do you know all that?"

"Do ye recall I told ye Morrigan tried to persuade me to become her consort in the beginning?"

She opened her mouth as if to say something but then closed it, nodding instead.

He couldn't help but smile at her restraint, knowing the urge to confront him with his supposed death drove her to *do him good*. He too refrained from commenting. He was cursed, *not* dead.

"Morrigan explained the void to me. She brought me to her castle, promising to remake it however I desired if only I'd agree to be her plaything for all eternity. She bragged about how the fae could change the void into anything they wished. With my own eyes, I watched her create a garden to rival Eden, and still I refused her." He flashed her a wry look.

"After that, she took away the island and the lake, leaving me stranded to wander in the mist for weeks. Were I not one of Fionn's best, my mind would have broken. The void is not a pleasant place, lassie."

"But you live on the island now, right? How did that happen?"

"Eventually Morrigan must have relented, because one day my island and lake were restored to me, and I've dwelt there ever since. 'Tis not overly large, and besides the plants and trees, I'm the only living thing there. Not even fish exist in the lake." His jaw tightened. "Still, I used to pretend. I'd go through the motions of hunting and fishing, just to occupy my time, ye see."

Regan's expression filled with compassion. "Sounds horrible. I'm sorry, Fáelán."

"My thanks. After some time, I set my mind to finding ways to leave the island, hence my ability to spend an entire day away." He grunted. "'Tis likely Morrigan tolerates my wandering so she can claim she's honoring the curse's only way out. If I'm to be free, I must seek one who sees me, aye?"

"I know we agreed not to talk about the curse, but doesn't it strike you as improbable that the way to end it is so simple?" she asked. "Given all you've told me about Morrigan, it doesn't seem likely that the minute you fall in love, zap, the curse will be over, and you'll go on your merry way." She shrugged. "I mean, there's the part about being willing to give your life for your lover's."

Had she been worrying over that bit for some time? "I expect there will be some sort of challenge, yet another test I must pass, but the fae have laws they must follow when dealing with mortals."

"Is it against their laws to commit murder?" Regan whispered, her voice shaky. "Because if it is, how did Morrigan get away with—"

"Aye, I take your meaning, *mo a míorúilt lómhar.*" It killed him that he couldn't hold her and put her mind at ease. "So many years have passed since Morrigan first cursed me. 'Tis my hope her wrath has diminished, for there was no cause for it to begin with. Let us put it aside for now. When the time comes, I shall endeavor to overcome whatever challenge she places afore me to the best of my ability. 'Tis why I still train."

Regan nodded slightly. "I've been meaning to ask you something. You said your family sees you and can talk to you. Does your family have fae blood? Are they gifted like I am? Because I really want to find out more about that." They'd reached Ballycarbery, and she parked alongside the lane. "If there's a way to turn my abilities off, I'd sure like to know how."

"Nay. 'Tis sorry I am to disappoint ye. After I was cursed, I sought Fionn's help. He'd been granted many gifts, so I hoped he'd be able to see me. More likely 'twas because he's part fae that he could. Anyway, I told him what Morrigan had done. He appealed to his fae kin on my behalf. Though they could not undo Morrigan's curse, one of them did grant me a boon and made it so my family could see me through the veil between the realms. Not all, but at least one or two in each generation, and they're able to help me."

"You have an answer for everything." Regan frowned.

"Newgrange," he reminded her before popping out of the car. "Ye are the one who brought all of this up, not I."

Regan snorted as she climbed out of the driver's side. "That's once for you, and once for me." She grinned. "We're still getting along, so the code word is working."

He laughed, and without thinking, he reached for her hand, dropping his arm when he realized what he'd done. "By the gods, both old and new." His heart thudded painfully, and he muttered a curse under his breath.

Regan stuffed her hands into her jacket pockets and set off for the castle, and he followed. She'd noticed what he'd done, but he didn't know what to make of her reaction. Did she feel as he did? Did she long for his touch as he burned for hers? They made their way up the hill toward the castle ruin.

"By the gods, both old and new," she mimicked, peering at him. "Why both the old and the new gods?"

"Hedging my bets, is all." He winked at her, pleased by the responding flare in her eyes. Aye, she wanted him. His blood heated, and he counted off the days until the solstice. Thoughts of Regan, naked and in the throes of passion, filled his imagination, and he fantasized about what he wanted to do with her.

They'd reached the summit where the ruins stood, and Regan closed her eyes and raised her chin. "I don't sense any ghosts here," she murmured.

"Are you disappointed, *mo Álainn*?"

"A little." She moved to peer down a set of stone steps leading to a chamber beneath the castle. "It would've been nice to meet Donal of the Feathers. Who knows? Maybe he's a cousin." She gestured toward the stone steps. "I wonder if there's a dungeon down there."

"More likely 'tis where the castle guard billeted. This is rather a small keep to have a dungeon."

"Mmm." She backed up several paces. "I think there's a hall above." She pointed. "Want to climb up there with me and take a look?"

He studied the decrepit steps, which were overgrown with weeds. "I'd rather will myself there. Climbing the stairs at the fort was no easy task, and these stairs are in much worse shape. 'Tis disorienting for me to climb anything in the earthly realm."

She canted her head and studied him, her gaze sharp. "How so?"

"I'm in the void. There is a boundary between the worlds. I cannot set my foot solidly upon a step for the same reason I don't get wet when it rains upon ye." His pulse raced with wanting her. "Or for the same reason I cannot touch ye. Though I long to touch ye, *mo a míorúilt*. Do ye doubt me in this?"

"Which part?" she asked, her cheeks blooming with color. "The boundary or wanting to touch me?"

"Both." He held out his hands, palms up. "As to the boundary, see for yourself."

Her expression skeptical, Regan turned to face him. She took her hands out of her pockets, held them over his and applied pressure. She sucked in a breath, and her eyes widened. "It feels like I'm pressing against an air mattress, only . . ."

"Press harder." She did, lifting her eyes to his in surprise. He flashed her an *I told you so* look. "Opposing forces. 'Tis similar to two like poles of magnets repelling, aye?"

"Oh, my God, this is . . . I've never encountered anything like this before, and I've had some pretty weird things happen." Her gaze bored into his. "But I've *seen* you lean against my car, Fáelán. How do you explain that?"

"Nay, ye only see a dysmorphic representation of what is truly happening." He paused, trying to come up with a way to explain what he experienced so she'd understand. He didn't fully understand himself. "'Tis like when ye look through thick glass, and things become distorted," he said, letting his hands fall to his sides. "Have ye ever dropped something into a pool of water, and when ye reached for it, ye missed the thing completely?"

"I have!" Understanding dawned, and her brow rose. "Refraction and distortion."

"Aye. 'Tis the best way I can explain the phenomenon. It only appears as if I'm leaning against your car, but what I'm really leaning against is the veil between the coexisting dimensions. Lean into me, Regan, and ye'll see what I mean."

Slowly, she let herself go, pressing against him from head to toe. The boundary between the two planes of existence separated and cushioned them. Not his best idea ever, because having her so close while not being able to hold her drove him to distraction.

She gasped. "The surface is not completely stable, is it? It's like lying on a waterbed."

The smallest movement caused ripples and waves between them. "I've never encountered a bed of water, but I get what ye mean." Thoughts of making love to Regan on a bed of water, the waves rocking them against each other, intrigued him.

"About the span of my palm separates us today. Two months ago, the boundary would've been twice that. As we get closer to the solstice, the space between us will decrease until there's naught left. Make no mistake, Regan. I will be with ye when the veil between the realms lifts." *And for the rest of my mortal life.* Hope swelled like the tide within him, and a lump rose to his throat. *"Mo a míorúilt ansa,"* he whispered. His dearest miracle.

She lifted her face to his, as if inviting his kiss. He leaned in to meet her, but doing so only caused a wave to push her back. Frustration, deep and sharp, sliced through him. He stepped away, crossing his empty arms in front of him. If only he could plunge through the boundary to her now. Never had the emptiness of his arms, his life and his very existence struck him as hard as it did in that moment. His lungs heaved, and his vision hazed.

68

"What causes the boundary?" she asked, studying the castle a little too intently. "Why does it decrease and increase in sync with the solstices and equinoxes?"

"The earth is magnetic, and it has a negative and a positive pole, aye? The earth's axis tilts toward and away from the sun at differing angles in its orbit, causing the seasons. Perhaps the tilt of the magnetic poles, in conjunction with the force of gravity, or the sun's pull causes the difference in the strength of the veil between the realms." He shrugged. "I can only guess."

"This is all a little too intense for me, sorry. I can't process any more right now." Regan stomped off down the hill, muttering to herself.

He hurried to catch up with her. "Ye must be hungry by now. Shall we take our midday meal, talk of naught but the weather for a bit and relax?"

She nodded but wouldn't look at him. "For a guy born in the third century, you have quite a grasp of physics, and an impressive vocabulary." One side of her mouth quirked up the tiniest bit.

"Aye, well I've had naught but time to learn." Now was probably not the time to tell his wee miracle he had a college degree, and that over the years, he'd studied a variety of subjects of interest to him. Once the Internet came into being, and with the help of his kin, the world had opened up in amazing ways. Still, Regan had been confronted with enough to challenge her wrong thinking for one day, and he far preferred pleasing his lady to confounding her.

Chapter Five

Regan sat at a small table in the dining area of the B&B in Tralee, sipping strong coffee and watching the other guests. One couple spoke German, and another group, a boisterous family of five, had American accents. She set her mug down and studied the two round patties left on her plate. They'd been described as puddings, one white, one black. Both smelled strongly of sage and onion sausage, but she had no idea what might be in them.

Black and white puddings were part of a full Irish breakfast experience, and she was on an adventure. She cut off a sliver of the black pudding with the edge of her fork, and Fáelán appeared in the chair opposite hers. "Augh!" she cried, dropping the fork on the plate with a clatter.

A few of the other guests looked her way, and she pretended she'd dropped something on the floor. She leaned over to pick up her imaginary dropped item and grabbed her phone from her purse as she straightened. "Hello," she said, her phone pressed to her ear. "Aren't you supposed to meet me at my car?" She kept her voice low and glanced at her watch. "In twenty minutes?"

"I couldn't wait," he said with a sexy, wicked grin.

Her pulse still pounded from his sudden appearance, and the intensity of his heated look added a belly flutter to her inner chaos. "It's just as well. I'm finished." She'd try the puddings another day. Pushing her plate away, she rose from her chair. "I'll see you in a few minutes. I have to get my things and check out."

"I'll come with ye." He stood and followed her out of the dining area.

Her ghost, if he was one, wended his way around the tables and chairs, while most would walk right through them without even noticing they were there. Once again, her mind worked on the puzzle of what he might be, and after yesterday's experiments with the boundary separating them, she was more confused than ever. "I'd prefer you meet me at my car," she said into her phone. "It's not like you can help me carry anything."

"Ye've a sharp tongue, *mo a míorúilt lómhar*," he said, his tone teasing. "I find I must invoke Newgrange, for though ye did not say the word *ghost*, the implication was clear."

"Invoke whatever you wish." She flashed him a look of annoyance. "So long as you go wait by the car." Honestly, having him crowd her in the tiny room with nothing but a bed and a small dresser was more than she could handle. The smoldering once-over he gave her only confirmed she'd made the right decision. "Go."

He made that rumbly, purring sound from deep in his chest. "Not long now, Regan MacCarthy, and I'll be able to hold ye in my arms." He winked and disappeared.

"And again . . . augh." She slid her phone into her purse and headed for her room to gather her things. How embarrassing. She wanted Fáelán in the worst way and hoped like hell his claims of a solstice furlough might actually happen. What was wrong with her? Sick in the head or hormones run amok, either way, this desire to tangle between the sheets with an apparition of unknown origin was not normal or healthy. It could only lead to the worst kind of trouble.

Barbara Longley

Shaking her head at her own insanity, she returned the key to her room and collected her receipt from the proprietor. By the time she got to her car, Fáelán had already made himself at home in the passenger side. Her heart leaped at the sight of him, and he grinned as if he knew exactly how he affected her.

Regan groaned under her breath and forced herself to look away. She should be doing genealogy searches in musty old churches, or finding magic she could access, not drooling over Fáelán.

The sun was shining, and fat white clouds drifted across the blue sky. A sheen of wetness glazed the narrow lane in the village where she'd spent the night. It must have rained earlier, though there wasn't a hint of rain or mist in sight now. Regan opened the trunk of her car and stowed her things. Then she slid in behind the wheel and started the engine.

"Gorgeous day for this," she said, pulling out of the parking space. "I looked up some places of interest. I want to see the Beehive Huts and Dunbeg Fort."

"Aye, they're not to be missed. We'll be wantin' to take Slí Cheann Sleibhe for the best views." He gestured toward a large green sign with Slea Head Drive written above the Irish name he'd just spoken. "Follow the signs."

Soon they were on the road that would take them around the peninsula, and Regan rolled down her window a bit. The air was so clear, and the sky so blue, it took her breath. The rugged, rocky cliffs against the sparkling ocean were awe inspiring. "Wow."

"Aye, wow." He nodded. "This is a place I traveled oft with my fellow Fenians. One of our responsibilities was to protect our island from foreign invaders. We worried about the Romans, for they'd already taken England by that time. The peninsulas offered a grand vantage point to keep watch."

Regan glanced at him, and her heart skipped a beat. He looked so happy and relaxed as he gazed out at the passing scenery. "Tell me what your life was like back then."

"'Twas a good life. If we wanted to eat, we hunted, fished and foraged, always sharing our bounty. We camped under the stars, making our beds of pine boughs, overlaid with the softest moss and topped with rushes. Quite comfortable. If we should ever get the chance, I'll take ye camping beneath the stars, and ye can see for yourself." He grinned.

"For safety's sake, we traveled in groups, and in the evenings, we told stories, composed verse and sang around the fire," he continued. "Did ye know we were called 'Fenians' after the way our campfires appeared to twinkle like stars in the night sky all across the land?"

"No, I didn't. I remember you told me you spent the winters lodging with families who took you in, but what about summer storms?" She loved hearing him talk about his life as a Fiann. He visibly relaxed, and his tone held pride, and when he shared his past, she caught glimpses of a much happier man. She saw no harm in encouraging him to remember better times.

"There were always those willing to give us a place beneath their roofs. We were welcomed by all, for 'twas our sworn duty to protect our people from those who would commit violence or theft. We also settled disputes and conflicts between clans."

"I read about your stringent code of conduct and ethics. With the army's mission to serve and protect, it sounds like the Fianna were the original knights of the realm."

"Aye, without the cumbersome weight of the metal armor." He slid her a brief look, his expression determined. "'Tis the fourth of June, Regan. A mere fifteen days away from the time I will bide in the earthly realm."

"So you keep reminding me." She squirmed in her seat.

"So much hinges upon those five days. I . . . ah . . . ye did agree to spend that span of days with me, and . . ."

Puzzled, she peeked at him. One of his knees was bouncing, and his face had turned red. "Oh, my God. The brave Fiann is blushing." She laughed, turning her attention back to the road. "What's on your mind, I wonder?" she teased.

"What is on my mind is the suffering for want of ye, *Álainn*. I desire ye with a fierceness ye cannot fathom."

The way he looked at her, like he might expire if they couldn't do the deed, nearly sent her into oncoming traffic. "Oh." Now her cheeks were burning.

"Do ye want me, my beauty? Am I alone in feeling thus, or—"

"Oh, I want you, Fáelán, but I'm still really confused. Put yourself in my place. I'm used to dealing with spirits, and though it's becoming more and more obvious you aren't a ghost, I still can't say for certain what you are. I can't deny my attraction, but until I know for sure your tale of faeries and curses is for real, I don't know if it's a good idea to go with whatever this is, or a really, really bad idea."

The tense way he held himself eased, and his knee quit bouncing. "'Tis a good idea to go with it—a really, really good idea. All I ask is that ye believe in me. Ye have my word I'll not let ye down. I swear I've told naught but the truth." His chin came up in what was becoming a familiar gesture. "We Fianna are honor bound to be truthful at all times."

Her insides melted, and she wanted so badly to have faith in him. "You're asking a lot of a twenty-first-century gal. Your tale of being cursed, not dead . . . how am I supposed to believe such a thing?" She glanced at him, and his expression of abject disappointment broke her resolve. "I'll try. I *am* trying. For your sake, I'll do my best to suspend disbelief."

"Nay, Regan. Not for my sake." His proud chin remained lifted. "Suspend disbelief for *our* sake, *mo a grá*."

Grá. Now there was a word she'd have to look up when she got home. "OK. For our sake. There's the sign for the Beehive Huts. Can we lighten the mood here and talk about something else?" Could he be telling the truth about being cursed? She was perilously close to crossing the line from wanting to help him pass over to desperately hoping his story was true.

"Let us consider the matter settled. I'll not bring it up again. I want ye; ye want me, and 'tis a very good thing for us both."

He winked, and wasn't she a sucker for his winks and hot looks? What the hell had she gotten herself into?

"I thought tomorrow we could visit the Clonmacnoise ruins?"

"How about the day *after* tomorrow. I need to do laundry and stuff." Honestly, she needed a break from the intensity of being with him. She needed time to process everything she'd learned about him, examine the evidence and come to a new conclusion.

"Hmm. I'd prefer to be with ye as oft as possible."

The curse, of course. She almost cried *Newgrange*, but technically speaking he hadn't mentioned falling in love with her or the word *cursed*. "I need a day, Fáelán."

"I'll settle for the eve then."

She pulled in to the car park for the Beehive Huts. "You are annoyingly persistent."

"'Tis one of my finer qualities."

Again, he lifted his hand as if to touch her, recalled himself and dropped it to his lap. Her poor heart lurched, and she capitulated. "The evening then."

"In your dwelling, if ye please. I enjoy watching the television."

"Of course you do." She huffed out a nervous laugh. "We can watch a movie." She'd gone and made another date with him. What if all his illusions came crashing down around him when the solstice finally arrived? It would also crash down around her.

75

"It was the oddest thing I've ever experienced." Regan paced around her living room while venting to her sisters that Monday afternoon. "No matter how hard either of us pushed or how we moved, the gap between us remained exactly the same width. Not only that, but I watched him eat." Fáelán's leather sack had held a hunk of cheese, brown bread, slices of some kind of roasted fowl and a leather container full of something to drink.

"Astral projection," Grayce cried. "He's a modern-day wizard or warlock who's really into history and likes to dress the part. He's projecting himself to you while he's asleep or in a trance."

"OK." Regan rolled her eyes. Leave it to Grayce to come up with the most outlandish possibilities. "But that doesn't explain the boundary; it only explains his presence." Did it explain the boundary? What did she know about astral projection? Nothing. "And if that's the case, why me? Wouldn't we have had to meet at some point in order for him to project himself to me specifically?"

"Not if your meeting at Newgrange was a random event, and he decided on the spot you were the one he wanted to stalk."

"That's—"

"Crazy?" Grayce laughed. "Yeah, I know. Really, I have no idea. I'm just throwing noodles against the wall, hoping one will stick."

"What do you think, Meredith?" Regan raked her fingers through her hair.

"There are two weeks until the summer solstice, and all you can do is wait until then. Either he'll prove he's telling the truth, or he'll have to admit he made it all up. If he made it up, my guess is he'll disappear from your life altogether."

Regan didn't like the sound of the disappearing altogether part. She chewed on the possibilities. "We both know there are ghosts and other beings who gain strength at certain times during the year." Come to think of it, those certain times coincided with solstices and equinoxes. The Celts believed the veil between the worlds lifted during those times—could they have been right all along? She'd read about all sorts of rituals performed during those times. The Celts wanted to protect themselves from whatever might walk the earth when the veil between the realms lifted.

"I've read about powerful spirits able to manifest as corporeal for short periods of time, or at least they give the appearance of doing so." Regan glanced out her window and stopped pacing. The day had turned blustery and wet, a good day to stay in. A perfect evening for a movie with a hunky Irish . . . ghost. She missed him, and no matter what he turned out to be, she loved spending time with the proud Fiann. "What about spirit possessions?"

"I don't know what to tell you," Meredith said. "Your guesses are as good as ours. None of us can say for certain what you're dealing with. We just have to wait and see."

"She's right," Grayce added. "I'm a little jealous I won't be able to see him the way you and Meredith can."

"If he really does materialize, I'll take pictures for you, and we can all do a Google Hangout chat together, so you can meet him." She'd take those pictures for herself, as proof of her sanity. Regan continued to stare out the window, her mind drifting to her past, puzzling over how it had led to her current predicament. Here she was, twenty-eight years old, and still alone. "I'd be perfectly happy if I didn't see ghosts or catch glimpses of other things that go bump in the night. Part of the reason I came to Ireland is to find a way to leave my giftedness behind when I head home."

"Regan," Meredith said in her stern sister voice. "You don't mean that."

"Don't I?" Her chest tightened, and a flare of resentment burst to life. She hadn't asked to be different. Who in their right mind would want to see the things she saw, or feel the things she felt when dealing with the dead? "Enough about my ghostly adventures. You two get to walk across a stage and pick up your diplomas next week. What are your plans?"

"We're going out to dinner with Mom, Dad and the grandparents, and after that, we have parties to go to." Grayce sighed. "I can't believe I finally finished my undergrad degree."

Meredith made a noise halfway between a choke and a snort. "And it only took you six and a half years."

"Hey, I had other things to learn first," Grayce said, her tone laced with feigned lightness. "There were things I needed to experience before I could do justice to earning a college degree."

"Like partying your brain cells away, you mean?"

"I prefer to think of it as my life-lessons-learned period."

"The past is the past, and I'm proud of both of you," Regan interjected. "Are you two still OK with my not being there to see you graduate?"

"We're fine," Meredith said. "Besides, even if we weren't OK with it, our trip to Ireland on your dime will more than make up for your absence."

"True," Grayce agreed. "And for the record, I know exactly what you mean about wishing you could stamp 'Return to Sender' on your giftedness, Rae. Sometimes I feel the same. It's not easy getting flashes of terrible things that are going to happen. And always knowing what someone is feeling about you while you're talking to them is no fun either."

"I can imagine." Regan's heart wrenched for her sister. In her search for an escape from her visions, Grayce had turned to alcohol and drugs. The chemicals hadn't worked, and Regan gave thanks every day that her sister had come through that dark time intact. "If I find a way, Grayce, I'll be sure to pass it along to you."

"Time to go," Meredith said.

"OK. I've kept you both long enough. Thanks for listening to me rant about my boasty ghosty." She had things to do too. Like vacuuming, dusting and laundry. She had a chicken stew going in a slow cooker, and the town house smelled delicious, which gave it a cozy, homey feel. "Later."

She ended the call and busied herself in domestic chores, the best thing she could do to keep her nerves at bay. How strange was her life? A man she found extremely attractive was coming over tonight, and there was no possibility of anything happening between them other than watching a movie. *Not fair, dammit.*

Fáelán picked at his supper, too worked up to eat. Finally, he pushed it away and poured the fae wine into his wineskin. Bathed, shaved and dressed in a clean tunic and trews, he'd done as much as he could to make himself presentable. 'Twas time to go. He'd never before left his island prison at night. What if the fae servant coming to take away the remains of his meal reported him missing? Worry dampened his excitement to be with Regan.

He strode to his lean-to, where he'd stashed the brush and boughs he'd gathered earlier. He bundled and tied everything into the rough shape of a sleeping man. Or that was what he hoped the result to be. Next he wrapped his cloak around the form and stuffed the hood with rolled cloth to look like his head. For the final touch, he threw his woolen blanket over the whole mess. Surveying the results, he grunted. "'Twill have to do." By the time he finished his preparations, his insides were churning. He couldn't let Regan down, but every instinct he possessed cried a warning that he shouldn't go.

The way he saw it, there were three possibilities: Morrigan no longer cared about him, and he had naught to fear; Morrigan would want him to fall in love with Regan, so the fae princess could incite more mischief; or Morrigan would put a stop to his wanderings for the sole purpose of continuing to keep him a prisoner out of sheer meanness. No matter which case might be true, his best course was to use caution whilst wooing Regan.

Should he wait until after the servant came? *Nay.* There was no telling when that might be. His food always arrived on a schedule, but the gathering up of the remains? On that the fae were unpredictable, and ofttimes the servant who brought his breakfast also took the supper tray away.

Moving to the shadows beneath the pines, he listened and watched for several long minutes. Certain he was alone, he focused his thoughts and his will upon Regan's home, which she'd allowed him to enter when they had returned from their travels. The whoosh and pull took him, and he appeared in her kitchen. She stood in the living room, staring out the front window. She shifted and fidgeted with the curtains. Regan watched for his arrival, and knowing so caused his breath to catch.

Could he hope 'twas anticipation that caused her to be so nervous? She'd admitted to wanting him, but wanting lived a far pace away from caring, and 'twas her caring he longed for. "What be ye looking for outside, Regan?"

She gasped and whirled around, her cheeks turning a most attractive pink. "God, Fáelán, you startled me." She put a hand over her heart. "Whew, I'll never get used to the way you pop in and out."

"'Tis sorry I am to have startled ye, but I cannot knock, and ye did invite me in when last we were together. 'Twas this room I fixed my mind upon when leaving my island. Would it not seem odd to open your door to no one should one of your neighbors happen to be about?"

"I guess." She gestured to the couch. "Have a seat. What kind of movies do you like? I suppose you've had plenty of opportunities to watch TV when visiting your family."

He approached, and her eyes widened, and she twisted her hands together. "There's no need to be so nervous, lassie. We've spent entire days together, have we not?"

"I know, and yet I *am* nervous." She took another deep breath. "This is so strange. You're here, and I can't touch you." The color in her cheeks deepened. "I mean—"

"Come to me, Regan. Let us see if the veil has thinned since last we tested the boundaries." She walked to him, her expression one of hope and vulnerability. His blood rushed, and longing for her nearly scorched him to ash.

"OK," she said, leaning into him.

Without thought he encircled her with his arms and tilted his forehead toward hers. "I have ye in my arms at last, but we're a world apart all the same."

She nodded, a half smile lifting the corners of her kissable lips. "Having your arms around me is like being surrounded with Bubble Wrap."

"I do believe the boundary has diminished a wee bit." Their gazes locked. Her eyes darkened with desire, and his heart pounded in response. "Can ye hear it, *mo a grá?*"

She blinked. "Hear what?"

"My heart beating so strongly. I fear 'twill burst." He tried to tighten his arms around her, tried like hell to get closer, but it only caused a shifting that nearly unbalanced the both of them. He let go of her. "Ye've no idea how badly I wish to kiss ye."

She groaned and walked into her kitchen. "Oh, I have a pretty good idea. I don't think I've ever been this frustrated or this . . . *Gah*, I don't even have the words for everything I'm feeling right this minute, but it's a shit storm, believe me."

Her shoulders bunched as she opened the bottle of wine sitting on the counter and poured a glass for herself. She placed a pouch of popcorn in the microwave and started it, watching the bag expand through the glass, her back still turned to him.

He wished he could smell the popcorn. Hell, he wished he could fill his lungs with Regan's unique scent. What might she smell like? Sweet? Spicy? Did she have a favorite perfume? "Faith, Regan. Ye have my word, I'll not let ye down."

"You don't owe me anything, so there's no possibility of letting me down," she said to the microwave. "Don't feel . . . obligated."

"Obligated?" He frowned.

"You know what I mean." Finally, she glanced at him over her shoulder. "I just can't see anything coming from all of this. No future, you know?"

The sadness and skepticism clouding her features nearly broke him. "How can ye think such a thing? We've not yet begun. We've the whole of our lives afore us, and if—"

"Newgrange," she whispered. "Let's watch a movie. A romantic comedy. How about *Leap Year* with Amy Adams?" Regan took her popcorn from the microwave and dumped it into a plastic bowl.

"Whatever pleases ye would be fine." Never afore had his chest ached with this heaviness pressing upon him as it did now. He couldn't tolerate seeing her unhappy, and his helplessness to do aught to ease her doubts smote him. Frustration surged, and hatred for Morrigan ignited.

Fáelán forced himself into a calmer state and took a seat beside Regan on the couch. She fiddled with the remote control until she found the movie she'd mentioned and pushed "Play."

"I used to watch the Irish version of the movie *The Secret of Roan Inish* all the time just to listen to the Gaeilge," she said.

"Did ye now," he said, unstopping his wineskin and taking a long pull.

She nodded. "And I have an Irish radio app on my phone that I listen to all the time while I'm driving."

"Ah." He hadn't realized how painful falling in love could be. Had that been the reason why he'd never given his heart? Was he a coward after all? While Regan watched the ridiculous movie, he sank deep into his own dark thoughts. Fáelán huffed out a breath, eliciting a curious smile from Regan. "'Tis a silly movie," he muttered.

"Do you want me to put something else on?" she asked, one delicate brow raised. "Something with exploding cars and fight scenes?"

"Nay. This will do, but the next time we watch a movie together, 'twill be my choice."

"Deal." She smiled, her eyes filled with amusement.

By God, her smiles and frowns could pierce through the toughest leather armor to find their mark—his heart. What if he gave her his love, and she refused to love him back? His curse would be broken, aye, but he would break as well.

Regan yawned and leaned into him, or into the Bubble Wrap border separating them anyway. His insides tumbled, and more than anything he longed to stroke her silken hair and kiss her brow. This tenderness filling him had naught to do with lust and everything to do with an overpowering desire to enfold her into his keeping, and to see her happy, safe and protected. "Clonmacnoise tomorrow?"

"Sure, and I read about a pub in Athlone that has been in existence for nine hundred years. Sean's Bar." She raised her head to peer at him, her expression hopeful. "There's a castle in the middle of town too. Can we visit both?"

"We can."

She yawned and settled back to resume watching the movie. Occasionally she sipped her wine, but the bowl of popcorn sat untouched. Fáelán lifted his legs and set his feet atop the table, his entire being focused upon the woman sitting beside him. It wasn't long before Regan's breathing steadied and slowed. She'd fallen asleep. He looked his fill, memorizing the peacefulness suffusing her beautiful features and the way her lashes fanned against the smoothness of her cheeks. A lump rose to his throat, and a wave of possessiveness overtook him.

He leaned close, trying like hell to catch even a hint of the heat and the scent radiating from her skin. Unable to sense anything, he had to content himself with watching her sleep.

That she existed at all truly was a miracle, and this nagging worry plaguing him was naught but anxiety about his cursed state. All he had to do was give his heart fully in order to be free. As Regan had pointed out, could it really be that simple? Why not? Morrigan had more to occupy her time than fretting over a mortal lover from ages past.

Chapter Six

Yoga had always been the cure-all for whatever ailed Regan, but today not even Ashtanga helped calm her. Still, she persisted, moving through the postures while her mind continued to twist and turn along its own chaotic path. Today was *the* day, the nineteenth of June. Fáelán had told her to expect him anytime after noon. He'd be with his family for a while first, and they lived in County Waterford, two and a half hours away from Howth. He'd said he had business to see to, and once he'd taken care of it, he'd come for her. She gave up on yoga and opted for a hot bath, hoping a good soak might help untangle the knots she'd tied herself into.

By the time she'd wasted an hour in a hot bath, dressing and applying makeup—on the off chance Fáelán really would show up—it was nearing lunchtime. Too bad she was too nervous to eat. She'd already packed a bag, since they'd be spending the night in Waterford. *Now what?* She fought the compulsion to stare out the window like a lovesick teen.

Restless energy sent her into a frenzy of tidying. She sorted through the pile of junk mail that had accumulated, making a game out of crumpling the pieces and trying to hit the trash can from varying distances. Then she reorganized one of the kitchen cabinets, all the while refusing to watch the clock.

She was in the middle of making a pot of chamomile tea when a firm knock resounded through the room. She jerked, spilling hot water on the counter. "Oh, God." Could it be? Biting her lip, she wiped her hands on a towel and tossed it over the spill. She hurried across the room, opened the front door . . . and lost her breath. Her jaw dropped.

There he stood, in all his hot magnificence. So much adrenaline surged through her system that all she could do was gape. Fáelán wore jeans and a tight-fitting T-shirt that showed off his sculpted torso. *Gulp.* His shiny auburn hair had been unbraided and brushed smooth. Today he wore it neatly tied back. She itched to set it free and mess it up.

They faced each other in silence, taking inventory. God, he was beautiful.

Once the adrenaline receded, her legs could barely hold her upright. "Come in," she managed to rasp out. The vein on the side of Fáelán's neck pulsed, and his face had turned a dusky red. Good to know she wasn't the only one finding the moment more than a little unsettling. He stepped across her threshold, closed the door behind him and slouched against it as if he needed the support. She could relate.

Regan reached out and placed her trembling hand upon his chest, needing tangible proof he was real. His warmth radiated up her arm along a path straight to her heart. He was warm, solid and breathing. His heart beat like crazy beneath her palm—not even remotely ghost-like.

She swallowed against the strangling lump clogging her throat. "I needed proof," she whispered, patting his chest. "You're here. You're really here."

"Did I not tell ye I would be, oh doubting one?" He placed both of his hands over hers where they rested on his chest.

Hers wasn't the only voice with a telltale quiver. Fáelán brought her fingers to his mouth and kissed the tips. Then he pressed her palm against his cheek. "*Mo a míorúilt lómhar*, is this naught but a dream? Are ye really here as well, or have I conjured ye from the depths of my despair?" he asked, his eyes misting.

His gaze roamed over her, coming back to stare into her eyes with such intensity she could hardly draw a breath. "Fáelán . . ." She needed him to hold her. She longed to feel his vibrancy, his aliveness. Inhaling deeply, she caught the earthy scent wafting from him, like he'd spent the day in fresh pine-infused air and sunshine. The space between them arced with pent-up sexual tension. "Would you—"

"I would." He drew her against him, his breathing ragged.

His mouth sought hers, and his kiss stole her ability to do anything but *feel*. Sensations coursed through her in a rush so powerful she trembled from the sheer strength of her response. The reality of his presence still stunned her. A mix of arousal, relief and happiness rendered her speechless. He moaned against her lips and plowed his fingers into her hair, sending need coiling low in her belly.

"I can scarce keep my legs beneath me, lassie. I've yearned to touch ye, to hold ye close for what seems like all the long centuries I've lived." He trailed kisses along her jawline and down to the sensitive spot between her shoulder and her neck. "'Twill be a trial indeed to keep my hands from ye, but we must be on our way. We've plans."

His erection pressed against her, and she throbbed and ached with wanting him. "Plans?" She wrapped her arms around his waist and snuggled into his warmth. The heat radiating from him, coupled with the way he smelled, drugged her senses. "Can't the plans wait?"

He kissed her forehead and set her away from him. "I'm taking ye to meet my kin as we agreed, and they await our arrival. There's to be a gathering at three." He tucked an errant strand of hair behind her ear and peered at her. "And later, I intend to take ye out on a date. We'll have a fine meal, listen to traditional Irish music, and there will be dancing. Ye deserve to be courted properly, love."

"Isn't that what you've been doing for weeks? I'm not suggesting we spend the afternoon in bed, Fáelán." She still didn't know if he'd told the truth about being cursed, but he was here now, and she'd wanted him since the day they'd met.

He did his deep chest-purring thing, and tendrils of desire unfurled within her. Breathless and needy, she rose to her toes and kissed him. She tugged his T-shirt out of his jeans and slid her palms up his bare sides. His skin was soft and warm, and he smelled so damn good.

His tongue circled around hers, and he drew her closer. "Ye tempt me away from my good intentions, woman," he growled into her ear.

A shiver of pleasure sluiced through her. "Give in." She took his hand and tugged him toward the stairs leading to her bedroom. He resisted for a moment. "Fáelán, honestly, I don't want to meet your family feeling like I do right now."

His eyes darkened, and his nostrils flared. "And how is that?"

"Hot and bothered. We've already had this discussion. I want you; you want me." She flashed him a disgruntled look. "Remember?"

"Aye, I recall, and we agreed 'tis a good thing indeed." He drew her back into his arms and kissed her again, crushing her to him. "Lead me where you will, *mo a grá*. I am yours to command."

Grá meant "love." She'd looked it up. Her eyes stung, and more than anything, she wanted him to love her, so he could be free. Then maybe they'd be able to forge a future together.

This time when she tugged at his hand, he followed. She'd never wanted anyone the way she wanted him. Breathless, her heart pounding, she led him to her bedroom. Fáelán scooped her up in his arms and carried her to the bed, laying her down gently before backing up a step.

Keeping his eyes fixed upon her, he kicked off his shoes, undid his belt and stripped naked in no time flat. Her boasty ghosty wasn't shy about his body, nor did he have a reason to be. He was a work of art. Tattoos covered his sculpted chest and broad shoulders. The man was perfect, freckles and all.

His gaze still drilling into hers, he lowered himself onto the bed beside her. "'Tis your turn, my beauty." He removed her shoes and socks, massaging one foot, then the other.

She sighed with pleasure, and he rose to undo her jeans, sliding them down slowly, kissing the bare skin along the way, then tossing her pants to the floor. He paused to gaze at her lacy, pink panties, a sexy grin lighting his features. He scooted down on the mattress and skimmed his lips over her belly.

"Ahh, that tickles."

"In a good way?" He peered up at her, one side of his mouth turned up.

She nodded. He tugged her panties down, kissed and nibbled her hips, moving to her thighs, sliding the pink lace lower. He tossed the panties to the floor and began working his way back up, kissing and nibbling every inch of her. Finally, he rid her of her blouse and bra in the same agonizingly slow, seductive manner.

Somewhere along the way, her bones had liquefied. She explored his body, sliding her hands up his back and then over his amazing chest. They came together, skin to skin, sexual energy and heat building between them. She was already wet and throbbing for his touch.

"Ah, gods, Regan, *Tá tú go hálinn, maise*, as beautiful as the dawn, and as soft as clouds." He cupped a breast, running his thumb over her sensitized nipple.

A shock wave of pleasure traveled from her nipple to her core, and she arched into him, wanting more, wanting his mouth on her.

"Ye drive me mad with wanting ye." He took a nipple into his mouth, sucking and nipping her into a frenzy. "I'm helpless against your charms, I tell ye."

She reached low between them, stroking him from the base of his erection to the tip, running her palm over the head. Regan reveled in the feel of him, his hardness and the velvety softness of his hot skin.

His sudden intake of breath, the way he moved into her palm, caused a surge of wetness.

Nuzzling his throat, Regan inhaled his intoxicating essence, and she nipped at the spot where his pulse pounded. He hissed out a breath, and the sound went straight through her. Tipping her face up to his, Fáelán kissed her deeply. She loved the way he kissed, like she held center stage in his wildest fantasies.

His hands were everywhere then, inciting a riot of desire. Never had she lost herself like this with anyone. Never had she melted, body and soul, like she did with Fáelán. She opened her thighs, needing him to touch her there, and clever man that he was, he caught on quick. Stroking her, he circled her clit, but not quite touching her where she needed him to. He tortured her into a fever pitch until she strained and writhed against him.

"Fáelán . . . ," she whispered. "Don't tease." He chuckled low in his throat, and she sucked his earlobe between her teeth and bit down in retaliation.

"Ahhh," he breathed out, trembling against her.

Finally, he brought his palm over her cleft and pressed, moving up and down, creating a delicious friction, while a finger entered her to touch just the right place deep inside. He kissed her deeply, his tongue swirling around hers. Pressure built, and she surrendered, completely immersed in the moment. She came in an explosive rush, shuddering and helpless in his arms.

He rose to his knees between her thighs and sat back on his heels. His gaze moved hungrily over her. She was completely open to him, vulnerable and boneless. His chest rose and fell, and he ran his hands over her breasts, an expression of awe suffusing his features.

"Like a wild rose, all soft and pink," he murmured, caressing her breasts. "And down here," he said, bringing his hands to her sex. "All dewy as ye are for me, 'tis a gift beyond imagining."

She swallowed against the tightness in her throat and the intensity of the bond flowing between them. "I want you, Fáelán." She reached for him, drawing him to her, and he thrust home, filling her physically and emotionally.

He made love to her slowly, taking her mouth in a demanding kiss. Regan held him close and wrapped her legs around his waist, bringing him deeper. His breathing came faster, and he pressed his face into her neck as he rocked into her. Pressure once again built in her core. She dropped her legs to dig her heels into the mattress, meeting his thrusts with hers, until she spasmed and tightened around him.

His muscles straining, Fáelán braced himself with his arms straight, threw his head back and came. He called out her name and shuddered with his release. Collapsing beside her, he gathered her in his arms and murmured sweet Irish endearments into her ear as they both recovered their breath and their heart rates slowed. Replete and overwhelmed by what they'd just shared, Regan couldn't muster a coherent thought to save her life. Fáelán stroked her back, occasionally pressing her close, so her breasts squished against his chest.

Sighing heavily, he backed up a bit to look at her, smoothing the hair from her face. "I told ye 'twould be a very good thing between us, did I not?" With a grin of total male satisfaction, he winked at her. "Ye see, lassie, as a Fiann, I am sworn to be a good and generous lover, and I'm particularly devoted to the art, ye understand."

She laughed, and he shot her a mock scowl. That only made her laugh harder, and tears slid down her cheeks. After weeks of tension and uncertainty, she'd built up plenty of steam that needed to be released. She widened her eyes. "Oh, you're being serious?"

"Hmph." He smacked her bottom. "As much as I'd like to tarry in bed with ye, we do need to be going. A quick shower, love, and then we must be off."

"All right. At least I'm much calmer now." She slid off the bed, stood up and raised her arms in a total body stretch. A languorous, sated contentment weighted her limbs. Fáelán's hot, appreciative stare brought a grin to her face. "Come on. You're right. We need to get going." She was curious to see how he and his kin interacted. Hopefully she'd be able to ask them about Fáelán's curse and their history with him. Though she still harbored doubts, with every fiber of her being, she wanted to believe his story.

After a hasty shower together, Fáelán urged Regan to get ready quickly. Once they were dressed, he grabbed her things and led her to his MINI Cooper, which he'd parked behind her car. He opened the back and tossed her bag and their jackets inside.

"You drive?" She flashed him a questioning look, pulled out her phone and snapped another picture of him. She'd also taken pictures of the two of them in bed, with the sheets pulled up to their chins and their heads touching close together.

"How did ye think I'd come for ye? Of course I drive." He couldn't remember a time he'd felt this good. Grinning broadly, he opened the passenger door for her. "I've had twenty days each year in which to learn to do many modern-day activities. I've a license, lassie. My kin . . ." He frowned. Did he really want to get into how he'd been born and died over and over—on paper anyway? "Well, I guess ye'd say they've helped me keep current."

"Huh," she said. "That's a lot of centuries of change and new stuff to learn, especially the technology. I can't imagine what it must be like to hold all of that in your brain."

"I hadn't thought of it that way, but aye, I've taken in more than my share of change."

Regan slid into the leather seat on the passenger side, and he closed the door. She watched him circle around to the driver's side. Truth be told, he rather liked the way she couldn't seem to take her eyes from him. He strutted a bit and threw his shoulders back, giving her a better showing of his fine form. She rolled her eyes as he settled himself behind the wheel and started the car.

"Boasty ghosty showing off?" she teased.

"Cursed Fiann showing off," he asserted. "Newgrange, love. After what we shared in your bed, isn't it well past time ye gave up the notion of my being a *scáil*?"

"Hmm." She sighed but said nothing to contradict him.

As soon as he had them on the road, he reached for her hand and placed it under his on the gearshift. "I love the way your skin feels, 'tis so very soft and warm. I cannot get enough." He squeezed her hand and glanced sideways at her. "'Tis odd, is it not? Weeks of getting to know ye, whilst not able to feel your warmth, detect even a hint of your sweet scent or to touch ye in any way, and now I'm overtaken with it all at once. I find I must touch ye in some way every second, or I might perish from the lack."

"I know what you mean. Watching you open the car door and climb in . . . such an ordinary thing to do, but after weeks of having you pop in and out of places . . ." She shook her head. "It's mind-boggling to say the least."

When he shifted gears, he moved her hand with his, and 'twas as if they'd been shifting gears that way forever. How could he feel this familiar and intimate with her after such a short span of time? Aye, he'd come to her every single day since they'd met, but they'd been worlds apart. Truly, he'd enjoyed acting as her tour guide, sitting beside her while she did Internet searches. Even more so, the way they'd argued about history, politics and religion. Ofttimes, they'd had long conversations about nothing at all. And they'd shared mealtimes together, he with food pilfered from his trays, she with whatever she'd cooked for herself. "We get on well, do we not?"

She shot him a wry look. "As long as I'm not herding you toward the light, and you're not telling me impossible tales of faerie curses."

"Do ye truly still harbor doubts?" He canted his head and frowned at her.

She shrugged and stared out the window.

"Regan . . ." His chest tightened, and the depth of his hurt at her skepticism stunned him.

"Mmm?"

Ah, but not even he could predict how things would turn out between them. Could he honestly say he'd given his heart fully into her keeping? A wrench to his heart stole his breath, and doubt flooded his mind. He couldn't say. The kind of love he desperately needed could not be forced. "Ah, never ye mind. We've five days, and I do not wish to bicker them away."

"Put yourself in my shoes for a minute, Fáelán. You have to admit this entire situation is bizarre."

"Not to me, but then I've lived with the reality of my curse for nearly eighteen hundred years."

"Hearing you say that doesn't make it any easier for me to accept." She shifted to face him. "Tell me who I'm going to meet this afternoon."

"Nephews, nieces and cousins, many, many generations removed."

"Do you go by a surname?"

"Aye. Fáelán Breck O'Boyle." He glanced at her. "Breck was my da's name. It means freckled one."

"Your name has a nice ring to it, and you obviously take after your dad with all those freckles." She grinned. "So, were you able to take care of all your business this morning?"

He'd crossed the realms at midnight. For the first time ever, it had been a struggle to fix his attention upon his home. He would rather have gone straight to Regan. "I did. I rose early to break my fast with family afore running a few errands. All is in readiness."

"What does that mean? What kind of errands?"

"Well, to court ye, I needed to lay my hands on some euros. Then there are always records needing to be updated, things to be renewed." He cocked an eyebrow. "Though I'm only able to spend twenty days per year in this realm, I must maintain a life of sorts, or at least the appearance of a life."

"Oh. I hadn't thought of that."

"Because ye believed me a *scáil* who made up a tale about being cursed by a mythical faerie princess?"

"Pretty much." She took her hand from beneath his and fiddled with the purse in her lap.

She was being forced to confront her doubts about him, and the struggle showed plain upon her beautiful face. She'd come around, especially if he fell in love with her and the curse broke at last.

"So, you have a place where you stay while you're here? Of course you do." She huffed out a breath. "That sounded strange, didn't it? Like you're visiting from another country, and not from a different plane of existence."

Fáelán reached for her hand and took it back without saying a thing, for there was no need to belabor the point.

"I didn't sleep well last night. Too nervous about today, I guess." Regan leaned her head back, lowered the backrest and closed her eyes. "Do you mind if I nap?"

"Not at all." She fell asleep quickly, and he stole glances at her when he could. The joy of having her near was something to be savored. In truth, their lovemaking had affected him more deeply than he thought possible. Sex had always been enjoyable but never the intense, soul-sharing experience it had been with Regan. Never before had thoughts of enfolding his lover into his keeping entered his thoughts like they had with her.

He drove on, replaying the best part of his day thus far—making love to Regan. A few hours later, he parked in front of his home. "Awake, my beauty. We're here." He leaned close and kissed her forehead.

She blinked, stretched and peered out the window. "This is where your family lives?"

"Aye, and where I stay when I'm able." He climbed out of the car and walked around to open her door. Fáelán tried to see the place through her eyes. The rectangular house of stone and stucco boasted two chimneys, one on either end, and a slate roof stretching betwixt them. Neatly trimmed hedges graced the front, and the first-floor windows all held flower boxes with red, pink and white geraniums and hanging ivy. 'Twas home, even in ancient times, and he did love the land.

He reached out his hand, and she took it. "I built this house for my kin in the early nineteenth century."

"How?" Regan asked. "I mean, it costs money to build houses and buy land. It's not like you were earning a paycheck while in the void."

"Early on, my da counseled me to look to the future and to what might aid me in my new life. Should I be fortunate enough to see the curse ended, I'd need the means to make my way." He shrugged. "Over the centuries, I gathered what small treasures I could, bringing them with me when I crossed from one realm to the other. Later, my kin stockpiled and protected everything for me, and when needed, we sold some of my horde. 'Tis how I purchased this land and built my home."

A wave of regret swamped him. "The armband ye saw in the museum, for instance." He'd hated selling his da's gift, but he'd needed a living far more than he needed an ancient ornament. "Private collectors and museums love antiquities, especially weapons and adornments made of precious metals and gemstones."

"Gathered what treasures you could, eh? Did you steal them?" she asked, her brow raised. "Other than what you owned, like your armband, I mean."

"Not all." His conscience nipped at him, and his face heated. "And the things I did steal were not taken from any who would suffer greatly from the loss—a bauble here, a dagger or a sword with a jeweled hilt there, books, coins, whatever might be worth something in the future."

"How did being a thief jibe with being a Fiann?"

He regretted the necessity, but he needed the means to protect himself and his people. "Ah, well, I only stole from our enemies, the English, mostly, or from arrogant, wealthy lords who oppressed us. I saw it as a continuation of my duty as a Fiann to protect the common folk." His declaration was met with a skeptical look from Regan. "I had no choice, lassie. I had to ensure this land remained mine."

"Are you still doing that, still stealing treasures?"

"Nay." He shot her a sheepish look. "Once my kin and I learned about investing, there was no longer any need."

Nodding, Regan shielded her eyes from the sun and looked toward the sea. "You have quite a view here."

"Aye, 'tis breathtaking." The front door opened, and his nephew stepped out. "Come, Regan. We are wanted." He gestured toward the elderly silver-haired man standing at the door. Regan's expression clouded at the sight of his nephew. He reached for her hand. "All will be well, sweetheart. Ye'll see."

"I'm always nervous about meeting new people." She tucked her hair behind her ear. "Because of who I am and the abilities I have."

Fáelán drew her close to his side and rubbed her shoulder. His heart ached for her. "These are my people, and they know there is far more to this world than meets the eye. Ye've naught to worry over."

"I know. It's a learned reaction from past experience. When most people learn that I see ghosts—and someone always spills the beans—they turn all judgmental. Then there are those who accuse me of being a con who preys on the grieving. Some are desperate to use me, while others are flat-out scared. I've suffered lots of rejection over the years." She inhaled a long breath and let it out slowly. "OK. I'm ready."

His chest ached with tenderness. Despite all her doubts and fears, she was willing to brave them for him. He fetched their things from the back of the car, and once again twining his fingers with hers, they walked to the front door. "Regan, this is Dr. James Ahearn, whom most call Jim. Nephew, this is Regan MacCarthy."

Jim's look bounced from him to Regan and back again. "Welcome, Regan, welcome. Come in!" He stood back to let her pass. *"Buíchas le dia,"* Jim muttered under his breath.

"Thank God, indeed." Fáelán chuckled and patted the man's shoulder.

"Not only can she bear your company, but she's lovely besides," Jim teased.

"Which are we thanking God for? That's she's lovely, or that she's willing to suffer my company?"

"Both." Jim grinned. "At last, there is hope."

Regan cast him a look over her shoulder. He winked in response. She rolled her eyes, but he caught the barest hint of a smile.

"Aye." He had hope, to be sure, but worry as well. Never one without the other, hope and worry always traveled as a pair. "There is hope."

Chapter Seven

Fáelán ushered Regan into his house, and the sound of voices and laughter drifted to her from a spacious room to their left. The wainscoting on the walls of the room were the same golden oak as the double doors opened wide. A sectional couch faced a large fieldstone hearth, and several other seating arrangements were grouped throughout the space. This room alone had to be close to the square footage of her entire town house in Howth.

Regan stood at the threshold, eyeing the twenty-plus individuals within. A bar took up one corner, and a young man bearing a remarkable resemblance to Fáelán stood behind it, pouring drinks for an older couple. The bartender's hair was short, more blond than auburn, and he didn't have as many freckles. Still, if his hair were darker, he and Fáelán could easily pass for twins, or at least brothers.

Fáelán set his hand at the small of her back and gently moved her forward. All eyes turned to them, and greetings flew like swallows, dipping and swooping through the air.

"This is Regan MacCarthy," Jim called over the din.

She was surrounded by smiling, happy faces in a wide range of ages. Hands took hers, someone patted her shoulder, and the younger children gamboled around the adults, picking up on the excitement. A surge of warmth spread through her. This was Fáelán's family, and they were welcoming her into their midst.

"So you're able to see Fáelán when he's . . . um . . . ," the young man who'd been behind the bar stammered.

"Aye, she can see me in the void." Fáelán put his arm around her shoulders. "Regan, this is Jeremy. He's Jim's oldest grandson." He went on to introduce everyone.

"It's nice to meet all of you." Her gaze darted around the circle of curious faces. "I'm afraid it's going to take me a while to remember your names."

"I told you we should've made name tags, Da." A middle-aged woman flashed Jim a reproachful look.

"Aye, so you did." Jim gestured toward the sectional. "Have a seat, Regan. Have a seat. Would you care for something to drink? A dram o' whiskey perhaps, or hard cider?"

"Cider would be nice, thank you." As soon as she settled on the couch, Fáelán's family gathered near her, some dragging chairs from across the room to place around the sectional.

"So," Dinah, Jim's daughter, began. "We're all grateful you're here. You've given us hope for Fáelán. Maybe you'll be the one to end his curse at last, Regan MacCarthy," she said, lifting her glass. "Here's to an end to the curse."

A chorus of toasts ensued, and Regan's mouth went dry. So it was true. Her boasty ghost was cursed and not a *scáil* after all? "How many of you are able to see him when he's in the void realm?" Six hands rose, including Dinah's.

"Being able to see him comes to us directly through his four sisters, and it's always been the way of it," Jim said. "Thanks to Fáelán, we've a family tree stretching all the way back to the year he was cursed. Would you like to see it?" He started to rise.

"Maybe later, James." Fáelán gestured for him to sit back down. "I know ye'll all be wantin' to hear the tale of how Regan and I met, aye?"

"That we would," Jeremy said, working his way into the circle of chairs and people. He placed a coaster and a glass of cider on the coffee table in front of Regan.

Regan couldn't help gawking. "You look so much like him."

"I do, and that's a fact." Jeremy winked. "Comes in handy."

What did that mean? Regan took a swallow, hoping it would relieve the lingering dryness in her mouth. The younger children came to sit on the rug at Fáelán's feet, their eyes sparkling with anticipation. Clearly, he'd told stories before, because the room quieted, and even the adults exuded an air of expectation. Fáelán must have amazing tales to share after being around for so long.

Her breath caught. He wasn't a ghost, and maybe, just maybe, she'd have a future with this gorgeous man. She too might get to hang on every word as he took on the role of storyteller at family gatherings.

He took her hand in his and rested them on his knee. "There she was, standing before Brú Na Bóinne, with her wee foot touching the back of her head, and her back arched. I wondered aloud what the daft lassie was about."

Entranced, Regan got caught up in his tale. He had everyone laughing as he related their shared banter, embellishing some things and downplaying others. Fáelán truly had a gift for storytelling. Hadn't he said to become one of the Fianna, a man had to be a poet in his own right? What must it have been like to sit around a campfire with him and a group of Fenians, each taking their turn to entertain the others?

After he finished the story, he shared with his family how the two of them had spent their time together since, including his need to go for a run while visiting Kilkenny because she'd vexed him so. "And here we are." He gazed around at his family. "Tonight, I plan to take her out on the town, and tomorrow we shall return to Howth."

"Will you not consider staying here, Fáelán?" Kathryn, Jim's wife, asked. "After all this time, we'd love to have you with us the day after the curse is lifted. We'll have much to celebrate."

"Nay. 'Twould be better if Regan and I had a bit of privacy."

His grip on her hand tightened, and he tensed beside her. *Why? What is going through his mind right now?* She looked at him in question, but he wouldn't meet her gaze.

"What were you doing at Newgrange that morning, Regan?" Jim turned to her, his expression avid. "If you don't mind me asking."

"It's a long story." She reached for her cider and took a sip.

"We've time enough, and we'd love to hear you tell it," Dinah said, her eyes lit with genuine interest.

"All right, but I'm not as good as Fáelán when it comes to telling stories."

"Makes no difference," a young woman assured her, one of the cousins whose names she couldn't recall. "Go on."

"All right. I come from a family of Irish descent, and many of us are born with . . . certain gifts. My sister Meredith and I can see and communicate with ghosts and other spirit beings. Meredith can also sense things that are happening to those close to her—family mostly. Then there's my sister Grayce."

Swallowing against the tightness in her throat, she took her hand back from Fáelán to run both sweaty palms down her jeans. Fáelán's family had been nothing but accepting, but old habits died hard, and revealing so much still made her nervous. "Like my dad, Grayce has visions and premonitions about things to come, and she's also an empath." Fáelán put his arm around her shoulders, and she leaned against him.

"There is a story that has been handed down through our family about an ancestor, a woman who helped one of the fae," she said. "I guess faeries can be bound by iron, and he'd been trapped. She set him free, and the faerie bestowed the gift of sight to the woman, and the abilities have been passed down one generation to the next." She gazed around the room, seeing nothing but acceptance and interest.

"I came to Ireland hoping to trace my family roots to that ancestor." She shrugged. "And maybe to find a way to give the gift of sight back, or at least to learn how to shut myself off from the ghosts." Trying to find a way to close herself off from the world of spirits had been at the heart of her attraction to yoga. When she meditated, she came close.

"Hmm." Jim frowned. "More than likely, the fae did not *bestow* the gift, but passed it along through the usual way. The two must've had a child together."

"Is that what happened with your sisters?" she asked, glancing at Fáelán. "Did they have children with one of the fae?"

"Nay, whilst your kin's gifts vary, and are passed down through your DNA, the ability my kin carry never changes. They see me. None have visions or see ghosts. Fionn's fae cousin, Alpin, described what he did as an opening of the mind for the sole purpose of helping me. He said the enchantment would follow only the direct bloodline of my sisters, and that it would echo through the ages."

Jim nodded. "I suspect the enchantment is triggered by a specific genetic marker passed on to a few us with each new generation."

"Aye, 'tis certain, though of course Alpin made no mention of DNA." Fáelán shrugged. "I see it as similar to the way Fionn became enlightened after he caught and ate the salmon of knowledge." He took her hand back. "Are ye familiar with the tale?"

She nodded. "I read about it when I did research on the Fianna."

"Why would you want to give your abilities back?" a boy of around twelve asked.

"'Tis a heavy load she carries, Michael," Fáelán said. "To see ghosts, and to be expected to help them depart this world, is no easy task. Imagine the toll it would take if ye were expected to deal with the dead day in and day out."

"Have you ever seen or felt a ghost's presence?" she asked the boy. He'd been one to raise his hand when she'd asked who could see Fáelán in the void.

He shook his head. "But I see Fáelán, and so do you. If you didn't have the sight, you wouldn't be able to help him."

"As far as helping him goes, there's really nothing I can do other than spend time with him," she said. "Even so, there's no guarantee that . . ." *He'll fall madly in love with me.* The words carried far too much weight, and pressed too heavily upon her hopes and dreams, to be spoken aloud. "Just because I'm with him doesn't mean his curse will end."

"True, but we've eyes enough to see he can't keep from touching you. We all see the way he looks at you," Jeremy added. "That's what gives us hope, Regan, not your presence or your ability to see him when he's in the void."

She risked a peek at Fáelán. His expression had closed, and his answering glance was brief but intense. Again, she wondered what might be going through his mind.

"Would you like a tour of the house, *Álainn*?" he asked, rising from his place beside her.

"I would." Grateful for the change of subject, she stood up.

He put a hand over his chest and faced his family. "As always, it does my heart good to see all of ye. Thank ye for coming today, and thank ye for your warm welcome toward Regan. We'll be back shortly, and ye can bring me up-to-date on all of your news." He took her hand and led her to the foyer.

His family hadn't shown any fear or repulsion after she'd told her story, only curiosity. In fact, more than a few heads had nodded when Jeremy wondered why she'd want to give back her giftedness. Their acceptance warmed her heart and soothed her nerves. "I like your family."

He grabbed her bag, and they climbed the stairs to the second floor. "Aye, 'tis blessed I am to have them." Slinging the strap of her bag higher on his shoulder, he took her elbow. "They're right. I cannot go a second without touching ye."

"Sure, but when's the last time you had a woman to touch?" She arched a brow. "It doesn't necessarily mean you'll fall madly in love with me."

"Nay, it doesn't," he said, his tone tight. "I'm still hoping the fae princess has forgotten all about me. The curse will lift, and naught will happen to test anything. Let us not think upon it overmuch today."

He led her to a door at the end of a long hall on the second floor. "I love this wing of the house, for 'tis mine and mine alone." He opened the door for her and stepped back.

Her curiosity piqued, she entered a large living room. Tall windows faced east and west, letting in plenty of light and fresh air. Regan moved to the eastern window and looked out at the expanse of land between the house and the rugged cliffs overlooking the ocean.

"'Tis a wonderful view." He came to stand behind her. "There is an identical suite at the opposite end of the hall, and four other bedrooms besides. James and Kathryn have lived and raised their family here, as prior generations have done afore them. My family maintains this home well, and for my part, I've done what I could for them. 'Twas the only way I could show my gratitude for their help over the years."

A large TV stood on a very antique-looking wood-and-iron trunk. A plush couch and two comfortable upholstered recliners had been arranged to face the makeshift entertainment center. "Is that a Sony PlayStation? You play video games?"

"Nay. My younger cousins, nieces and nephews like to play, and I have it here for them. I've never acquired a taste for video games. Having fought in real battles where real men, many of them my friends, bled and died, I find I do not enjoy pretending."

Regan wandered around the room, stopping now and then to study a painting, or to get a better look at the objects displayed on the built-in oak shelving. She picked up an ornate clock with gold edging and turned it over in her hands. "Is this an example of stolen treasure?" She held it up.

"Nay. I paid for that piece after selling a more ancient treasure I'd . . . er . . . *collected* long ago."

"Collected." Regan snorted. "Meaning pilfered, purloined, lifted, pinched—"

"What would ye have done if the accursed shoe had been on your wee foot?" He walked across the room and opened another door. "Come see the rest, oh judgmental one."

She followed him into a luxurious bedroom with a hearth identical to the one downstairs only smaller. This room faced south, and sunlight poured in through the windows. Fáelán obviously favored bright colors, because the room was done in crimson, gold and hunter green. It fit his bold personality.

An enormous four-poster bed dominated the room. "That is some bed," she said. "How old is it?" She ran her hand down one of the intricately carved wooden posts. It had a frame for a canopy, but no curtains hung from the top. Was this piece stolen? How did one whisk away a heavy four-poster bed to the void, then bring it back again to the material realm? She grinned, trying to picture Fáelán stealing this particular antique.

"Sixteenth century, and don't think I can't see plainly on your face what's going through your mind. Not everything I own has been pilfered. This bed came to me through my family."

"OK. If you say so," she teased.

He dropped her bag upon the mattress and drew her into his arms. "Would ye like to test the mattress, my beauty?"

Her heart turned over, and desire coursed through her in a flood of heat. More than anything, she wanted to make love with him again . . . and again. "While twenty of your family members continue to party downstairs, waiting for our return? Maybe later." She ran her hands up and down his chest and stepped out of his embrace.

"*Maybe* later, ye say?" He did that chin-lowering, peering-at-her-from-beneath-his-brow thing she found so sexy.

"Exactly. We need to pick up some protection if we're—"

"Protection?"

"Condoms," she said. "Haven't you ever—"

"Nay, nor do I wish to." He crossed the room to yet another door. "The loo is through here."

"Now that I know for certain you aren't a ghost or some other kind of spirit being, we're going to have to use some form of birth control, whether you wish to or not."

She joined him to take a peek. An elegant marble floor, a shower and an equally elegant vanity filled the large bathroom. And even better, there happened to be an old claw-foot tub, which would be a great place for one of her nerve-calming soaks. "I can't take another chance like we did earlier today, Fáelán."

"Do ye not want children, Regan?"

"Sure I do. Someday." How would she bear it if he disappeared after his brief reprieve? "But being a single parent doesn't appeal to me, and—"

His jaw tightened. "Aye, we'll pick up protection in town. Would ye like to put your things away, or would ye rather return to our guests? And we've much to face afore we can even speak of such things."

Her heart thumped, and icy fingers of dread laced her stomach into a tight corset. If Fáelán did fall in love with her, what would the fae princess do to test his willingness to give his life for Regan's? At the moment, she wished she had her sister's ability for precognition. A vision would come in handy right now. But she didn't, and she doubted anything Morrigan might do could possibly end with "and they lived happily ever after."

"I don't have much to put away. It can wait. Let's go back downstairs and spend time with your family. I want to get some pictures of you with them, and of you and me in front of the fireplace. You can show me the rest of the house tomorrow morning."

⟦⟨⟨⟨⟨⟨⟩⟩⟩⟩⟩⟧

Fáelán gazed at Regan across the linen-covered table as he took another mussel from its shell and popped it into his mouth. "Mmm." He winked at Regan. "Delicious, aye?"

She nodded while buttering a piece of the rosemary-garlic bread. "Really good."

"My cousin Daniel went to Ballymaloe Cookery School in County Cork. He worked for a restaurant in Shannon for several years before coming home to Waterford and opening his own place. We should take a tour of Ballymaloe sometime."

Fáelán had financed his cousin Dan's ambition to open this restaurant, and he was deeply gratified to see it doing so well. Earning a tidy sum from his investment didn't hurt either. "The school is quite impressive," he continued. "They've their own organic gardens, and, of course, there's a castle. I know how much ye love castles."

"I'd like to visit Ballymaloe," Regan said around a mouthful. "The sauce on these mussels is amazing."

Fáelán left the last mussel for Regan and tore off a piece of the fresh warm bread to soak up some of the buttery white wine sauce she'd mentioned. Gods, but she looked lovely in a dress. She wore her hair swept up, showing off the graceful curve of her neck and shoulders. Other men had ogled her as the two of them were led to their table. Ah, but she was here with him, and seeing all that admiration turned her way filled him with pride. Thankfully, they'd had the good sense to stop at a pharmacy on their way to the restaurant because thoughts of making love to her consumed him.

Regan pried the last mussel from its shell and put it in her mouth. The pink tip of her tongue darted out to catch a drip on her lower lip.

108

She sighed and half closed her eyes. His blood rushed to his groin. The hint of cleavage peeking from the V in her dress wreaked havoc on his self-control, and the memories of making love to her earlier that day flooded his senses. He was supposed to be impressing her with his good manners and charm, and he was finding it difficult even to speak.

He'd always been lustier than most, but he'd also prided himself on his self-discipline. Searching his mind for something to say, he tried to clear the haze of lust enough to start a conversation. Thankfully, their waiter came then, refilling their wineglasses and clearing the appetizer away.

"Shall we share our entrées?" Fáelán placed his elbows on the table. "I'd love a taste of the lamb ye ordered."

"Absolutely. It was hard to decide, everything sounded so good."

"The musicians are beginning to set up." He tipped his head toward the bar area, where a small stage stood before a dance floor. Brilliant conversationalist he turned out to be. "Will ye dance with me after supper, Regan?"

"I will, but I can't guarantee I'll be any good." She glanced at him from beneath her lashes. "I haven't done a lot of dancing."

"Ye'll do fine, for I'll be leading." He leaned back and sipped his wine, pleased when his boast brought forth her laughter. "Music to my ears." Fáelán couldn't keep his eyes from her, no matter how hard he tried. The candlelight brought a sparkle to her fine eyes, and her skin glowed in the soft light. "*Tá tú go hálinn, mo a grá*, so very beautiful, and being with ye this eve . . . well, 'tis proud I am to have ye by my side."

"Thank you, Fáelán." She gifted him with one of her heart-piercing smiles. "You don't have to flatter me, you know."

"The Fianna do not flatter, and I speak only the truth." He reached for her hand and held it between his. "Tell me why ye doubt my sincerity, love."

She shook her head, her features softening. Her expression held a tender kind of sadness he'd not seen afore, and his heart dropped. More than anything, he wanted to see her smile again. The need to know she felt secure, the desire to see her confident of his regard . . . when had these things become his driving force?

"I just know how hard you're trying to fall—"

"Ye know I'm sworn to speak only truth, and your doubt cuts me to the quick." Even he was surprised by how true his words were. "I would never tell ye false. I'll not say what I do not mean. Ever."

Her brow creased, and her smile disappeared. She slid her hand out from beneath his and rearranged the linen napkin on her lap, keeping her eyes downcast. "I didn't mean to hurt you, Fáelán. But my take on things is a little different from yours. I understand how much you want to love me and why. Let's face it. The only reason we're together is because of a stupid curse, and because I happen to have the ability to see you when you're in the void. Not the best foundation on which to build a relationship, is it?" Her eyes met his. "Our being together has nothing at all to do with who I am, and everything to do with ending your captivity."

He cut loose a string of curses under his breath and scrubbed his face with both hands. Lowering his hands, he leaned as far across the table as he could and fixed her in his gaze. "How can ye dismiss what is between us so easily? Do ye not feel the same quickening pulse, the same breathless gladness when ye set eyes upon me that I do when I lay eyes upon ye?"

She opened her mouth as if to speak, and at that moment, their dinners arrived. Regan's eyes were overly bright. They waited in silence as their plates were set before them and the waiter left.

"Have you given it even a second's thought how all of this is affecting me?" She pushed the roasted vegetables around her plate with her fork. "I'm not dismissing what I feel for you, Fáelán, but it's . . ." She cleared her throat. "It's going to crush me if you disappear after our five days together. I'm trying to be rational about all of this. I'm trying to—"

"Protect yourself." *Feck.* He'd considered only himself and what he needed. He hadn't spared even a fleeting thought for her feelings. "I beg your forgiveness, *mo a grá.* 'Tis clear I've been selfish." A fierce yearning rose within him. He wanted a future with Regan. He wanted to give her children, a home and a lifetime filled with love. "Can we set the matter aside for now and enjoy this fine meal?"

"I don't think you're selfish, Fáelán. If the accursed shoe were on my wee foot, I'd be desperate too." Her expression filled with sympathy. "I want you to know I'm here for you, and even though I can only imagine what it's been like, I can empathize."

He couldn't speak past the prickling at the back of his throat. Nodding, he cut a portion of his salmon and placed it on her plate. He struggled to gain control over the powerful emotions churning through him. Her compassion humbled him, and he was in awe of her beauty, both inside and out. "Eat, lassie, and then we'll dance."

"Here," she said, placing one of her lamb chops on his plate.

They ate in silence. Regan was a rare woman indeed. In all his long life, he'd never met her equal. Brave, caring and generous, she fairly shone with goodness and beauty. "Ye'd have made a grand Fiann, Regan, and I would have been proud to serve with ye."

"I don't think so." She huffed out a laugh. "No way could I bind my hair and run for miles without a single strand coming loose. I wouldn't even try."

"I want ye," he rasped out.

She stilled. "I want you too."

"How would ye feel about going home early?"

"I'd like that."

They finished their meal to Irish music being played in the bar. They'd dance another night. Right now he wanted to take Regan home and show her how he felt about her. Fáelán signaled their server for the bill. The waiter disappeared into the back, then reappeared, accompanied by Fáelán's cousin.

"How's my favorite investor?" Daniel asked, clasping Fáelán's hand in a hearty shake. He glanced curiously toward Regan.

"Daniel, this is Regan MacCarthy. Regan, this is Daniel O'Boyle, another one of my many cousins. We missed ye at the gatherin', boyo."

"Sorry I couldn't make it, but I knew I'd be seeing you tonight." His gaze swung back to Regan. "You have no idea how glad we all are to meet you, Regan. In honor of this momentous occasion, tonight's meal is on the house." Daniel rubbed his hands together. "Dessert is on the way."

"Everything we had was outstanding, but I don't have any room for dessert." Regan placed her hand on her midriff. "I am full."

"We'd like to retire early this eve, but we'll be back soon," Fáelán told him. *"Go raigh maith agat."*

"Yes, thank you," Regan added.

"You are both more than welcome, and I look forward to future visits." He sent Fáelán a meaningful look. "May the rest of your week go without a hitch. Safe home to you both. *Slán abhaile.* I'll have the dessert boxed and brought out right away." With that, Dan left them.

Their waiter brought them the to-go box. He and Regan gathered their things, and Fáelán dropped a generous tip on the table. He could hardly wait to have Regan in his bed. Tonight he'd fall asleep with her in his arms. He'd be surrounded by her scent with her sweet curves pressed against him the whole night through. Placing his hand at the small of her back, he guided her out into the warmth of a fine summer's eve.

He couldn't remember a time when he'd felt quite this happy or this optimistic.

"Thank you for the wonderful dinner, Fáelán," Regan said as they reached his car.

"Ye are most welcome." He couldn't get them home fast enough, and for the first time, he missed his ability to will himself where he wished to be. He took Regan by the hand, fixed his mind upon his bedroom and gave it a try. Naught happened. "Hmph." He opened her door for her.

"Hmph?" Regan repeated.

"I wanted to see what happened if I tried to will us into my bed to save time." He flashed her a wry look. "Didn't work."

She laughed. "It's not a long drive." She settled into the MINI Cooper.

"Is it not?" He hurried around to the driver's side and got them going down the road toward home. "May there be many more dinners out yet to come for us," he said under his breath. Regan placed her hand over his on the gearshift, and his insides melted. He switched so that his hand rested atop hers. "I have not told ye enough how very beautiful ye are, Regan, and 'tis not flattery, but the truth."

"Yeah, you're just trying to get me into your bed," she teased, a sweet smile playing across her kissable mouth.

"Aye, that too." He squeezed her fingers. Her laughter washed through him, dispelling his worries and gladdening his heart.

By the time he pulled the car in to the driveway, he was breathless with his need for Regan. Fáelán grabbed the bag from the pharmacy, and Regan took the to-go box. Thankfully, they found the house quiet as they entered. "I'll put this dessert into the fridge," he said, trading sacks with Regan. "Go on. I'll be up in a moment."

"All right." She started up the stairs.

Transfixed, he watched the way her hips swayed, the graceful way she ran her hand along the polished banister. She glanced back, catching him ogling her.

She arched a brow. "How long do you plan to stand there?"

"Not a second longer." He turned on his heel and strode to the kitchen, put the dessert away and jogged back to the stairs. Far be it from him to keep his beauty waiting. He opened his door to find Regan's dress pooled upon the rug just over the threshold. His pulse raced as he caught sight of her shoes, and beyond them, a flash of something lacy in front of his bedroom door. He groaned and followed the trail she'd left him, unbuttoning his shirt along the way.

He found her naked and lying on her side upon his bed. "What a sight ye are, *Álainn*, a feast for the senses." He kicked off his shoes and stripped. Her sultry gaze ran over him, and his cock twitched. Climbing onto the bed, he stared into her eyes and growled, stalking her. "Your wolf is about to take a bite."

Laughing, she welcomed him into her arms, and their mouths came together in a scorching kiss. He learned her body with his hands and his mouth, reveling in each delectable bit of her luscious curves. "Mmm." He kissed his way down her neck to her soft, plump breasts. "Delicious." He took a hardened nipple into his mouth, sucking and nipping until she moaned and arched into him.

For the second time that day, he lost himself in Regan's beauty. They were perfect together, and making love to her was like coming home to a warm, welcoming heaven on earth. Drawing her closer, he flipped them so that she was on top. He slid his palms down her back to cup her bottom. "Ah, Regan, ye amaze and humble me, ye do." He gazed at her, smoothing her hair back from her face. By all that was holy, she was beautiful, beautiful and precious beyond imagining. Fáelán was nearly brought to tears as feelings of possessiveness, tenderness and desire to protect her washed through him in a deluge.

Regan kissed his forehead, then both of his eyelids, his cheeks and finally his mouth. "You're pretty amazing yourself," she whispered before nipping his neck.

The sound of her breathing, she soft way it touched his skin, sent a cascade of shivers down his spine. He ached to be inside her. She shifted to lie by his side and took him in her hand, stroking and fondling his cock until he thrust helplessly into her touch, wanting more, wanting her. "Condom."

"Right here," she replied, reaching under a pillow. "Do you need help?"

"'Tis certain I can figure it out for myself." He took the foil wrapper from her and tore it open. He'd been around long enough to know of them and how they worked. "I'm more clever than ye think," he muttered, rolling the sheath over himself. "'Tis like wearing a slicker on a sunny day," he grumbled.

She caressed his aching balls, and he forgot all about how much he disliked protection. "I've the desire for dessert after all." He took her nipple into his mouth again, first one then the other. "Open for me, *mo a grá*."

She did, and he found the sensitive nub of her sex. Her slick readiness drove him mad. He worshipped her body with his hands and kissed his way down her torso. Seeing her so open to him, he lost the ability to think. Instinct took over, and he made love to her with his mouth, flicking his tongue over her clit until she cried out and pressed herself against him. He plunged a finger into her welcoming heat, nipped, licked and teased until she came apart. Before the last pulse of pleasure receded, he entered her.

Forcing himself to think of other things, he remained still for a moment, lest he come at the first thrust. Regan moved beneath him, drawing his attention to her.

"What's wrong?" She slid her hands up his arms to his shoulders.

Fáelán touched her forehead with his. "There's naught wrong, my beauty. I need a wee bit of control, is all."

"What if I don't *want* you to be in control?" She thrust her hips against him again.

He chuckled. "Have it your way." Fáelán made love to her, slowly at first, increasing his pace as the groans and gasps she made drove him over the edge. This was more than sex, more a merging of souls, and he shattered with his release, coming together again as a new man. He dropped to the mattress beside her, wrapped his arms around her, unable to speak.

Snuggling up to him, Regan traced his tattoos with her finger, occasionally dropping kisses here and there. "Do your tattoos mean anything, or are they purely decorative?" she asked, touching the leaping salmon over his heart.

"Aye." A sigh of utter contentment escaped. "The salmon identifies me as one of the Fianna. It's Fionn MacCumhaill's symbol. The other on my chest is my clan's symbol, and upon my back ye'll see another that identifies me as the son of Breck." He peered into her eyes. "See, if I'd been slain far from home, I'm stamped with my return address. That way, my remains would make it home to my kin without difficulty."

"That's . . . macabre." She yawned.

"Nay, 'tis but good sense." He ran his hand up and down her back. "The tattoos on my shoulders are to commemorate victories in battle."

"I love your tattoos." She yawned again and snuggled closer. "Your cousin, the one who looks just like you, mentioned the resemblance came in handy. What did he mean?"

"When my appearance is needed, he darkens his hair with dye and stands in for me."

"When would your appearance be *needed*?" Regan lifted herself slightly to peer at him.

"I wished to get an education, which is not easy when one can only walk in the earthly realm twenty days out of the year. With the help of my kin, I did what I could online, dictating research papers, whilst they entered my words into the computer. I'd read the textbooks whilst one of them turned the pages for me."

He shifted and drew her back down against his chest. "But many classes were not offered online, so Jeremy attended them for me." He arched a brow. "'Twas I who did all the work, though. He recorded the lectures for me, and in return, I paid for his education."

"That's fair. So, you have a degree?"

"Aye, in anthropology and ancient history. I want to continue and get a PhD in archaeology."

"Really?"

"Aye. Since I actually *know* where significant sites can be found, just think what I might be able to accomplish."

"Wow. I'm impressed."

"Perhaps I'll also be a professor."

"Sounds like a good plan." Regan sighed and closed her eyes. "Comfy bed."

"Comfy woman," he whispered, cupping her breast. As soon as she fell asleep, he turned to his side and wrapped himself protectively around her. Nothing in this world compared to having Regan in his bed and in his arms. He'd waited nearly two thousand years to feel like this, and the thought that he might lose her could not be borne.

Her warmth seeped into him, and worries plagued him. Why had he not realized sooner? 'Twould not be him Morrigan would harm, but Regan. Hence the part of the curse where he'd be willing to lay down his life for hers.

More than anything, he needed Regan to be safe. If ending the curse meant trading her well-being for his, he'd refuse. He clenched his jaw against the ache in his chest. These five days might be all he'd ever have with Regan, for he would not put her life in peril for his freedom. He would not give her his heart fully, because to do so meant putting her in danger. Once again, he'd thwart Morrigan, and there was no telling what she'd do or how she'd react to his defiance.

Chapter Eight

"You want to lean your hips back to find the sweet spot where you can hold the pose without strain." Regan corrected Fáelán's downward-facing dog. Any excuse to touch him worked for her. He'd asked her to teach him yoga, and since he insisted on practicing naked, of course she'd agreed. Because of the naked part, she'd suggested they practice in her bedroom with the blinds closed. She didn't need her neighbors getting an eyeful of her gorgeous Fiann, and the curtains over the living room windows never closed completely.

"On your next exhale, go from downward-facing dog into the lunge. Let me demonstrate again." She moved into the lunge, conscious of his appreciative stare. Of course, he'd insisted she be naked too. Coming to standing, she gestured. "Now you try." She slid her hand down his back to fondle his fine butt as he moved into the asana.

"Regan . . ."

"Yes, Fáelán?"

"Ye are distracting me."

"Am I?" How could this already be the end of day three together? Panic careened through her at the thought of how quickly their time together might end. She forced herself into a calmer state. They had right now, and she didn't want to miss a second with him because of what might happen in the future.

"From lunge, bring your feet together, toes pointing in slightly, heels apart. Inhale, straighten your legs and go back to touching your toes again. Well, eventually you'll be able to touch your toes," she teased. "For now, let your hands dangle. On your next exhale, release a bit deeper into the pose."

Fáelán groaned. "Why do I want to touch my toes again?"

"To stretch and open your spine and your joints, that's why. You're not there yet, and that's OK. You don't want to injure yourself, so don't force it. Exhale, and roll up slowly, stacking one vertebrae at a time. Then move into the standing backbend again, with your arms raised over your head. Good. Inhale and come back to the mudra pose with your hands over your heart. You're doing really well. Hatha Yoga is the basis of all forms of yoga, and once you've mastered the basics, we can explore other more challenging disciplines."

"Grand. First let's have sex, and then we can fall asleep in each other's arms. My favorite thing in all the world is falling asleep with you beside me."

She snorted. "Sex first, though?"

"Aye—first, second and third." He scooped her up and carried her to the bed. "I've centuries without ye to make up for."

"Is that what you're trying to do? Make up for centuries without having sex with me?" She snuggled closer against him.

He laid her on the bed and stretched out beside her. "Aye, though I know 'tis impossible." He kissed her forehead and then her eyelids. "Do ye mind?" he whispered into her ear, causing a pleasant tickle.

"Not even a little bit," she said, drawing him to her for a kiss. He was a generous lover and sensitive. He picked up on her responses quickly, intuitively understanding what she needed. When it came to loving, Fáelán possessed his own kind of giftedness.

His touch was more tender tonight, almost hesitant. He took his time, as if he meant to commit every second to memory. The emotions flowing between them were deeper somehow, more intimate, bringing a sting to her eyes. Or maybe the sting came from worrying about their uncertain future.

Her passion built, and she strained to get closer, trying to feel every inch of him against every inch of her. Fáelán whispered Irish words of endearment into her ear and loved her more fiercely. After they were both spent, he wrapped himself around her—this was her favorite part too—and nuzzled her neck.

"Regan." Her name came out on a sigh. "I fear to say aloud what I feel for ye. I've no idea how Morrigan might come to know. Is she privy to my thoughts, or must I speak them aloud?" He squeezed her close. "'Tis of no matter, for I cannot give ye my heart fully, *mo a grá*. I *will* not. 'Tis too dangerous."

"What do you mean?" She closed her eyes tight against the ache his words caused.

"See, I cannot bear the thought of anything happening to ye. I'd rather remain cursed for all eternity than give Morrigan cause to harm ye."

She twisted around in his arms to face him. "How is refusing to love me because you fear I might come to harm any different from being willing to lay down your life for mine? By refusing to love me, you remain cursed and face endless suffering; if you do admit you love me, you're free, but one or both of us must risk our lives. The sentiment is the same either way, isn't it? And Morrigan is going to see it that way."

"Hmm. I hope not."

Regan tangled her fingers in his hair and kissed him. "So you . . ." What if the faerie could hear them? "You've fallen?"

"I have, but I will not—"

"I love—"

"Hush. Do not say it aloud."

"We've two days left, Fáelán. We need to figure this out, prepare." *He loves me!* Oh, God, and she loved him, passionately, deeply. *Now what?* "If I'd focused on magic instead of touring, then maybe we might already know how to defeat your faerie princess."

"Ah, but ye saw no need, aye? Ye thought me a *scáil* who'd spun a tale. Besides, playing tour guide gave me time to be with ye, and I don't regret a single moment." Fáelán kissed her forehead. "But now we've come to the point, and I'll not have ye fight the fae on my behalf. They cannot be defeated by mortals, no matter what magic ye might possess."

"The Milesian wizard Amergin managed to defeat the Tuatha, and he was a mere mortal."

"Aye, but that was a different time, and the world was a different place then. The knowledge Amergin held is no longer."

She frowned. "I don't believe it's gone, only forgotten, and even if it's just to protect myself, I need to learn whatever I can. I felt the magic and heard the echoes of spells and wards being cast while at Newgrange. I have to at least try in case Morrigan comes after me."

Whether he wanted her to fight for him or not, she intended to do whatever it took. "Have you heard of any places other than Newgrange where someone like me might be able to pick up on magic?"

"'Twould ease my mind if ye had some way to protect yourself, and not just from the fae. We can return to Newgrange if ye wish, and perhaps the Hill of Tara still holds magic." He smoothed her hair away from her face and kissed her neck.

"Tara?" A wave of panic sent her heart racing at the thought of a face-off with Morrigan. She traced the tattoo over Fáelán's heart, wishing he had a few of his fellow Fenians here to help them.

"Aye, 'tis where our kings were crowned and where they held court. My king, Cormac MacArt, made his home upon that hallowed ground.

Though I could not sense it, others oft remarked on the hill being the source of mystical power for our people."

"Good." Regan pushed herself up and peered down at him. "I'm willing to try again to somehow gain access to that power. I thought my desire to come to Ireland had everything to do with seeking out the source of my gifts. I was wrong, and now everything makes sense. You drew me to Ireland, Fáelán. *You're* my reason for being here, and I have to do whatever I can to—"

"It matters not what you think. I will not allow ye to put yourself in harm's way."

Regan stared into his eyes, her resolve strengthening. "It's not your choice; it's mine."

He ran a knuckle down her cheek. "Think, Regan. Even if I remain cursed, each year we'll have twenty days together in the earthly realm, and I can still be with ye whilst I'm trapped in the void—same as I have been this past month."

"Twenty days a year is enough for you? Because I have to tell you, it's not enough for me. Besides, you'll remain the same, while I grow older each year. Not looking forward to that." Even so, having him for whatever time they could share together would beat not having him in her life at all. "I'd rather make a stand and put an end to whatever it is between you and Morrigan once and for all. If the curse ends, does that mean you won't be immortal anymore?"

"I've no way of knowin', do I?" He drew her back down into his arms. "Ye own my heart, Regan," he whispered. "Do ye not see? Your safety means far more to me than freedom."

"You just said we shouldn't say that out loud, and now you've gone and done it anyway. I feel the same, and I can't even think about any-thing bad happening to you without having a panic attack. Something, some force we don't understand, has brought us together and led us to this point. My sister even said as much. She sensed you're significant to me, and I'm supposed to help you. The way and place we met, it all has to mean something."

She laid her head over his heart, needing to hear its reassuring beat, needing to feel his warmth. "We're meant to be together, and I'm willing to fight for what we have. Aren't you? Between your skills as a warrior, and my ability to—"

"See ghosts?" He grunted and ran his hand up and down her arm. "Or do ye refer to your ability to touch your toes?"

"Not helpful." She glared. "Tomorrow we're going to the Hill of Tara. If there is magic there, I *will* find a way to take it, and if I don't sense magic at Tara, we'll go back to Newgrange. With magic, we might be able to protect ourselves from Morrigan, even if it's only to hide our whereabouts so she can't get to us. I know I'm grasping at straws here, and it might be unrealistic, but if force of will has anything to do with wielding magic, I'll make it happen."

"Your bravery touches me in ways ye cannot imagine," Fáelán said, his voice strained. "Like ye said, we've two days in which to prepare. Tara is not far from here, and perhaps we might find something there to aid us. No matter what, we'll face what comes together, knowing our hearts are pledged."

He shifted and wrapped himself around her again. "Sleep now, love. Ye'll need to be well rested if ye are to find a way to grasp hold of Tara's magic, aye?"

Now that things were settled between them, her panic receded and determination rushed in to take its place. They'd find a way; they had to. Regan yawned, drugged by Fáelán's enveloping warmth. "Are there ghosts at Tara?"

"'Tis likely."

"Maybe they can help, or at least one of them might have information we can use."

"Perhaps."

Held within Fáelán's arms, Regan drifted into sleep, even as her mind worked on a solution to their looming problem.

⁂

Fáelán could scarce breathe through the tightness in his chest. Regan had it aright. He loved her, and he'd only fooled himself into believing he could hold back even a portion of his heart, when all along she'd owned him body and soul.

A familiar tugging sensation assailed him, and adrenaline surged. Fully alert, his heart pounding, he listened and waited. When naught happened, he blamed it upon nerves and settled himself again. Another tug, this one stronger, and before he realized what was happening, he was wrenched from Regan. Fáelán landed with a thud—not upon his island, but in the midst of the fecking grayish-green mist.

"Morrigan," he shouted. "This cannot be. Ye swore to free me once my heart was given. Ye cheating, heartless bitch, by Tuatha law, your oath cannot be broken." For what seemed like hours, he shouted, ranted and railed against her until his throat was raw.

He sank down to the bare ground, engulfed in the dreaded fog, naked and helpless as the day he'd been born. By the gods, to be so close, only to have that conniving, duplicitous faerie break her word . . . Fáelán closed his eyes and shuddered.

Grief and anger broke what control he had left, and sobs racked his entire being. He cried for Regan, for the heartbreak his abandonment would cause her. He cursed Morrigan for the years of injustice perpetrated against him, and he wept bitter tears for his part in poor Nóra's murder so many centuries ago.

A sense of futility gripped his heart, compressing the organ into a hard, heavy stone in his chest. Confusion hazed his mind. He'd been robbed over and over again, and for what? What about the time he should've had with his family? That too had been cruelly ripped away.

He hadn't been there for his ma when his da died, and he'd never known the joy of holding a child of his own in his arms. Ah, gods, he'd never know a life with Regan, the one love of his long, long life.

Scalding tears of anger, sorrow and self-recrimination poured forth until he was emptied, and his roiling emotions ceased. The sound of his own breathing was all he had left to hang on to in this desolate place. His head throbbing, he lay on his back and stared blindly into the gray-green void. How could he ever forgive himself for the heartbreak he'd cause Regan? Once again selfishness—his and Morrigan's—affected an innocent in whatever this was that lay between the two of them.

He had nothing, not even a bit of cloth to cover his nakedness. How could he fight one of the fae? How could he bear this loss? His sanity would surely forsake him now, for 'twas clear Morrigan had never intended to set him free and never would. Fáelán curled himself into a ball and fell into a fitful slumber.

Startled alert, he sensed Morrigan's presence. The air around him smelled of summer rain, and the mist became charged as if a storm threatened. Fáelán pushed himself up to standing and prepared to fight in whatever way he could. The mist parted, and Morrigan stepped forth. He glared.

"Fáelán." She smiled, her eyes filled with cold derision. "How nice to see you again."

Time had not altered her in any way. She still possessed the same ethereal, unnatural beauty. Her complexion was impossibly pale and her hair so light as to be almost colorless. It hung to her waist, and she wore a long, diaphanous gown.

Repulsed by the very sight of her, he averted his gaze. "Ye broke your word." Gods, what he'd give for a weapon right now, any means to strike out at her. The instant the thought formed, his body turned to lead. He couldn't raise his arms or move his legs, no matter how much he struggled to throw off the force she exerted over him.

A cold sweat added to his misery, and humiliation at his helplessness against her galled him to the depths of his marrow. "Your sire, King Lir, will learn of this," he managed to grit out. "By reneging on your word, ye've broken fae law . . . again. He'll sense your crimes."

"Have I broken my word?" She circled him. "Perhaps I took you from your mortal lover a bit early, but I've not acted against Tuatha laws in any way."

"The curse—"

"Aye? What of it?"

"Ye granted me a way out, and I met the conditions set forth."

"Did I grant you a way out?" She stroked his cheek and traced a finger down his torso.

Bile rose up the back of his throat, and his skin prickled with disgust. Try as he might, he couldn't move away. "Aye, by wind, water, earth and fire ye swore, once I gave my heart fully—"

"I know what I said," she snapped. "The terms I set forth were ambiguous at best, and purposefully so. Not without mercy, a daughter of Danu be, I grant ye one path by which ye *might* be free," she recited. "*Might*, as in at my discretion. And what of the last line?" she asked, tapping her chin. "How did it go? Ah, yes, in the earthly realm *may* ye once again live." Shaking her head, she tsked. "*Might* and *may*—do these words not suggest things could go either way? It *might* be this, or it *may* be that—either an end of your curse will come to pass, or it may not. I choose *not*."

"Why? After all this time, why concern yourself with a mere mortal? 'Twas ye who came to me in falsehood, not the other way 'round. I'm the one wronged here, Morrigan, by your deceit. What did I ever do to warrant your eternal wrath?"

"I offered you a life of immortality as my royal consort, and you insulted my generosity with your refusal. *You*, a puny human, rejected *me*, one of the Tuatha Dé Danann and a direct descendant of the goddess Danu!" The blue of her eyes glowed, and the mist around her darkened and eddied. "I need no other reason." She lifted her hand, and a portion of the mist parted and cleared to form an oval, a window of sorts.

The surface rippled, and Regan came into view, still sound asleep in her bed. Peaceful in slumber, she was unaware he no longer slept beside her. Fáelán's heart split in two, and fear unlike any he'd ever known closed over him. Again he struggled to free himself from Morrigan's hold. His fight yielded naught but an evil look from his captor.

"Don't hurt her," he rasped out. "I beg ye, do not harm Regan."

"Foolish mortal that she is, did she not swear she'd fight for you? I'll not lift a finger to harm her, but neither will I prevent her from casting herself into troubles of her own devising." She shrugged. "If she possesses an ounce of sense, she'll realize she's powerless against me, and she'll do naught. In which case, no harm will come to your lover by my hand. Besides, 'tis your misery I wish to savor, and so I shall for as long as it amuses me. Here you shall remain for all eternity, and here you will watch your lover age and die before your eyes."

For an instant, he considered capitulating. He'd swear to be her consort, but to what end? Regan wouldn't know, so he couldn't prevent her from searching for him or trying to find a way to defeat Morrigan. Nor was there anything he could do to prevent his love from aging and dying, while he remained eternally five and twenty. "Damn ye to hell." Fáelán closed his eyes and his mind. He refused to pay the fae princess another second's heed.

The air around him changed, and he was released from the paralyzing force. Morrigan had left him, and once again he was alone to face the unending emptiness. Why had he not reasoned things through before courting Regan? He knew Morrigan's treacherous nature well enough. Aye, but he'd been greedy for freedom, wanting to believe life in the earthly realm was finally within reach. He'd believed at long last he'd live a real life with a woman he loved by his side. He'd selfishly ignored what he knew to be true, and yet another innocent would pay the price. The rending of his soul brought a piercing sting. Hardening his heart, he clenched his jaw, determined to defy Morrigan in any way possible.

His back to the portal, he lowered himself to sit, drew up his knees and rested his forehead upon his forearms. He'd refuse to participate in Morrigan's twisted game. He would not look through the portal, not even once, and in this small way he'd deny Morrigan the satisfaction of watching him suffer. By the gods, both old and new, 'twas likely his future held naught but this dismal view from now on—gray mist, loneliness and remorse were his only companions from this day forward, and here he'd thought he'd run out of tears.

Regan awoke and stretched, every inch of her a prime example of one well-loved, satisfied female. Fáelán must have already been up, because his side of the bed was empty. His down pillow still held the indent from where his head had rested. Sighing, she turned to her side, pulled the pillow close and inhaled his lingering scent. If she stayed in bed long enough, perhaps he'd come back upstairs and join her. Smiling, she nestled under the covers, listening for him over the patter of rain against the windows.

She didn't hear the shower going, or any noise or movement from downstairs. She couldn't detect the scent of coffee or tea from the kitchen either. In fact, her place was too quiet. Empty. Throwing the covers back, she rose to sitting and swung her legs to the floor. Fáelán might have gone for a run. Rain didn't bother him. Or he might've gone to the bakery in the village. Her hopes pinned on the latter, her mouth watered at the thought of fresh scones for breakfast. The thought of food propelled her out of bed. At least she could have the coffee ready and waiting for his return.

Regan got up, took her robe from the hook on the back of her bedroom door and slipped into it. She picked up the pile of Fáelán's clothes from the floor, exactly where he'd dropped them, and tossed them into the hamper before heading downstairs to start the coffee.

By the time she'd had breakfast, showered and dressed, with no sign of Fáelán, worry consumed her thoughts. He hadn't left a note, hadn't called or texted, and his car was still parked in front of hers on the street. She grabbed her phone from the kitchen counter, where it was recharging, and punched in his number. Her heart thudding, she followed the sound of his ringtone to the nightstand in her bedroom. Her mouth going dry, she ended the call and stared.

The oppressive silence amplified his absence. Regan walked across the room and peered out the bedroom window into the pouring rain. They'd made plans to go to the Hill of Tara today. He wouldn't just disappear without a word, would he? She sucked in a breath. He would if he believed abandoning her might protect her from Morrigan.

"Dammit, Fáelán!" She brought her phone up and looked for Jim's number in her contacts. A death grip on her cell phone, she pressed it to her ear. If Fáelán was hiding out in Waterford, she'd give him a piece of her mind in blistering detail. They'd agreed to face whatever came together, and then he'd left her once she'd fallen asleep? *Coward.* Maybe not cowardly, more like playing the martyr when he didn't have to.

"Dr. Ahearn here," Jim answered.

"Hi, Jim. It's Regan." She swallowed a few times. "Is Fáelán there?" There was a long pause, and her gut twisted.

"Nay. Is he not with you?" he answered, his tone filled with concern.

"No, and I don't have any idea where he is. He was gone when I woke up this morning." She bit her lip for a second, trying to get control over the way her voice quavered. "I haven't heard a word from him. I'm afraid he left out of some mistaken notion about protecting me."

"It's happened then, has it? He loves you."

She nodded, then realized how stressed she was, because of course Jim couldn't see her nod. "He does, and I love him too. We have today and tomorrow left, and now he's gone. If you hear from him or see him, call me immediately."

"Aye, of course, but—"

"Tell him I'm pissed, and he needs to come to Howth ASAP."

"Wait, Regan. Is his car still there?"

She brought her hand to her forehead. He'd left not only his car and his phone but his clothes too. "It is, but he could've called someone to come get him."

"Perhaps, but I'd be the one he'd call, aye?"

"OK. What are you suggesting?"

"I fear—"

"You think Morrigan took him?"

"It may be. The Tuatha Dé Danann are selfish creatures by nature, and they see no need for fairness where mortals are concerned. Years ago, I did warn Fáelán this might happen, but he insisted Morrigan had made a vow, and fae law prevents them from breaking their oaths."

She closed her eyes. Certainty settled in her gut like a load of gravel. After their declarations of love last night, Morrigan had taken Fáelán from her. Regan needed her sisters, if only for emotional support. "Are we completely screwed here?" Tears of frustration filled her eyes.

"That I cannot say, but Fáelán told me once that any action undertaken by one of the fae was known to all of them through some kind of collective awareness."

"OK, so how does that help us?"

"Their kings and the law keepers will know a wrong has been committed, though not exactly what the act entailed. Morrigan's father is one of their kings, and he'd be more sensitive to any transgression on his daughter's part because of their bond of kinship."

"So, her father will know she's up to no good, that she broke her oath to Fáelán?" Did that mean there was hope? If so, she'd clutch the slim possibility to her and never let it go. "Her father might intercede?"

"A slim bit of hope, aye. The fae follow their own whims and love nothing more than their intrigues, deceptions and plots within plots. If Morrigan was not clever enough to get around their laws somehow, King Lir might become involved. That doesn't mean Lir will restore Fáelán to our time. He may put him back in the third century, where he belongs. In which case, things would go on for Fáelán as they were originally meant to, and we'd likely lose any knowledge of ever having known him at all."

"I don't want to lose my memories of Fáelán," she said, her voice hitching. "I don't want to lose him." She shut her eyes. "Right now we don't know what's going on, or where he is. Will you call me if you hear from him?"

"Of course."

"Great. I have to go. I'll let you know if I hear anything. I'm not . . . I can't sit here and do nothing. I'm going to look for some way to help him while I still can." *While I still remember him.*

By the time she ended the call, tears were spilling down her cheeks. She headed downstairs and sank onto the couch. Regan hit the picture icon on her phone and scrolled through the many pictures she'd taken of Fáelán with his family, and those she'd taken of the two of them together. Finding the pictures still there reassured her. It meant he hadn't been returned to the third century, and there was still time for her to do something. What that something might be, she had no idea.

Regan leaned back and closed her eyes again. She needed a few minutes to calm down, and then she'd call her sisters. With their abilities combined, they might be able to help her at least locate where Morrigan held Fáelán. He was her destiny, and she'd been drawn to Ireland to help him, hadn't she? God, she hoped so.

Chapter Nine

It was already late afternoon, and Regan had hardly moved from the couch since her phone call with Jim. She still hadn't pulled herself together enough to come up with any kind of rescue plan for Fáelán. She still hoped it was all a mistake, and he'd walk through the front door any minute.

A jarring ring startled her out of her lethargy. She grabbed her phone from the coffee table, checked the ID and had to swallow a few times before she could answer. "Hey, Meredith. I was just about to call you."

"Rae, what's going on?" Meredith asked. "Grayce and I are both picking up on your distress, and we were supposed to be having our Google Hangout date with you and Fáelán now. We got worried."

Since the day Fáelán had appeared at her door, Regan had been texting photos to her sisters and keeping them up-to-date, and today she'd arranged for them to meet. "Oh, God. He's gone, Meredith. Fáelán is gone."

"What do you mean he's gone? Start from the beginning. Wait. I'm going to put my phone on speaker, so Grayce can be part of this conversation."

Regan cradled the phone against her ear. "OK. So." Tears clogged her throat and filled her eyes. "Just a sec."

"Take your time," Grayce said, her tone gentle.

Regan grabbed a few tissues from the box on the coffee table and blew her nose. "Last night, Fáelán told me he loves me, and . . . and this morning he was gone—and I mean really gone. His clothes, phone and car are still here, but I can sense he's no longer in this world. I talked to his nephew. Jim thinks Morrigan discovered her curse was about to end, and she stole him back to the void."

"Wait," Grayce said. "I thought he had five days of freedom. This is only day four, right?"

"It is, but . . . obviously that doesn't matter." Regan grabbed another tissue and swiped at the tears on her cheeks. "Besides, the curse doesn't specify a number of days. I need you two here. Are you close to a computer, so we can book your flight?"

"Yeah. Hold on," Meredith said.

While her sister went for her laptop, Regan strode over to the kitchen table and grabbed her purse from the chair. She pulled out her wallet and returned to the couch, where her own computer sat on the table in front of her. "I don't suppose you've had any visions that might lead me to Fáelán, have you, Grayce?"

"No, but if something comes to me, I'll call you immediately."

"Please do, or maybe when we're together, we can join forces and make something happen," Regan said, wishing it was true. Could they combine their abilities in a situation like this? They weren't facing a spirit needing to be exorcised here. This was completely out of the realm of their prior experience.

The next twenty minutes were spent arranging their flight to Ireland. After that, Regan went over every detail of her last evening with Fáelán. "He said he'd rather remain cursed for all eternity than put me in harm's way, because my safety is more important to him than his freedom." She wiped her nose again. "It could be Morrigan took him at his word, and zap, he's her prisoner again. Only now it's forever." A fresh tear slid down her cheek.

"Not only is he gorgeous, but he has a true Celtic heart." Grayce sighed. "He's a romantic."

"Yeah, well," Regan croaked. "I wish he'd been a bit less romantic and a lot less dramatic. Then maybe he'd s-still be—"

"We'll be there Monday morning," Meredith assured her. "Hang in there."

"Do I have a choice? Go. Pack. Call me when you land, and I'll pick you up at the Dublin Airport." They said their goodbyes, and ended the call. Once again, the silence closed in around her, and Regan turned on the TV. Background noise was better than emptiness.

Regan forced herself to make something to eat, and then she cleaned up and moved back to the couch and her computer. How did one defeat a faerie? She typed it into the search bar, surprised when things actually came up. She read the first entry. "To kill a faerie, you must trap it in a microwave oven." Regan glanced at the compact appliance on her kitchen counter. "Yeah, I don't think so."

She scrolled down to the next link. "They can be trapped or harmed by iron," she read, "but killed only by weapons of their own making." *Great.* How could she get her hands on a fae weapon? Even if she did, she'd have no clue how to wield such a thing. Besides, the faerie on the receiving end would surely have a weapon as well. Chances were good it would know how to fight, while she did not. All those years she'd studied yoga, chanted om and namaste she should've spent learning martial arts. This was getting her nowhere.

She and Fáelán had planned to visit the Hill of Tara today. She brought up the park's website and glanced at the time. It was already 7:00 p.m., and Tara closed at 6:00. She could trespass like she had at Newgrange, but it was pouring rain, and she was still too emotionally wrecked to function well enough to concentrate. The site opened at ten o'clock tomorrow, which was Friday. She'd go to bed early and start the day searching for magic, information and a faerie weapon. Yep. Things looked entirely hopeless.

Friday proved to be the clearest day she'd encountered since arriving in Ireland, which made missing Fáelán all that much worse. He should be with her now, spouting historical facts about the Hill of Tara. Missing him hurt like hell, and she wanted him back, dammit.

Regan pulled in to the car park at Tara, relieved to see there were only two other cars present. That would change. Soon the tour buses from Dublin would arrive, and the tourist attraction would be swarming.

With everything she'd learned about Tara, a fragile hope had taken root. When the wizard Amergin had defeated the Tuatha Dé Danann, he'd banished the fae to dwell beneath this very hill. There had to be a reason why the wizard had chosen this spot. Fáelán's theories about metaphors embedded into Irish mythology made sense, and Tara had long been recognized as the center of all things mystical to the ancient Celts who'd settled here.

Regan climbed out of her car and followed the path to the small parish church that had been converted into a visitor center. Already her pulse raced in response to the energy and mystical power radiating from deep within the land, and she wasn't anywhere near the top yet. She paid the admission fee and left the visitor center.

The path leading to the top of Tara ran behind the church and led her past a statue of Saint Patrick, the church's patron saint. Pausing, she stared out over the rolling landscape spread out under the saint's benevolent granite gaze. She needed a minute. Strong magic permeated the site all right, along with lines of energy triangulating the area. *Ley lines?*

Never before had she experienced anything like this, and her fragile hope grew by leaps and bounds. She continued along the path to the summit, drawn by those invisible threads of power. *Trust in your abilities.*

Regan took in a long, slow breath, released it, and opened herself to the energy coming at her from all directions. This time it worked, and she trembled from the onslaught. Closing her eyes, she tried to separate the threads crossing through her. Would one of them lead her to answers? How would she know? She opened her eyes and started walking. As she grew closer to the top of the hill, the threads of power increased in strength and exerted a pull.

A frisson of fear traced through her. She was caught in a spider's web of magic as ancient as the earth itself. Whatever this was, she was being drawn in a specific direction, held by a current she wasn't sure she could escape. Did she want to escape? Not if the pull led her to Fáelán. She came to a stop in front of a mound, a miniature passage tomb with stones guarding the entrance.

These stones bore the same ancient designs etched into the slab of rock guarding Newgrange's entrance. Every cell in her body tingled, and the hair on her arms and at the back of her neck stood on end. She even had goose bumps on the calves of her legs.

The Mound of the Hostages, she read on the plaque before her, Duma na nGiall, dating back to 3000 BC, built of boulders and covered with earth. Exactly like Newgrange and more than likely built by the same ancient inhabitants. Her heart tattooed against her ribs. This had to be the way into other dimensions and the reason Amergin had chosen this place to banish the fae from the earthly realm.

The Mound of Hostages sat atop the pinnacle of Tara, the place where fae magic and the ley lines of earth's energy intersected and combined. Those powers and energy combining must form a vortex of some kind, and she'd find it.

An iron gate blocked the entrance into the mound. She needed to find a way around the barrier. Circling the mound, she searched for any sign of a magical door. What was she thinking? Even if she did find a way in, then what? Fáelán had said he focused his will on a particular location and there he'd go. But he had to have already been to the place before the process worked. How many planes of existence were there? Her knees went a little weak, and she trembled. How the hell would she find one Fiann in a haystack of dimensions?

She returned to the entrance and read more of the plaque. Humans had been cremated here—was that code for sacrificed?—yet she didn't sense a single ghost, only currents of energy, power and magic, a cosmic layer cake of things she knew nothing about and couldn't hope to control.

A group of tourists were coming up the hill and heading toward the mound. Regan forced herself to move toward the Stone of Destiny, Lia Fáil. She could almost see the ley lines connecting the mound and the stone. The path was that electrified, and once again she was being drawn in a specific direction. Trusting her intuition, she followed the current, and came to a stop within reach of Lia Fáil. Had this stone really made noise when the rightful kings of Ireland touched its cold surface? Judging by the waves of energy, the vibrations, she believed it was possible.

She'd read that the stone had been brought to Tara by the Tuatha Dé Danann themselves. It had to be the key that would unlock the door to the fae realm. All the energy, power and magic converged here between the mound and the stone, as if this piece of rock was the conduit for everything.

An overwhelming compulsion to touch the stone gripped her. She struggled against the urge. *Not now.* Not until her sisters were with her, and they'd figured out where Fáelán was and how she might help him. She fisted her hands and held them at her sides. She wanted to step back but couldn't. Her heart climbed to her throat, and a fine sheen of sweat covered her face and the back of her neck. Regan tried like hell to move away, but the current held her fast. Even scarier, the harder she resisted, the stronger the compulsion to touch the stone grew.

Her hand came up, as if on a string pulled by someone else. Try as she might, she couldn't force it back down, and she watched in horror as her fingers inched closer and closer to the stone. Sweat dripped down her temples, and she couldn't breathe.

Her hand connected with the stone. Shock waves nearly knocked her on her ass. The stone was not cold at all, but warm and pulsing with life. She was caught up in a whoosh of movement, and the world flew by in a rush of color. Dizzy and disoriented, she closed her eyes. As quickly as it began, the sensations ceased, and she came to a sudden stop. Regan toppled forward, hitting her shin against something hard. Somehow she managed to stay upright.

Frozen to the spot, afraid to open her eyes, Regan assessed her surroundings. The smell of impending rain filled her nostrils, and the air around her held an unnatural chill. Regan shivered and wrapped her arms around herself. "Oh, great. A ghost."

"Do not fear." A soft, feminine voice surrounded her, bringing warmth and a sense of peace. Regan cracked an eyelid to take a peek and gasped. She'd landed inside her town house in Howth, and her shin had connected with the coffee table in the living room. "OK. I heard the laughter. You may as well show yourself."

A young woman appeared out of thin air. She wore a long, flowing gown of pale green, like something found in one of those ancient tapestries from the Dark Ages. Her hair, a shiny light blonde with a hint of red, hung to her waist. Lithe, delicate and so beautiful it hurt to look at her, the being glided closer—did her feet even touch the ground?—and again the sense of peace washed through Regan.

She didn't trust the sense of peace or the warmth. Nothing about this creature struck her as natural, and her nearness set off Regan's fight-or-flight instinct. Fear churned through her. This creature had to be fae. "Morrigan."

"No! Oh no." The woman shook her head and waved her hand. "My name is Boann. I am Morrigan's daughter." Her neon-blue eyes met Regan's. "And Fáelán is my sire."

What? "I need to sit down," Regan muttered.

"Please do."

How she managed to get herself around to the couch, she had no idea, but she sank onto the cushions, leaned over and put her head between her knees.

"I mean you no harm," Boann said, her voice soothing and altogether otherworldly.

Prickles of unease crept up her spine. Regan forced herself back to sitting upright. Her mind had completely short-circuited. The Hill of Tara's force, the way she'd been brought here, and especially the ethereal creature before her . . . it was all too much, too big and impossible to take in. Thoughts and feelings crashed together, until she couldn't think straight. Regan slid her sweaty hands down her jeans and swallowed against the dryness in her mouth and throat. "What do you want?"

"To help you . . . and my sire."

"Fáelán never mentioned he had a daughter." That too caused a swirl of conflicting feelings. Why had he kept that from her?

"He has no notion I exist."

"Ahh . . ." Regan frowned. "I can't . . . I'm having trouble . . . processing."

"Take a moment to gather your wits, so that we might speak." Boann glided toward the kitchen. "I'll make tea."

Hysteria bubbled through Regan, bursting forth in a bark of laughter. "*You're* going to make tea? Like . . . like that's going to make all of this seem . . . normal?"

"Would you prefer coffee?"

"I'd prefer a Xanax, if you really want to know the truth." She plowed her shaky fingers through her hair.

"That I cannot give you. Would you prefer I bespell you into a calmer state?"

"No! Oh, God, no." She leaned back, closed her eyes and rubbed her temples. "Tea would be great. Chamomile." Regan focused on the ordinary sounds of an extraordinary being making tea in her kitchen—Fáelán and Morrigan's daughter no less, half Tuatha Dé Danann, half human.

"Does your mother know you're here?" She snorted. Even to her, the question sounded ridiculous. Boann wasn't some teenager who'd snuck out of the house to party with friends.

Regan opened her eyes again as Boann set a teapot and two mugs on the coffee table. Then she kind of floated over to the chair across from Regan and sat down.

Regan's ability to think was coming back to her in small increments. To buy time to recover, she poured tea into the mugs. Lifting hers, she sipped while stealing peeks at the fae princess. Boann had Fáelán's mouth and chin, and her fine, straight nose was a smaller version of his. Morrigan had kept Fáelán's daughter from him, and knowing him as she did, Regan ached for the new hurt this would cause him when he found out.

Boann reached for the second mug. She leaned back in the chair and wrapped both hands around the ceramic cup. "To answer your question, nay, my mother does not know I am here, and she must not learn of it. I have masked my whereabouts from her."

She canted her head and scrutinized Regan. "Normally, I would not involve myself in the affairs of mortals, but because of the innocent new life you carry, I find I must intercede."

"What are you talking about?" Oh, and just when she'd recovered her capacity to think straight, there it went again.

"New life has quickened within your womb. You and Fáelán have conceived, and I—"

"You can't possibly know that." She stiffened, and hot tea spilled onto her lap. "I haven't missed . . . Fáelán and I only spent a few days together." She couldn't be pregnant. Could she? They'd had unprotected sex once. She hadn't actually counted days on her calendar, but she'd been pretty sure she'd been in the safe zone. Oh, God, was it true? *Am I ready to be a mother?* Morrigan lied, why wouldn't her daughter do the same? "I don't think so, and anyway, it's too soon to know."

"Nay, 'tis not too soon." A pitying look flitted across Boann's features. "The moment conception takes place, a new and unique ripple enters the astral plane. Mortals have lost the ability to detect such things, but at one time, you too would've known the very instant a new life began within you."

"I need a minute." She couldn't deal with this additional stressor. Regan's hands were shaking. She set the tea on the table and lowered her head between her knees again.

"I understand. While you gather yourself together, I'll explain a little about what is going on. My grandsire King Lir is aware something is amiss with Morrigan. Our actions send energy trails through the astral plane, and when we do wrong, the vibrations alter. Our energy patterns are as unique to us as fingerprints are to your kind. 'Tis how we identify ourselves and others."

So what Jim had told her was true. "How can you help, and why would you want to? Why did Morrigan keep you a secret?" Regan asked, coming back up to face the faerie. Could she trust her, or was Boann here to lure her into danger? This might be part of Morrigan's plot to test Fáelán–or to torture him.

The smell of rain intensified, and Boann's eyes took on a definite glow. "'Tis a long story, but one you must hear, for I am at the crux of my sire's curse, and oft my mother and I quarreled over his fate."

Her voice carried a deep sadness, and Regan didn't doubt the truth of her words. Her defenses lowered the tiniest bit.

"When a Tuatha Dé Danann woman becomes pregnant, she bonds irrevocably with the sire of her babe. Unbeknownst to Fáelán, I was conceived during his brief tryst with my mother. 'Tis why she became obsessed with him, and why she remains so today. When Fáelán rejected her, Mother's obsession and disappointment turned to rage. She set out to punish him for his impertinence, and she kept me a secret from him out of wounded pride and spite."

"But . . . Morrigan deceived him from the start. None of what happened can be laid at his feet."

"Aye." Boann sighed. "Morrigan's wishes were thwarted by a mere mortal. To her, that is all that matters."

"Why did you wait until now to help him?" None of this made sense to her. "Couldn't you have ended his curse yourself?"

"Nay. 'Tis not possible for any of us to end a curse or an enchantment laid by another. Otherwise I would've done so eons ago. Even so, 'twas I who returned his island to him after my mother abandoned him to the mist."

Again Regan sensed a deep sadness within Boann. "I'm sorry you never got to know Fáelán. He's . . ." Her eyes filled. "He's funny, smart, honorable and—"

"Oh, I have come to know him a little, though he's been unaware." A wistful smile played across Boann's features, and her eyes ceased glowing, softening to a clear blue. "Despite my mother's edict that I not reveal myself to him, I oft posed as a servant and brought him his meals. I also watched him through a scrying bowl." Her smile grew. "'Twas amusing, seeing him pretend to hunt and fish, and to watch him train so intensely, as if he fought a real foe instead of a tree. He's quite determined. My sire's mind is exceptionally strong for a mortal."

Her heart broke for Boann, who obviously longed for a relationship with her dad. Regan propped her elbows on her knees and rested her forehead on her hands. The mother of all headaches throbbed painfully at the back of her skull, and she really, really wanted to crawl into bed and sleep for a week. *Rescue Fáelán first, and then you can sleep all you want.* "So, if you can't end his curse, how do you propose to help?"

"There was naught I could do until the terms of my sire's release came to pass, and Morrigan reneged on her oath, which is against our laws. 'Twas wrong of my mother to interfere with a mortal, and her deceitfulness in masking her true identity makes her actions all the worse. That she hid all of this from my grandsire will go against her."

"So, your king doesn't know you're part human?" Regan asked, her head still in her hands. "That seems—"

"Of course he knows, but that minor transgression was ignored. To conceive at all has become rare for our kind. Because of me, my grandsire was willing to overlook Morrigan's involvement with a mortal. Morrigan hid all else from King Lir. I am bound by laws of kinship, and because of that binding, I could not bring any of this to my grandsire's attention. Fáelán is not one of us; the fae court would not view Morrigan's keeping me from him as a wrong done against me. On the contrary, they would view it as appropriate. 'Tis you who must plead your case to my grandsire. You must go to King Lir's court."

"Me?" Regan squeaked.

"Aye, for 'tis you, my sire and your unborn child who have been grievously wronged by Morrigan's machinations. My mother has broken more than one of the covenants between our kind and yours, which gives you the right to seek redress." Boann lifted her chin, and the gesture gave her such a striking resemblance to Fáelán that Regan's breath hitched.

"As to my motives," Boann continued. "I grew up without my sire. He was forbidden to me, and I from him. I will not allow my half sibling to suffer as I have."

How could Boann's mother be so cruel? A lump rose to her throat, followed by a rush of anger. If what Boann had told her was true, Regan's child might also suffer the same fate because of Morrigan. Not if she could help it, dammit. "I hope we have the chance to get to know each other better once all of this is behind us," Regan said, pushing herself to standing.

"I hope so as well." Boann rose from her chair.

"So, what do we need to do now?"

"I will take you to Prince Mananán, my uncle. He has a magical boat, *Ocean Sweeper*, which will transport you to King Lir's kingdom, and there you must present your case at his court."

Panic sent her pulse pounding. How could she, a mere human, face a faerie king? "Will you come with me?"

"Only as far as I am able. Your cause will be better served if I return home as if naught out of my ordinary routine has occurred. There I can distract my mother and hide your actions, so you will have the chance to present yourself to King Lir."

Another wave of panic swamped her as new worries flared, clamoring for attention. "If I do manage to reach your grandfather's court, how will I get back? What if my presence in the faerie realm is unwelcome? What if your mother somehow catches wind of this?" By the time she'd voiced her newest fears, more surged to the front of the line. So many things could go wrong.

"I cannot offer you any assurances, Regan. I wish I could. I'll do my best to keep my mother's attention away from you."

"Do your best, because I'm completely defenseless against your mother. Though I can feel magic all around me, I can't use it in any practical way. I've tried to . . . to somehow tap into the power I sensed at Newgrange, and again at Tara. I failed at Newgrange, and at Tara the magic controlled me, rather than the other way around."

"'Twas I who took you from Tara." Boann moved to one of the windows and thrust her hand into a beam of sunlight. "You believe magic is outside of you, that it is something to be caught in a glass jar like you humans do with fireflies? Come," she commanded. "Watch."

Regan moved closer. Was it her imagination, or were the dust motes gravitating toward Boann's palm?

"Magic exists within all sentient beings. It is innate to the Tuatha, and to humans."

Sure enough, the dust began to coalesce, becoming more and more dense by the second. Regan blinked, rubbed her eyes and looked again.

"Do you really think you could perceive magic's presence if you didn't already possess its essence within yourself?" Boann asked, keeping her gaze fixed upon the emerging shape.

"Hmm." That hadn't occurred to her, but it made sense.

The faerie held out her hand and presented her with the finished product, sliding it from her palm to Regan's. Regan studied the shape, the long ears laid back against the fluffy form, its tiny feet peeking out under its chest. "A dust bunny." She shook her head. "Cute, but not much help against an angry faerie princess. I can't imagine Morrigan running away in terror from"—she lifted the bunny—"this mighty beast."

Boann chuckled, and the sound splintered apart, appearing throughout the room as tiny bits of light in rainbow colors. "I meant it only as a demonstration. You possess magic, Regan. Your mistake was to look for it from without rather than within. Magic is everywhere, and using it is simply a matter of exerting your will."

"Can you teach me?"

"Alas, there is no time."

Regan's desperate hope dissolved, and at the same time, the dust bunny in her hand fell apart and drifted to the floor.

"See?" Boann pointed to the pile of dust. "*You* did that."

"Not consciously." She swiped the remnants of dust from her hands.

"Aye, well . . ." The faerie glided to the door. "Mayhap your abilities will be greatly enhanced whilst you are in the fae realm."

"I have a few things to do, and a few things to gather before I go anywhere." She grabbed her phone and texted her sisters that she might not be there when they arrived. If she didn't answer her cell phone, they were to take a cab to her town house, and she told them where to find a key she'd hidden outside her front door. "I'll be ready in fifteen minutes."

It took her ten minutes to put everything in place. Regan stuffed her phone into her day pack, right next to the police-grade stun gun her parents had insisted she take with her when traveling alone. She tossed in a couple of protein bars and two bottles of water, then zipped her bag shut and slung it over her shoulder and across her chest. Squaring her shoulders, she faced Boann. "OK. I'm ready." What the hell was she doing? Facing impossible odds against any chance of success was insane, yet when Boann reached out her hand, Regan took it. The crazy rush and whoosh took them away.

Chapter Ten

No matter how far or how fast Fáelán ran, Morrigan's accursed window into the earthly realm kept pace beside him. He refused to look, lest he be drawn in by what he might see. His lungs heaved, and sweat dripped from his bare skin to combine with the gray mist of the void. Though his muscles burned and cried for mercy, he kept moving.

Options were few as to how to spend his time. He'd chosen to expend his energy through physical exertion, working his body until exhaustion dulled the cutting edge of his pain. 'Twas the only way he knew to stay sane. Only in sleep and dreaming could he be free, and then he dreamed of a life with Regan.

Shortly after his confrontation with Morrigan, he'd inadvertently caught a glimpse of Regan crying herself sick whilst sitting on the couch in her town house. That brief look had set off an unbearable inferno of grief and rage, and he'd quickly learned to be more careful. He'd tried to will himself elsewhere, but Morrigan had put a stop to his wandering. He'd even tried to go through the window itself, to no avail. Fáelán's entire life had been reduced to two objectives: remain sane, and thwart Morrigan in every way possible.

Coming to a stop, he leaned over and gasped for air. His limbs shook with fatigue, and he sank to the ground. Now that he'd completed the physical exercise, he began the mental drilling. Fáelán brought to mind all the training he'd received in Fionn's army. He relived every battle he'd fought, studying his opponents' moves, countermoves, feints, parries, grapples and holds. With no weapons to hand, or sparring partners, all he had were his memories to help him keep his skills sharp. Soon fatigue overtook him, and he dozed.

Someone's presence woke him, and he once again found food and drink had been left beside him, though whoever had brought it was gone. Morrigan no longer risked having a servant bring his meals to him whilst he was awake. Did she fear he'd somehow convince one of the fae servants to help him? If so, was that not proof of her guilt, and that she had indeed broken her oath? That might lead King Lir to intercede. Then again, it might not.

Even if King Lir chose not to act, over time Morrigan's guard would slip, and Fáelán would be ready. He'd catch one of her servants bringing his food, and he'd beg for their aid. Aye, he'd throw himself at their feet if need be. All he had to do was feign sleep and wait—not now while Morrigan would still be vigilant, but in time.

Sighing, he sat up and drew the tray to him. Gods, he was tempted to look through the fecking portal, if only to assure himself Regan was safe. Surely she'd realized by now he hadn't left her by choice. He prayed she'd do naught to provoke Morrigan. His skin crawled at the thought of Regan being anywhere near Morrigan or any other of the Tuatha.

"Regan will forget about me, and she'll go on with her life, Morrigan," he shouted, his voice still hoarse from his last bout of shouting. "I'll not put on a show for ye."

"Perhaps, but you will not forget her. Think you I cannot feel your suffering even now? Seeing you so utterly defeated gladdens my heart."

Though he sensed she was nowhere near, Morrigan's words came to him through the mist from all directions. He let loose a string of curses.

"*Speaking of your mortal lover, I've a bit of news that might be of interest to you. Do you wish to hear what I have to share?*"

Ever so casually, he lifted the water goblet and took a drink, refusing to give her the satisfaction of a response.

"*Nay? Well, I shall share it regardless. Regan is with child, a child you will never know and who will never know you.*"

His grip tightened around the goblet. Was it possible his and Regan's love had borne fruit? Aye, 'twas possible, but Morrigan was deceit incarnate, and he and Regan had only forgone protection once in the brief span of days he'd dwelt in the earthly realm. "Ye lie," he shouted into the mist.

"*Do I? I've provided you with the means by which you may see the truth for yourself. Now you shall also watch your child age and die before your eyes.*"

He couldn't get any air into his lungs, and his insides shattered into a million pieces. Fáelán squeezed his eyes shut, lest a single tear escape. Concentrating his will, employing all his self-discipline, he began reciting the saga of ancient Irish history aloud, just as he'd done before Fionn so many centuries ago. If he erred, he'd stop, go back to the beginning and start over.

Morrigan's laughter reverberated around him. Fáelán continued with his recitation, moderating his tone and volume, giving no outward sign that he was dying inside.

Regan's hand was still held in Boann's as the two of them came to a stop. "Where are we?" she whispered into the pitch blackness surrounding them. Wherever this was, it held the same warm, pulsing energy as Lia Fáil and smelled of earth. A still, humid warmth enveloped her.

"Beneath Tara."

They were in a cavern under a mountain of dirt and in complete darkness. That explained the unease traipsing down her spine. "So I was right, and the Hill of Tara *is* a gateway into other dimensions."

"'Tis but one of many thoroughfares between the realms." A tiny orb of light appeared above Boann's palm. "Even in the darkest places, light and heat can be drawn forth. Hold out your hand, Regan."

She did, relieved by the light Boann had created. She'd expected Boann to give her the glowing sphere, like she had with the dust bunny, but she didn't.

"Concentrate upon the smallest bits of . . . I believe you would call them leptons or neutrinos."

"What would you call them?" Regan tried to imagine the plastic models of atoms she'd studied in high school.

"Hmm. It matters not, for I wish to speak of what flows between. In the language of the fae, what flows around the smallest particles of matter translates into something like 'life force,' or 'life essence,' and that is what you must seek." The orb in her hand cast a silvery light into the domed cavern of earth and stone. "I fear it doesn't translate well at all in terms you might understand. Nothing in the universe is still or empty, and the friction from that constant movement creates energy that can be harnessed."

No matter how hard she thought about atoms moving and what might be between them, nothing appeared in her palm. "By you— not me."

"You can reach for it as well," Boann chided. "Stop talking, and allow yourself to—ah, how to explain? You must be an observer, separate from your thinking self, with nothing on your mind except the essence of light and life."

"Trancelike?"

"Exactly. In that state, you can draw the energy and bend it to your will."

"You said we didn't have time for a magic lesson. Shouldn't we be finding your uncle?" *Or rescuing Fáelán from an eternity of hell?* Her stomach lurched at the thought of how he must be suffering right now.

"Aye, but we are about to enter my grandsire's kingdom, and I cannot take the journey with you to the end. I don't want to leave you without your having at least the means to illuminate your way."

"All right." She drew in a long breath and adjusted her posture. "I'm guessing the state of being is like meditation?"

"Aye."

Regan stared at her palm, centered herself and stilled her thoughts. Stepping back from her conscious mind, she became an observer. Engulfed within the thrum and pulse of Tara, her heartbeat synched with the hill's rhythm, and the essence of life Boann spoke of not only surrounded her but flowed through her. Or had it always been there, and she just now became aware of it? Regan's breathing slowed, and she merged with the flow of energy. *Come to me.*

She pictured the smallest particles of matter in a river of something she had no name for. She imagined the tiny bits vibrating and colliding, generating energy. She focused on the space above her palm and willed the light to her. A tiny spark appeared and hovered above her hand. "I did it!" The spark disappeared. "Almost."

Boann laughed. "Did I not tell you? You lost your concentration in your excitement, but at least now you know how it's done. Even in the worst places, you can draw forth light and warmth to you. Doing so will come easier with practice."

The faerie drew a rune in the air, and a door-size portion of the cavern wall shimmered. "Follow me." She stepped through and disappeared.

Fear of being left alone under tons and tons of earth propelled her forward, and Regan followed. Passing through the shimmer was no different than walking through an open door, and she found herself in a sunlit meadow with soft grass beneath her feet. A variety of colorful wildflowers waved in a soft summer breeze, and the air held a sweetness and purity unlike anything she'd ever encountered anywhere. The sky was a pale shade of blue with wisps of pink and gray clouds streaking the horizon. Awestruck, she gazed around her.

Boann beckoned to her from a path leading up the hill. "Come, my uncle's keep is just beyond this rise."

Regan hurried to catch up. "I thought this was the void. It's so beautiful here, and peaceful. Is all of your world like this?"

"More or less."

"It's not at all like I imagined the void would be."

"Mmm. 'Tis not so very different from the earthly realm, aye? You have continents surrounded by vast oceans. We have continents surrounded by mist."

"I guess. Fáelán told me the Tuatha Dé Danann project magic onto the void to create whatever environment you want, while ours just exists the way it is with or without us. Is that true?"

"'Tis complicated. We have our own society, culture and a ruling hierarchy. We are monarchal, and our world is made up of several kingdoms, with a high king over all. Though those of the aristocracy may create whatever homes they wish, our world is created by the consensus of our monarchs and a council of aristocracy."

She stopped and turned to Regan. "There are certain protocols you must follow in dealing with my uncle. Mananán is a master illusionist and a trickster. He's very powerful. You must not look directly into his eyes, even though he might command you to do so."

"All right. I won't look him in the eyes." Her heart pounded. It was easy to think of Boann as half human, but Regan was about to come face-to-face with a completely nonhuman demigod, who might not welcome her presence. "What would happen if I did look him in the eyes?"

"He would enchant you, and you would be powerless to refuse any request he might make. Trust me in this, should you come under my uncle's thrall, he will make the most outrageous requests. Be respectful and humble, but never forget who and what he is, a direct descendent of the goddess Danu."

"Thank you for the warning."

"Do *not* look into his eyes, Regan." She started up the hill again.

"I won't." She frowned. "Can I look at his feet?"

"Best keep your eyes upon your own."

"Can you look at him?"

"Of course. He's my uncle. Because of our blood tie, he cannot enchant me. For our kind, to transgress the bonds of kinship in that manner would be a punishable offense, even for a prince."

They reached the top of the hill, and Regan surveyed the valley below. A pastoral green meadow dotted with grazing sheep and cattle surrounded a medieval-style castle with a village spread along the outer wall. Beyond the village, fields had been planted with ordinary crops, and grapevines covered a terraced hill. Her gaze returned to the castle, which had turrets, ramparts, a moat and a drawbridge leading to a barbican and an outer bailey. "Your uncle farms and raises sheep?"

Boann flashed her a wry look. "Aye, and beeves, chickens and pigs. We have all manner of animals within our realm, including horses and game animals. We love to hunt. Our world is as real as yours, Regan. Do humans not shape the environment to their will? You humans build dams, blast through mountains to make roads. You too change the landscape and the environment through your actions and your will. Is this not so?"

"I suppose it is." She frowned, thinking about the ways in which humankind impacted and altered their world. "But . . . Fáelán said he was the only living thing on his island, and there weren't any fish in the lake."

"'Twas all I could do to give him back the illusion of the island, and I didn't push any further than I dared." Boann began walking toward the castle. "I shall stretch the truth a bit whilst pleading for Mananán's help. Pay no heed."

Her nerves taut, Regan nodded and followed Boann to the drawbridge. She hadn't known what to expect when it came to fae dwellings, but she never would have guessed a fae prince would live as a medieval lord. Flowing waterfalls, moss-covered knolls and open airy pavilions maybe, but a castle, village and farming? She shook her head.

They crossed the drawbridge and entered an outer bailey teeming with activity. People dressed in medieval peasant garb went about their business in the midst of a marketplace of open booths and wagons. The ground was covered in cobblestones, with the occasional evidence of horses having passed through. Again, not what she'd imagined for magical demigods. She took it all in, the smells of roasting meat, fresh bread being baked, the wares being offered and the faeries, who were all impossibly beautiful, pale and blue-eyed.

The crowd bowed and parted to make way for Boann to pass, some offering respectful greetings. Regan garnered a few curious looks but no alarm. "No one seems too surprised or concerned about my presence."

"All sensed your entry into Summerland, which is what we call our world. None have any reason for concern. We are the Tuatha Dé Danann." She glanced at Regan, her expression radiating superiority. "You pose no threat."

Regan's gut twisted, and despite the illusion of ordinary life all around her, her complete powerlessness and vulnerability among the fae hit home. They continued on through the nearly deserted inner baily. The door to the castle opened at their approach, and Regan lowered her gaze to the ground in front of her.

"'Tis only a servant," Boann assured her, taking her by the arm.

"I'm not taking any chances." She had her Fiann to rescue. She wasn't about to become ensnarled in any faerie's spell, even if he was a prince. They passed through the threshold, and Regan studied the wood plank floor beneath her feet.

"My dear Boann, how gracious of you to visit." A man's voice filled the entire hall. "I see you've brought a sweet morsel for my enjoyment. Is she meant as a gift?"

His voice held the timbre of deep seductive enchantment. Regan fought against the lure of being drawn in.

"Nay, Uncle. She is my sire's mate. Regan's plea for help reached me through the astral plane. I would not have involved myself but for the blood tie binding me to the babe she carries." Boann crossed the hall, drawing Regan with her. "A grave wrong has been committed against this woman and the innocent soul she bears. I have brought her to you, because I know you are her best hope for help."

"Ah, yes. Quite fecund, and delightful to the beholder." Mananán circled Regan, and his perusal moved over her in a very physical way, as if he touched her skin . . . only not with his hands but with his senses. "You've a beautiful aura about you, my lovely."

He stood in front of her now, and Regan's heart thumped wildly. Desperate to put some distance between her and the impact of Mananán's nearness, she closed her eyes and stood her ground. Wave after wave of his unmistakable sexual desire lapped over and through her. He took her hand, and an electric tingle arced through every single nerve in her body.

"Welcome to my home, Regan. Ah . . . I sense you carry a trace of fae blood." He brought her hand to his lips and kissed her knuckles, lingering over the act.

She nearly came from the contact, and her entire being recoiled at the unwanted sensations. "I do, yes." She bowed her head and slipped her hand free, relieved when he didn't insist on keeping it in his grip.

Mananán chuckled softly. "Let us sit, and you can tell me all about the wrong that has befallen you. Perhaps I can be persuaded to offer my help."

"We would be grateful of any aid or advice you might offer, Uncle Mananán." Boann once again took Regan's arm, squeezing it for an instant.

"Yes, thank you, Your Highness," she murmured, hoping she'd addressed him correctly. Boann led her to a thronelike carved wooden chair, one of a grouping of four set before a hearth fire burning cheerfully away with no logs or fuel of any kind. At least the dancing flames gave her somewhere safe to look. Regan sank into the chair, careful to keep her gaze off the prince, fighting against the compulsion to peek. He had to be devastatingly gorgeous.

What harm can come from looking? Gaze into my eyes, my lovely, and I shall grant you pleasure beyond imagining. His voice whispered through her mind.

Regan shook her head, and continued to focus upon the flames. Did creating fire like this happen the same way Boann taught her to draw light and heat from the essence flowing between particles of matter? If so, how did the fae keep it going so effortlessly?

Mananán grunted. "You are strong for one of your kind, and I do so enjoy strong females of your species," he purred. "Tell me of your plight."

Regan dug in her mental heels, resisting the sexual pull Mananán exerted over her, and launched into Fáelán's story from the beginning of his encounter with Morrigan to his present imprisonment. "When Fáelán met Morrigan's conditions for breaking the curse, when he gave me his heart completely, your sister stole him from me. Morrigan broke her word, and now I am without my mate, and my child will be without a father." Her heart thudded painfully. She, Fáelán and their little one might never have the chance to be a family, and all because of one selfish, vindictive faerie. The unfairness of it all staggered her.

"It does sound like something my sister would do," Mananán said with another enchantment-infused laugh.

"Mother reneged on her vow to my sire, thereby breaking the covenant the wizard Amergin formed between the Tuatha Dé Danann and mortals," Boann added.

"Think you to lecture me on the covenant formed long before your birth?" Mananán asked, his tone mocking. "What has any of this to do with me?"

Good question. Why would he help? Regan glanced at Boann, hoping like hell her arsenal of faerie magic included the power of persuasion.

"Morrigan's breach gives Regan the right to bring her complaint to our king. She wishes for an audience at King Lir's court, but she lacks the means to get there. I am your blood kin, and her mate is my sire. On their behalf, I am asking you to grant Regan passage on *Ocean Sweeper*, and—"

"You wish me to lend my boat to send this . . . this *human* to Father's court?"

"Aye, and do not forget, she carries fae blood."

"But a trace. My dear niece, our kinship aside, what do I stand to gain?"

Once again, the prince's gaze, a physical, covetous pressure, centered upon Regan. She gritted her teeth and did her best to repel the seductive force. A new appreciation and understanding dawned for what Fáelán had endured with Morrigan. *Please let there be a future for me and Fáelán, and I'll apologize for doubting him every day for the rest of my life.* She placed her hand protectively over her womb.

"I ask it as a personal favor, Uncle. It grieves me to think of my sire being tortured for all eternity. He has committed no wrong against Morrigan, and her treatment toward him is a cruel injustice."

"Hmph."

Silence stretched on for several moments, and Regan's hopes plummeted. "Please," she whispered.

"Perhaps we can come to an agreement. It has been too long since I took a mortal to my bed. Stay with me for a fortnight . . . nay, a month, and I shall escort you to King Lir's court myself and aid you in pleading your case."

"Uncle . . ."

Tears welled, and the more Regan thought about how these creatures had dealt with Fáelán, and the way this prince behaved toward her, the hotter her indignation burned. Mananán's seductive magic lost some of its power over her. "Look." She gripped the armrests of the chair. "I'm begging for your help. Morrigan has committed a crime. No argument there. You're a prince among your people. Aren't you honor bound to . . . to uphold the law? With all due respect, Your Highness, your suggestion is not only insulting, but it's another wrong heaped on top of the first. I won't stay with you, or . . . or—"

"Then I have no help to offer." His tone no longer held any trace of the seductiveness from before. "I doubt Father would be the least bit interested in one puny human caught in my sister's sticky web. Morrigan has managed to keep her pet a secret all these centuries, and—"

"And though I have pleaded with you repeatedly, you have done naught to ameliorate my sire's suffering. Or mine." Boann's voice took on a determined edge. "As I have oft said, my mother has denied me contact with my sire, and it grieves me deeply. Breaking her vow to Fáelán is not Mother's only unlawful transgression. She gave a mortal the Elixir of Life without his knowledge and without the sanction of the royal council."

"Again, none of this has aught to do with me."

"Except you knew of it and did naught to dissuade her. 'Twould pain me to cause strife between us, but if you will not grant Regan some sort of aid, so be it. Now that Fáelán has met the conditions for his freedom, I *will* find a way around our kinship bond to bring this to Lir's attention myself. Your complicity will not be looked upon favorably by our council or by our king. In fact, I shall see that Regan's case reaches our high king's court. 'Tis certain Dagda Mór will be displeased to say the least. Perhaps he'll banish you and Morrigan from Summerland for a century or two."

Boann rose from her chair and moved to stand before her uncle. "As our covenant decrees, Morrigan provided my sire with a way to free himself from the curse. Fáelán met the conditions to be released from the curse, and Mother reneged. 'Tis a case without defense, and a situation you have had knowledge of since its inception."

"Hmm."

Regan held her breath as another long silence stretched between the three of them.

"'Tis best that I not be involved at all—"

"Uncle . . ."

"*However*, there is a way in which all interests might be served without involving Dagda Mór, Lir or myself."

"What do you suggest?" Boann asked.

"What I've in mind would solve everything, including Morrigan's unlawful use of the Elixir of Life. Send this woman back through time. Have her interfere with the Fiann before the curse can be cast, thereby righting the wrong before ever it occurred."

"You can do that? Would you send me back to before he and Morrigan—"

"We cannot stop Morrigan from being with Fáelán. 'Tis strictly forbidden, but we can allow you to interfere with mortals such as my sire and Nóra. If you can keep Fáelán from his lover the night he was cursed, then—"

"But . . . but . . . Fáelán won't know me," Regan stammered. "If I manage to prevent the curse from happening, then he and I will never have met, and . . . he won't . . . We won't have . . ." He wouldn't know her at all, much less love her. She'd no longer carry their baby.

Her heart breaking, she wrapped her arms around her midriff. "Fáelán and I won't be able to communicate well enough for me to convince him. I'm sure ancient Irish is much different from the modern-day version. Why would he listen to a complete stranger, even if he could understand what I was saying?"

"Your understanding into the workings of time and the universe is astonishing in its paucity," Manánan said, his voice dripping with derision. "I find I no longer have any desire for you at all."

Fine by her. Regan's gaze flew to Boann. "What does he mean?"

"It means he's not going to try to seduce you into his bed anymore."

"Thank you, Boann. I got that. I meant the paucity of understanding part."

A corner of Boann's mouth turned up for the briefest moment. "Time is not linear, nor does it move in only one direction. Between past and present . . . there is no difference. Fáelán's existence in your perception of the present, his time with you, none of it can be erased whether you prevent him from being cursed or not."

"I don't understand."

"'Tis far too complex to explain at present. But before now, you believed in only one world, aye?" Boann arched a brow. "Yet you now stand in an altogether different reality, and there are so many more. You must simply accept what I say for now, and mayhap in the future we might have the chance to discuss this further."

"I'll try." *Many more worlds? Different realities?* How was any of this possible, including time travel, and yet here she was, considering going back through time. But then, she hadn't believed anything Fáelán had told her either, and look how *that* had turned out. "So, he might know me if I go to him?"

"That, I cannot say." Boann shook her head. "'Tis possible he'll recognize you on some subconscious level, and 'tis possible he'll understand your words whilst not knowing why."

"I'll keep my baby?" she asked, her voice shaky.

"You will." Boann crossed the room and reached for Regan's hand. "Of that I am certain. Fáelán will be confused, and he will very likely be defensive and fearful. You must prepare yourself."

She nodded. Fáelán had been willing to sacrifice his freedom for her. The least she could do was try to undo Morrigan's curse for him. "Will I be able to return? Can I bring him with me to the twenty-first century?"

"As to the first, aye." Boann squeezed Regan's hand and let it go. "As to the latter, that will be up to him."

Could she convince Fáelán to listen? She'd do her damnedest, and she had the pictures on her phone to help him remember. "You can place me where I need to be, exactly when I need to be there?"

"I can, for I have oft watched that night unfold through scrying." Boann's expression clouded. "I sought a way to change my sire's fate, you see, but until Fáelán gave his heart, there was naught I could do."

"All right. If traveling back through time is the only way I can help him, then I'm willing." Regan straightened. "Let's go."

"Uncle, may I show her—"

"Do what you must. I've business to attend to." He rose abruptly. "You will both sup with me before you depart."

"Of course. Thank you for your hospitality," Boann said. "Come, Regan. We must form a plan, and to do that, you must see the events of that night."

Boann motioned to a woman hovering in a doorway. Speaking in what must be the language of the fae, she gave the servant instructions. Then Boann led Regan upstairs to an alcove on the second floor of the castle. In the center of the space stood a pedestal of marble, and a silver bowl covered in gold-chased runes etched on the outer surface sat on top. The bowl held clear water. Boann stirred the liquid with a finger and said something in her native language. "Let us watch together."

Her throat tightening, Regan stepped closer and peered inside. Images emerged, and the night of Fáelán's curse and Nóra's murder

161

unfolded before her like a silent movie. She closed her eyes during the lovemaking part, unreasonable jealousy burning through her. By the time they reached the end, tears streaked down her face. "Isn't it a crime for a faerie to commit murder?"

"Aye, and let us hope you are successful, for 'twill be two lives you save that night. Watch again, and this time, pay attention to every detail of the landscape. We will choose a safe place where I might leave you, and where you will find the way back."

"All right, but is there a way to skip the part where Fáelán and Nóra make love? Even though they're under the furs, and you can't see anything, it really . . . It's difficult for me to get past the feeling he's betraying me. Which makes no sense, I know, but—"

"Of course. Forgive me for being so thoughtless."

They went through the scene six more times before they'd worked everything out, including the sun's location on the western horizon. Regan needed to be able to judge the time when Morrigan would appear, so she could meet Fáelán on the path before he reached Nóra's cottage.

"'Tis time for us to rejoin my uncle. You did well with him, Regan." Boann walked out of the alcove. "He respects you for resisting, believe me."

"He still scares me."

"'Tis wise to remain so, for he is unpredictable."

Delicious smells wafted up the stairwell, and Regan's mouth watered. The woman from earlier met them halfway up the stairs, a bundle of clothing in her arms. "For you, my lady," she said, handing Regan the bundle. "Safe journey." She bowed slightly and turned back down the steps to disappear around a corner.

"Do you suppose she overheard the conversation we had with your uncle?"

"Without a doubt." Boann nodded. "And by now the tale will have reached everyone, and it is rippling through the astral plane on its way to the keepers of our laws and to our kings. It is the way of our people and will only aid you in your quest."

She and Boann joined Man03nán in the great hall, where he already sat at the head of a table set upon a dais. Regan held the garments close to her chest and kept her gaze on her own feet.

"Come. Sit. You are welcome at my board," Man04nán beckoned. "You've naught to fear from me, Regan. No harm will come to you should you deign to look upon me." His tone held none of the seductiveness from before.

Regan glanced at Boann.

"Aye, he means you no harm." She gestured toward a chair. "You may relax."

She gave in to the urge and met the fae prince's amused gaze. He was indeed gorgeous and extremely masculine. Still, he didn't appeal to her nearly as much as Fáelán did. She lifted her chin and smiled. "Thank you for your hospitality, Your Highness," she said, attempting a curtsy. "And thank you for not attempting to enthrall me anymore."

His glacier-blue eyes held warmth as he gazed back. "Don't think I am not sympathetic to your cause." He gestured toward the chairs. "Despite what my niece believes, I have had words with my sister about your Fiann. Oft I have pushed her to find another human lover, and perhaps to have another child. 'Twould rid her of her obsession with your mate." He sighed. "But she refused to heed my advice, and would not let him go."

"That I can understand. I'm not willing to give him up either." Placing the clothing on an empty chair, Regan took a seat, and a woman appeared at her side with a pitcher of wine. She put her hand over the goblet set before her place. "I don't think I should drink anything other than water."

"Uncle, I've had another thought."

"One that will prevail upon my generosity, I trow."

Regan watched as silent, beautiful fae servants placed plates in front of them and filled their goblets. Hers now held water. She took a drink and eyed the meal, roast beef with potatoes and vegetables. Her stomach rumbled.

"All of the Fianna will know of your magic swords, will they not?" Boann asked. "My sire will have heard the legends and seen the illustrations Fionn has in his possession?"

"I suppose." Mananán paused in cutting his beef. "Why?"

"'Twould help Regan convince my sire of the truth if she carried Little Fury, or perhaps The Retaliator. 'Twould be a ward against Mother as well."

He frowned, looking from her to Boann. "Will you give your personal guarantee of its return, Boann?"

"I will."

"The Retaliator, then. 'Tis far more impressive in appearance than Little Fury, and none can mistake the Tuatha runes etched upon the hilt. The Retaliator is fae forged, Regan, and you'll find it is not nearly so long or heavy as those of human origin of that era."

"I'm grateful for anything either of you believe will help." She dug into her meal, her mind spinning. Here she sat at a table, eating roast beef and potatoes while sitting beside a Tuatha Dé Danann prince and Fáelán's half-fae daughter. If everything went well, she might become Boann's stepmother. She glanced at the princess, wondering how she might take having a puny mortal for a stepmother.

If things turned out as she hoped. Given the time period, and his lack of memory of the future, Fáelán would likely see her as a threat. After all, he was a product of third-century thinking. She'd make him listen, dammit, and hopefully the pictures on her cell phone would loosen bits of memory from deep within his subconscious. "I'm going to need cord or rope," she said between mouthfuls.

"Whatever for?" Boann's eyes widened in question.

"You said Fáelán is likely to be defensive and afraid," she said with a shrug. "If he refuses to hear what I have to tell him, I'm going to knock him out with my stun gun and tie him up. When he comes to, I'll sit on his chest and force him to listen."

Mananán threw his head back and guffawed, and the sound bounced off the walls. "Ah, I am reminded why I desire mortal women. You humans are so very . . . unexpected. Unpredictable." He chuckled again. "I can see why Morrigan's pet lost his heart to you."

"He's not the only one who lost his heart." Memories of the morning they'd met flooded her mind. He was so funny, self-assured, sharp. She'd believed they were together only because she could see him. Now she knew better. They were meant to be.

The back of her throat got that pre-tears tightness. Even if he didn't return with her, she'd make sure he got to live his life fully, and she'd have their child. Her insides fluttered at the thought. Would she have a girl or a boy? Would their baby have their daddy's freckles? She hoped so, because she loved every single one of Fáelán's. At least she'd have their child to give her comfort in the future.

Chapter Eleven

Third century, Ireland

Fáelán drew his cloak close around him and hurried down the path toward Nóra's cottage. When he'd left to bathe in the stream, she'd been stirring a savory stew, and the scent of wood smoke and their supper hung in the air, enticing him to hurry. What should he have first—her or a hot meal to fill his belly? He grinned, grateful for his good fortune. He'd been taken in for the winter by Nóra's kin. Luckier still that her family had gone to visit their son, whose wife had recently given birth to a fine, healthy boy.

Of course, he knew her parents had left their daughter behind with the expectation she and Fáelán would grow closer in their absence. Her da had made it clear they all hoped the association would lead to a wedding, and perhaps it would . . . someday. 'Twas well past time he took a wife, but did he love Nóra with his whole heart? Nay. Perhaps that would never happen for him. He was quite fond of her, and he did find her pleasing to the eye. Would that be enough to sustain them over his long absences as a Fiann? Not likely. Mayhap 'twould be best not to marry until he left the service.

A figure stepped out from shadows between the trees, a woman. Nóra? Nay. Even in the gathering dusk, he could see her clearly enough. She was tall, comely and dressed in the garb of a lady. She wore a cloak of the finest fur-trimmed wool about her shoulders. Something about her niggled at him, and his pulse quickened. Odd that she wore a sword strapped to her waist, and odder still, she carried a small pack slung over a shoulder. Lassies of high birth did not travel alone. Perhaps she needed his aid. He hoped not, for he anticipated a night of ease between the warm furs with his even warmer lover.

"Good eve to ye, my lady," he said, bowing slightly even as he veered to the left to go around her. Nóra's home was not far from the village. Mayhap this woman was kin to their chieftain.

"Fáelán," she said, blocking his way. "Don't go to Nóra tonight. It's a trap. Morrigan will catch you with her, and she will curse you to dwell in the void realm, where you'll remain for almost eighteen hundred years."

Had she just called him by name? His blood surged, and he tensed. Her words were foreign to his ears, yet he understood everything she said. And what she said filled him with unholy fear. Could she be a witch, or one of the accursed fae? "How is it ye know who I am, yet I've never laid eyes upon ye afore this moment?"

"You know me, Little Wolf. Please listen. There isn't much time." She glanced toward the setting sun, then back at him.

Little Wolf. The name, spoken in her tongue, echoed deep within the recesses of his mind, as if familiar, but . . . not. He shivered, and his need to be away burgeoned, yet a small part of him wanted to stay. Witchery, 'twas certain. "If I'd met ye afore, I'd surely remember, and I do not."

"It's me, Regan," she cried. "Try to remember. You have to remember," she pleaded.

He was a logical man, aye, but he also had a healthy suspicion and wariness when it came to anything unnatural. He understood her speech, though he'd never heard its like until now. 'Twas cause enough for fear. Even more so that he answered her in kind. She must have placed an enchantment upon him. Best listen to his gut and ignore the part of his nature urging him to stay. "Nay. I know ye not at all. I bid ye good eve."

"Wait. I'm here to prevent you from being cursed." She gripped his tunic and gave him a shake, her expression desperate. "I'm here to save Nóra's life."

"Ye must be mad." He removed her hands, stepped back and crossed himself. "I will listen no more to your raving." Again he tried to step around her, and again she moved to block his way, this time grabbing hold of his wrists.

"Morrigan is one of the fae, a Tuatha Dé Danann princess. She's King Lir's daughter. She came to you disguised as a human. Think, Fáelán. Who were you with before you came to stay with Nóra?"

"Hmph." A little over a fortnight ago, he'd spent a se'nnight with a woman he'd met at an autumnal gathering. Deirdre, she'd called herself, and she'd been most eager to have him. For the duration of the gathering, they'd been lovers, but . . . fae? Nay, he'd have sensed something, surely.

"You and Morrigan spent a week together," the woman continued. "You told me all about her, and how she seduced you into her bed." She looked down the path behind her, as if expecting someone any minute. "Morrigan is insanely jealous and obsessed with you, because . . . well that part can wait."

Her grip on his arms tightened. "What you need to know now is that she's going to be here soon. If you go to Nóra tonight, Morrigan will murder your lover and curse you to dwell in the void realm. You and I won't meet until the twenty-first century, and—"

"Enough! I do not believe your blather." The fae princess Morrigan was well known for stirring trouble. Could this woman afore him be

Morrigan herself, come to wreck his life? An icy finger of dread swept down his spine, as if he'd walked over his own grave.

Even if she wasn't the fae princess, what was she saying? They'd met in the twenty-first century? Not possible. Surely the new god's Apocalypse and Second Coming would occur long afore then. Gods, he wanted to be away from her and her disturbing words, so why was he still standing afore her?

"It's true." She let him go, brought her wee pack forward and reached inside. "I have pictures of the two of us together. You swore you loved me, and that broke the curse, but then Morrigan stole you away from me, and—"

"How is it I understand ye, when I've never afore heard the language ye speak? What have ye done to me that I can speak it as well?" How could this stranger know about his previous lover, or about Nóra for that matter? Something about this woman, some sense about her hovered at the edges of his awareness. She must be fae, and all knew the fae loved to meddle with mortals for their own amusement. He placed his hand upon the knife at his belt, even though his blade would be useless against her if she was one of the Tuatha.

"You told me once—it was the morning we met at Brú Na Bóinne—you said you'd had centuries to learn all forms of English, French and German." She brought something out of her bag and touched the surface a few times.

An unholy light came forth, and she thrust the thing at him. Fáelán couldn't help himself. He peered at the glowing object only to see himself in bed with this stranger in his arms. Lest there be any doubt, the mark of a Fiann shown clearly over his heart. All the air left his lungs, and his mouth went as dry as chaff. "Leave me be," he rasped out. "I want no part of this witchcraft. I want no part of you."

Uncertainty roiled in his gut. The fine hairs on his forearms and at the back of his neck standing on end, Fáelán put his hands on her shoulders and moved her from him. Giving her his back, he strode down the path. By the gods, he prayed he'd not lose his legs afore he reached the safety of the cottage.

"I didn't want to have to do this, Fáelán, but you leave me no choice."

What now? He was but a hundred paces from the cottage, when a buzzing, clicking sound filled the air behind him. He pivoted, his posture defensive. Something hit him in the chest, jolting him off the ground and paralyzing his limbs. He dropped like a felled tree, and the back of his skull smacked against something hard. He groaned, and the world around him went black.

Regan retrieved the wire of her discharged Taser, and stuffed the weapon back into her day pack. "I'm sorry. I'm so sorry, Fáelán. I didn't mean for you to hit your head. I only wanted to immobilize you long enough to bind and gag you." That didn't really sound any better than what had happened, even to her own ears.

Regan moved the sword at her waist out of the way and crouched down beside her unconscious warrior. Gingerly, she touched the back of his skull where he'd connected with an exposed root. No blood, but already a lump was forming. Then she checked his pulse, which was as strong as ever. Relieved, she grabbed him under his arms and dragged for all she was worth. Grunting with the effort, she half dragged, half carried him down the path until she'd put more distance between the two of them and Nóra's cottage.

Now that she'd prevented him from sleeping with Nóra, did that mean Morrigan wouldn't show up? God, she hoped so. The alternative was that Morrigan would now see Regan as the threat, and the faerie might then come after her. She veered off the main path onto a narrow trail into the woods, dropping him to catch her breath.

Regan glanced through the woods. What if Nóra came looking for Fáelán? Then what? She huffed out a breath, straightened and arched her back for a second. At least Nóra was a mere mortal like herself. She'd deal with her when and if she had to. Crouching to get a better hold of Fáelán, she continued on. Regan hauled him along until she found a small clearing not too far from her escape route.

It was growing darker fast, and she had to tie his hands and feet while she could still see. She found a tree small enough for her to get his arms around the trunk and made the last exhausting effort to pull him across the clearing to the sapling.

How much time did she have before he came to? Her back aching, she lifted Fáelán to sitting and propped him against the trunk as best she could. Breathing heavily, sweat pouring down her face, she grabbed the rope out of her day pack and snatched the knife from Fáelán's belt.

He groaned, and she nearly jumped out of her skin. Regan sprang into action. She cut the rope in two, hurried around to the back of the tree and tied Fáelán's wrists together behind the trunk. Then she scanned the ground for a place to secure his feet. A gnarled root stuck up through the soil. *Good enough.*

She tied his feet together at the ankles and fastened the extra length of rope to the root so he couldn't kick her. Regan's mind raced with everything that could go wrong. What if Morrigan came after him anyway? Her throat worked convulsively at the thought of facing Fáelán's tormentor.

Regan drew her pack around and pulled out the clean washcloth she'd brought. She stared at the unconscious man she loved with all her heart. "Sorry about this," she muttered, stuffing the gag into his mouth.

He groaned again but didn't wake. She huddled upon the cold ground and drew her cloak around her. Another thing she hadn't planned for, a night outside in the cold with no way to build a fire—which she wouldn't do anyway, because a fire would make it easier for them to be found. At least it was above freezing. Regan did her best to bring Fáelán's cloak around to cover him, but with his arms tied behind him, her efforts didn't do much good.

He wore the same thing he'd had on the morning they'd met, and the aching familiarity nearly broke her. She ached all over, and tears filled her eyes. He didn't know her at all. He might not ever remember her, but at least she'd prevented tonight's tragedy. She hoped so anyway. No sign of Morrigan.

Regan scooted closer and snuggled against her captive to share their combined body heat. Spreading part of her woolen mantle over the both of them, she settled against his side. His warmth seeped into her, and she hoped hers warmed him as well. She rested her head against his chest and took his scent deeply into her lungs. This might be the last time she ever had the pleasure of being beside him. She'd accomplished her goal, and for now Fáelán was safe. "Well worth the sacrifice," she whispered, listening for any signs of the faerie or Fáelán's girlfriend. All was still and silent, not even a ghost stirred. Sighing, she tried to relax.

She must have fallen asleep, because Fáelán's stirring woke her. Sometime during the long, cold night, she'd draped herself over him, and if his attempts to twist away were any indication, he wasn't happy about their current positions. She sat up and met his hostile glare.

"Sorry I used my Taser on you. I'm even sorrier you bumped your head. I bound and gagged you," she whispered, "because this was the only way to save your stubborn ass, since you refused to listen to me."

Early-morning light filtered through the clearing. Regan pushed herself up from the hard ground. "I'll be right back," she muttered, fishing in her pack for a few tissues and one of the bottles of water. Hunger, cold and thirst didn't come close to the misery of her disappointment at Fáelán's reaction to her. After all she and Fáelán had shared, his hostility and suspicion were too much to bear. How could she get through to him, dammit?

Regan stalked off to a private spot in the brush and took care of her body's needs. Listening for signs of anyone searching for the missing Fiann, she rinsed her hands with a bit of the bottled water and then took a drink. Fáelán was probably hungry and thirsty too, and once she'd said her piece, she'd let him go. Her shoulders weighted with sadness, she returned to the clearing.

"If you promise not to call out for help, I'll take the gag from your mouth." She pulled the protein bars from her pack. "I have water and food, and I'm willing to share if you're willing to listen to what I have to say." She shoved her disappointment and hurt aside. Once she was back in Howth, she'd have plenty of time to weep. "That's all I want, Little Wolf. Just hear me out, and then I'll let you go. Do we have a deal?" She met his gaze. He was still angry, but she also caught a hint of resignation in his expression. He gave her a single nod.

"I can always stuff this gag back in place if you break your word," she said, taking the cloth from his mouth. He didn't call out, and she brought the bottled water to his mouth and let him drink. Then she tore the wrappers from the protein bars, and while she ate hers, she fed him bites of the other. All the while, she began the story of how they'd met.

"I was doing yoga and meditating at Newgrange, and you made a comment. Turns out, I was able to see and hear you while you were in the void," she said, her voice cracking. "I was sure you were a ghost, and you kept insisting you were not dead but cursed." A tear slipped down her cheek.

All impossible and unbelievable experiences she couldn't have imagined in a million years. Yet here she was in third-century Ireland, trying like hell not to fall apart. Judging by his skeptical expression, the man she'd given her heart to didn't remember a single thing she had mentioned. They were going to be parents, and not a glimmer of recognition registered in his gaze.

"You even recited Morrigan's curse for me." She repeated what she could remember, watchful for any sign she was getting through to him. His expression gave nothing away. "So you see," she whispered, "I've come to you from the twenty-first century for the sole purpose of saving you from centuries of captivity and oppression under Morrigan's thumb."

She sat back. "For now anyway. I don't know what you can do to protect yourself in the future, but you need to figure it out. Believe me, Morrigan isn't going away, and you won't be free until this thing between the two of you is resolved."

He grunted but didn't say a word. Sometime during the night, she must have taken off the belt holding Mananán's magic sword, because it now rested on the ground beside the sapling. "There's more," she said, picking up the scabbard and drawing out The Retaliator. "You and Morrigan conceived a daughter together, which is why the princess is obsessed with you. She will keep your daughter from you out of spite."

"The hell you say," Fáelán hissed. He'd kept silent and sullen throughout the tale. His expression was as hard as granite, and his eyes were filled with wariness, but this at least got a reaction.

"It's true. Her name will be Boann, and she will have your nose and mouth. I guess fae women bond irrevocably with the biological father when they conceive. That's why Morrigan has held on to her anger and won't let you go."

Fáelán leaned his head back against the trunk and closed his eyes. Tension radiated from him. His jaw muscles twitched, and his mouth was drawn into an angry, straight line. She'd known hearing he would have a daughter he would never meet would get to him, and it hurt that she'd been the one to cause him fresh pain.

"Boann has been helping me in the twenty-first century, and it was her uncle Mananán who suggested the best thing to do would be for me to come to you in your century. This way, I could prevent the

curse from happening in the first place. Which I did. You're welcome."
Thank whatever powers that be, Morrigan hadn't appeared last night.

Regan placed the sword in his lap. "Do you recognize this? It was
loaned to me, so that I'd have some kind of proof if I couldn't convince
you."

He opened his eyes and stared at the weapon. "Aye, 'tis Fragarach,
a fae-forged blade, belonging to Mananán, son of King Lir Beneath
the Sea. *If* what ye say is true, then ye consort with the fae and carry a
sword belonging to one of their princes. How do I know ye aren't fae
yourself? Why should I trust ye?"

"I'm not fae, though I have a trace of fae blood. You should trust
me because I was willing to put my life at risk to warn you. I'm here to
save you from the agony of being cursed for nearly two millennia. Is
anything I've told you helping? Are you convinced yet?"

"'Tis a fantastical tale," he said, his tone flat. "Though it may be
true, I've no recollection. And, as you say, your coming here has prevented any of it from happening." He let out an audible breath, still
avoiding eye contact. "I am grateful to ye, for 'tis a good turn ye've
done me. But . . ." His Adam's apple bobbed, and he turned to stare
into the forest. "What is it ye want from me? I've a bit of gold and some
amber, and ye are welcome to all of it."

He wanted to pay her like she was some stranger who'd helped
him out of a jam? That stung like hell. "Fáelán, when you told me you
loved me, you said you'd rather remain cursed forever than to see me
in harm's way. My welfare was more important to you than your freedom." Her voice came out strained. "Since I love you just as much, I
had no choice but to do whatever I could to . . . to save you."

Her heart aching, she forced the words past the choking rejection.
"And now you're asking me what I want as payment. Not your gold
or your amber, Little Wolf." She swiped at the escaping tears on her
cheeks. "I was hoping you'd remember me, and that I could convince

you to come back to the twenty-first century. You have a life there, a family and a home."

"Do I?" He grunted. "If, as you say, ye've altered my fate, all I have in the future would cease to exist, for I was never there, aye?"

"No." She shook her head. "No. Boann explained there's no difference between the past, present and the future. They exist simultaneously. The time we spent together, the time you spent with your relatives . . . none of it can be erased, only forgotten. I think if you came back with me now, it will be as if you'd never left, only you'd finally be free."

Sliding her day pack to her front, she pulled out her phone and brought up all the pictures of their time together. "Here's proof. If my preventing the curse made everything else disappear, then I wouldn't still have these pictures." She sat beside him and held her phone for him to see.

Fáelán peered at the screen. This time he seemed more interested than afraid, and hope rose swiftly enough to steal her breath. "Here you are in your house in Waterford with your relatives. This is your nephew many generations removed, James Ahearn, and this is his wife, Kathryn," she said, before naming everyone else in the photos she'd taken of Fáelán surrounded by his family. "Here we are at your cousin Dan's restaurant in town, where you took me out to dinner. The waiter took this picture for us. I had the lamb, and you had salmon, and . . . and we shared."

Fáelán's gaze was riveted to the images now, and she scrolled through the pictures a few times for him. "Do any of these photos jog your memory? Will you come home with me?"

He shook his head. "'Tis sorry I am, but whatever may have occurred between us in the . . . uh . . . in the future, it matters not. I've a sworn duty to my king and to Ireland. I'm pledged to serve Fionn MacCumhaill himself. As long as ye are giving me the choice, I choose to remain here."

"*Giving* you the choice? Of course it's up to you."

He stared pointedly at his bound ankles and wiggled his feet. "Is it? Have ye not already taken me away against my will, rendering me unconscious with whatever weapon ye brought with ye from the future?"

"You hit your head. The Taser only stunned you." She tucked her phone back in her day pack. "I had to get you to listen." A gaping tear opened in her soul, and grief bled out. It was over between them. He felt nothing but fear and suspicion toward her. The only man she'd ever loved this deeply no longer knew her at all. "The choice is yours, and I understand why you wish to stay. This is your home and your era. You were born in this century, and it's where you were always meant to be. Morrigan messed with your life, and now you have it back."

She hated to play the "I'm pregnant" card, because it was far too close to what had happened between Fáelán and the faerie. While Morrigan was all about manipulation, Regan had no desire to play on his emotions. "I wasn't going to say anything, but if this is the last time I'll ever see you, there's something I have to tell you. What I'm about to say . . . I'm not telling you this because I expect you'll change your mind; I'm telling you because you have the right to know." She blew out a shaky breath. "I'm carrying our baby."

His chest heaved, and he strained against his bonds, twisting away from her. "Ye *lie!*"

His denial cut fresh welts across her heart, but at least she'd been up front. Regan stood up, reached for his knife and went around the tree to cut him loose. "Whatever you do, no matter what you believe or disbelieve, if you care anything for Nóra, then *don't* go to her. Doing so will likely cause the curse to happen after all, only a little later. Morrigan will kill her, or any other woman you sleep with for that matter. Find a way to end things between you and Morrigan before you climb into bed with another woman. OK?" She couldn't help the bitterness seeping into her tone.

He brought his hands in front of him and rubbed his wrists while she cut the binding on his ankles. "You're free to go, Little Wolf." She straightened and handed him his knife. "Maybe someday you'll remember what we had together. Maybe not. Either way, I did my best."

She didn't wait for a response. Another denial of everything they'd been to each other would destroy her. Regan's vision blurred with tears as she stumbled through the forest toward the path. Boann had given her a twenty-four-hour period in which to cross through the portal she'd created for her, but Regan couldn't bear to remain in the third century another second. She hurried down the trail, veering off on the path leading to the stream. Crashing through the brush, she headed for the copse of rowan hiding her way home.

Just then Regan heard a woman calling Fáelán's name, and she froze. It had to be Nóra. Two more voices, both male, joined the woman's. Nóra must've gone to the village for help once she'd realized Fáelán was missing. What if Fáelán went to them? What if he reunited with his girlfriend?

Indecision tore at her. If she returned and tried once more to convince him to stay away from Nóra, she'd face third-century strangers whose minds were superstitious and fearful. They'd be apt to kill her first and ask questions later. Not a safe situation. If she didn't return, would the cycle start over? Fáelán might still be cursed, despite her efforts.

Dammit, she had told him what he needed to know, and he would either heed her warning or he wouldn't. As difficult as it was to accept, she had no control over what Fáelán chose to do. Regan set out once again, heading for the portal that would take her back to her own time.

She'd done what she could. Fáelán had made his choice, and no matter what happened from this point forward, it was time for her to leave. Her reason for being in Ireland had been fulfilled. All that remained was learning how to continue on with her life now that she'd left her heart behind with a proud Irish warrior who happened to live in the third century.

Chapter Twelve

Fáelán followed the woman through the woods to the trail and watched as she disappeared around a bend. Regan, she called herself, and she had claimed to love him. Even more outrageous was her claim that he loved her. Never once did she look back as she fled, and for some inexplicable reason, his chest tightened and ached. He continued to gaze down the trail in case she might return. She didn't.

Ye lie! That was what he'd cried out when she'd told him she carried his babe. *Impossible.* She had to be lying, didn't she? Then why did those two words strike at him so grievously, and why did regret bite into him the way it did? Mayhap 'twas due to the hurt his denial caused, which had shown plainly upon her lovely face. He shook his head at the strangeness of it all, of her incredible tale—none of which could be true.

Still, *ye lie* echoed through his mind as if he'd shouted the very same words to someone else but a short time ago—and for the same reason. He hadn't. He couldn't have. By the gods, she'd said she was from the twenty-first century! He blew out a breath and returned to the clearing where Regan had forced him to look at images that made no sense—on a device that made even less sense.

Nay, that wasn't entirely true. She hadn't forced him, for he could easily have turned away or closed his eyes. He'd *wanted* to look, but try as he might, he couldn't summon a single recollection of any of the folk she'd claimed were his kin—his family in the far-too-distant future, or so she'd claimed. A shudder racked through him. 'Twas devilry and naught else, and he was well rid of her.

Fáelán crossed the clearing and lifted the fae sword from the ground. He examined the runes etched into the hilt. What magic did the symbols hold? Naught that he could sense, and none that he cared to. Still, he couldn't help but admire the fine workmanship and the lightness of the weapon. He doubted Regan realized she'd left Fragarach behind. She could not have known what power he now held in his hands. Only a fae-forged weapon such as this could kill one of the Tuatha Dé Danann. And with this sword, Fáelán could not be defeated by any human foe—unless they too wielded a fae weapon. But then, they'd have to be more skilled than he, and there were few who could make the claim.

He reached for Fragarach's scabbard and belt just as Nóra called his name. Soon other voices joined hers. What was he to do? He couldn't ignore what Regan had foretold, yet he couldn't quite believe her either. Nor could he pretend to himself his encounter with the stranger was naught but a dream. Rope burns circled his wrists, and a magic sword hung at his waist. Best not tempt fate.

Fáelán set out in the direction of the voices, and Nóra met him upon the path. As a Fiann, he was bound by an oath of honesty, and even if he weren't, he cared enough about her and her kin that he had no wish to cause a rift of any kind. Yet, for Nóra's sake, he'd need to skim close to the truth, whilst protecting her from the worst.

"Fáelán," she cried, hurrying toward him. "When ye did not return last eve, I worried myself sick for ye, I did." When he failed to open his arms to her, she stopped, and her eyes narrowed. "What is it? What has befallen ye?"

Two men from the village joined them. He nodded a greeting but stayed well back from the three facing him. "I've had an . . . encounter," he began, holding out his wrists for them to see the reddened marks from his bondage. "By one of the Tuatha Dé Danann, I fear." Better to say his visitor had been fae than to say Regan came to him from the future, warning him Nóra would die if he lay with her. Besides, though Regan claimed otherwise, he was not entirely convinced she was not fae. How else could she travel through time?

Nóra gasped. "What does it mean? What did he want with ye?"

"'Twas a she, love, and she warned me of great danger to come. I must leave here at once." 'Twas close enough to the whole story without causing her more fear or hurt than need be.

"Are ye off to warn Fionn MacCumhaill then?" one of the men asked. "What is the danger? Are we to be invaded?"

"Aye, I must go to my captain, but I cannot say what the danger is until after I've spoken with him." He started down the path, resting his palm against the fae blade's hilt. "I cannot tarry. The faerie left me Fragarach, this fae-forged sword, as proof of her visitation." *Close enough to the truth, aye?* She'd brought the blade as proof of her veracity, and when she'd left the weapon behind, the proof transferred to him. Heat rose to his face. When had rationalizing become so easy?

"I must gather my things." As he passed, Nóra reached out her hand, and he took it. Yet doing so set off a twinge of wrongness. "'Twould be best if ye wait outside whilst I gather my belongings. 'Tis fair shaken I am, and I want no taint of the faerie's magic to fall upon ye, lest some mischief follow." He slipped his hand from hers.

"Once the danger is past, ye'll come back to me, aye?" she implored, her gaze searching his for reassurance.

He nodded. "If I'm able, I will return." Saying so also felt wrong, as if he was betraying another. He knew not what to think, nor what to make of the conflicting emotions churning in his gut. He entered the cottage and stuffed his things into his rucksack. Then he gathered his weapons and strapped them to his waist and back. Slinging the quiver holding his bow and arrows over one shoulder and his rucksack over the other, he walked out into the clear winter morning.

"Wait but a moment," Nóra said. "Ye'll be hungry. I'll pack ye something to break your fast." She hurried into the cottage.

"I'd be most grateful," he called after her.

A short time later, she emerged and handed him a linen-wrapped bundle. "Fare thee well, Fáelán. I'll await your return."

"Do not wait for me, love, for I know not where Fionn might send me once I tell him what has happened."

Nóra's mouth turned down, and her eyes shone with tears. "Safe journey, Fáelán, and may a fair wind bring ye back afore long. Send word if ye can."

"That I'll do, and gladly." He nodded again to the two men. "My thanks to ye both for coming to Nóra's aid. Look after her until her kin return, aye?" With that, he turned south and strode off. First he'd travel to Fionn's stronghold. If Regan spoke the truth, who better than his captain to help him find a way to put a stop to Morrigan? After all, Fionn was kin to the fae, descended from King Nuada of the Silver Hand himself.

After relating what had happened to his captain, Fáelán would continue to his clan's village to spend the winter with his parents. In the meantime, he'd live a celibate life, for he could not dismiss the facts. Even though he couldn't recall ever having laid eyes upon her afore, Regan would not have appeared to him without good reason, and she'd brought proof. The images she'd shown him on her wee window box haunted his thoughts and would for some time to come.

By midday he planned to stop to fill his waterskin at a spring, rest a bit and eat. This grotto and spring were well known to all the Fenians as a safe, well-hidden place to rest. But as he approached, the fine hairs at the back of his neck stood on end, and a prickling sensation overtook him. His heart leaped to his throat, and his palms grew damp. Something unnatural, a malicious presence, filled the grotto.

Alarm pulsed through him, holding him to the spot. Fáelán gripped Fragarach's hilt as he listened and scanned his surroundings, seeking any sign of who or what awaited him beyond the rock walls jutting from the earth. He was being watched, that much was certain, but by whom? Soft, feminine laughter reverberated through the air, and he tensed.

"Come to me, Fáelán. I offer you immortality, a life of ease and pleasure. Come to me, and I will grant you riches beyond your imagining."

The siren's alluring voice echoed around and through him, enticing and seductive. She called him by name. Tendrils of desire wrapped around his heart, and he took a step forward.

"Aye, come closer, I ache to hold you in my arms."

Regan's warning came back to him, but still, a burning need to go to the siren compelled him forward. Morrigan? *The fae princess will curse you and kill your lover*; that was what Regan had told him. She'd prevented the curse but not the time he'd spent with the fae princess. Was it Morrigan who called to him now?

His skin crawled, and a bone-deep instinct for survival surged. Summoning all his will, he fought the creature's compulsion. Whoever beckoned, she could not get to him unless he heeded her summons and willingly entered the grotto. How he knew this he couldn't say, but he did. He clenched his jaw and tightened his grip upon Fragarach's pommel.

Keeping his eyes upon the path leading toward the spring, he fought the compulsion and backed away on cat's paws, careful not to turn over even a pebble. By the gods, both old and new, his life had been simple, and he'd been happy enough afore Regan appeared with her strange tale of curses and faeries.

Once he was well away, he turned and jogged farther down the trail. All along he kept his hand upon the hilt of Fragarach, his talisman against the unnatural being who'd called to him. "Feck." *Feck?* 'Twas a word he'd never heard afore, yet it rolled off his tongue as if he'd used it oft.

Dread chilled him to the very marrow of his bones, and he picked up his pace. He had no wish to confront whoever or whatever had set a trap for him. Gods, the siren had called him by name! There were other springs, clear streams where he might take his rest and fill his waterskin. And if those places were haunted as well, he'd move on and do without. 'Twould not be the first time he'd eaten on the run or suffered deprivation whilst avoiding an enemy.

***

Fáelán rubbed the weariness from his eyes and slumped in his chair. He sat at Fionn's table, with Fragarach resting between him and his captain. He'd traveled without stopping to his commander's stronghold, and he had just told him the entire tale of Regan's appearance and the hauntings he'd encountered every time he attempted to stop to rest along his way. Now that the tale had been told in full, Fáelán could barely keep his eyes open.

"I know not what to do, my lord. If the woman spoke the truth, then it had to be Morrigan attempting to draw me to her on my way here. Unless I find a solution, I fear she will not cease."

"Hmm." Fionn rubbed his bearded chin and studied the sword. "I do not doubt your visitor spoke the truth, and I suspect the curse has been delayed, not prevented after all. What Regan told ye about fae women bonding with the men who sire their children is a fact."

Fionn slid the sword closer to Fáelán. "I'll not take Fragarach back to its rightful owner just yet, for ye have need of it still. This sword acted as a ward against Morrigan, and as long as ye carry this weapon, she cannot take ye, for ye hold the means to kill her. The magic Fragarach holds also binds her powers, so Morrigan cannot defeat ye in battle with magic. However, having the fae sword is sure to bring ye even more trouble. Mananán will want it back, aye?"

"I have thought as much. I don't believe Regan meant to leave the blade behind." The memory of the hurt his denial had caused twisted him into a knot. *Mo a míorúilt lómhar.* The words came to him from

184

the far edges of his awareness. He shook his head. *Another haunting?* Fáelán shifted and propped his elbows upon the table. "My lord, is it really possible to travel back and forth through time as the stranger said?"

"Aye. I did so myself during my enlightenment. The fae oft pass through time, both forward and back. Sure, and ye've heard tales of people disappearing, only to reappear decades later, not having aged at all. Where do ye think they've been? Caught in a Tuatha's wake as they leaped through time, they were." He shrugged. "Or held in Summerland, the realm of the fae."

"I have heard the tales." Fáelán sighed. "But I thought they were made up to scare children away from places known to be frequented by the fae, lest they be stolen and replaced with changelings."

If he accepted Regan came to him from the future, then must he also accept everything else she said? Had he loved her? Mayhap she did carry his child after all. He might never know. His throat tightened at the thought, and he frowned with the effort of trying to remember aught about her.

Why should he feel so torn, or even try to remember her when his time was here? He was a warrior, and he carried great responsibilities. He'd pledged his fealty to Fionn and to their high king, Cormac MacArt. As a Fiann, his vows to king and country superseded any other, even to blood kin. He had a sworn duty to his people here and now, and not in some distant century.

"Most warnings have some basis in truth, do they not?" Fionn remarked, bringing Fáelán back to the present. "I shall dream about your situation this night, and by morn, I'll know better what is to be done. For now let us sup together. Ye'll sleep in my hall this eve, Fáelán. Morrigan cannot enter here without my permission." He clasped Fáelán's shoulder. "I'll have a pallet brought to ye."

"'Tis grateful I am to ye, my lord." At least he now had help, and he was safe from the faerie princess's pursuit for the time being.

Fionn signaled to a servant and gave him instructions. Other Fenians began to trickle into the hall for the evening meal, and Fáelán spent some time greeting those he knew and sharing news. He took a place at the table with his fellows and ate what was placed afore him, too exhausted to taste aught.

By the time he'd finished, 'twas all he could do to drag himself to the pallet that had been set out for him. Several braziers with burning peat and coal warmed the hall. His belly was full, and his thirst had been quenched. More important, he had the prospect of several hours ahead without worry. Despite the drinking, storytelling and laughter going on all around him, he fell into a deep sleep.

Fáelán woke with a start, gripped in terror and covered in a cold sweat. He labored to catch his breath as if he'd been running for hours. He'd dreamed he was lost in an endless gray, swirling mist, with no hope of finding a way out. The rage and frustration from his dream lingered. Echoes of a curse reverberated all around him, along with the taunting, evil voice of the faerie who had trapped him in that hellish place. Were these memories, or simply a bad dream caused by the unsettling events of the past two days?

His heart pounded so hard, his ears rang with the force. Fáelán sat up and surveyed his surroundings. The braziers in Fionn's hall still glowed red, and the rush-covered floor was littered with sleeping Fenians. 'Twas their heavy snoring that had awakened him no doubt. Surely it had been naught but a bad dream, set off by his encounter with the stranger claiming to be from the future. Yet Fionn accepted her story as truth, and Regan had said Morrigan held him prisoner in the void realm. Could the foul place he'd dreamed of be the void?

Fáelán once again strained to remember any detail of a life other than the one he knew in this time and place. Naught came to him. 'Twas like trying to reach for smoke, attempting to hold it in his hand. It could not be done. He shook his head and let out a long breath.

He checked to see that the fae sword still rested between him and the wall, half hoping 'twas not. The blade was still there. He lay back down, rested his hand upon the scabbard and soon fell back to sleep.

This time he dreamed of a woman standing atop a hill, her back to him. She wore naught but hose and a tight-fitting chemise, and seeing her thus filled him with desire. She'd contorted herself into a pose, whereby she balanced upon one leg and touched the back of her head with her other foot. Her supple back arched like a bow, and he grew hard with wanting her.

The sun was just rising, and they stood before the tomb of the ancients near the River Boyne. Though her back was to him, she was familiar. Something about her tugged at his heart. *"Turn around,* Álainn. *Face me."* In his dream, he called to her over and over, but she didn't turn, and he never saw her face.

The whoosh and rush of movement stopped, and Regan landed painfully on her bottom. "Ow." She opened her eyes to total darkness. Oppressive warmth, humidity and the scent of dirt pressed in all around her, while a pulsing energy thrummed through the walls and the ground.

"No!" Something had gone very wrong. She recognized these currents of power. Instead of her town house in Howth, as she and Boann had planned, Regan had landed in the cavern beneath the Hill of Tara. She crab-walked backward until she hit a wall. Panic, swift and all consuming, seized her by the throat. Her pulse pounded, and she couldn't breathe. She was trapped, enclosed in this space, under tons and tons of earth and stone. She swallowed against the dryness of her mouth and throat.

Was she back in the twenty-first century or still in the third? She had no way of knowing. "Boann, help!" she cried out into the darkness again and again. *Fáelán, I need you.* Oh, but he wouldn't come to her. He couldn't. Besides, he'd chosen to forsake her. She blinked against the tears filling her eyes. It was over. She'd never see him again, and now she was trapped.

"Boann!" She shouted again and again until her voice grew hoarse. Her pleas went unanswered, and fear sluiced through her. Had she misplaced her trust? Had the fae mother and daughter planned to kill her all along? Why? She'd done nothing to either of them—nothing other than win Fáelán's heart and make a baby with him anyway. She could see why that might piss Morrigan off, but had it made Boann jealous enough to wish her harm? Regan bit her lip hard enough to draw blood. The possibility she'd been betrayed galled her. Damn the fae; if she could tear out that part of her DNA she would.

Despite the heat, her hands and feet had gone cold, and she still couldn't get enough air into her lungs. "I don't want to die in this dark, damp place," she rasped. Hell, she didn't want to die at all. What about the tiny soul she carried? Her heart shattered.

Her baby deserved the chance to be born, to grow up and experience all that life had to offer. Her child deserved to live. Regan drew her knees to her chest, rested her forehead on her forearms and wept. She'd lost Fáelán, and now she and their unborn baby would die alone in this dank place deep underground. No one would ever find their bones. She cried until despair dulled her terror. Swiping at her cheeks, she fought to pull herself together. "Dammit. It's not over yet, and I'm not giving up."

She still had a bottle of water, but no more protein bars. Her phone! If she was in the twenty-first century, would she have a signal? *Oh, God.* She couldn't even tell anyone exactly where this cavern was located. Was it at the heart of the hill, or was she close to an outer slope? If she did manage to reach someone, could anyone get to her?

Wait. She had air to breathe, so there must be an opening somewhere. Regan brought her day pack around to her front and fished out her phone. She unlocked the screen, and again panic sent her heart pounding. No signal. Of course not. Even if she had returned to the twenty-first century, she'd landed deep underground.

Her hands shook so hard, she could hardly hold on to her phone, much less scroll for the flashlight icon. The icon appeared, and Regan managed a single, shaky tap. The phone's beam of light filled the space, and she searched the stone walls and hard-packed dirt floor for any hint of an opening where air might enter. When nothing stood out as the source, she took a tissue from her pack and rose to her feet. Holding the Kleenex by a corner, she brought it close to the wall, centered the beam of light on the white square and walked around the cavern.

The tissue fluttered in front of a crevice the width of her little finger. She studied the narrow fissure, and again despair steamrolled her, deflating all hope. She had no tools, and even if she did, who knew how thick the wall might be before she reached the outside? Like she had the strength to break through solid granite anyway. She had no food and only the one bottle of water. She'd die of dehydration long before she made it out of her underground prison.

Sinking to the ground, Regan huddled into a ball and tried to think. *Look for the positives.* At least she wouldn't run out of air. And . . . and she had a trace of fae blood. Now that she knew what it was like to be transported from one place and time to another, could she do it on her own? Fáelán had no fae blood, and he'd managed to figure out how to wander around at will while he was in the void. Maybe her fae genes would be enough to make it possible for her to whoosh herself out of there.

New resolve stiffened her spine. After all, she had managed to conjure a spark of light over her palm. Regan moved into a half-lotus position and began *ujjayi pranayama*, the breath of victory. Calming herself enough to meditate took time. Panic kept rising, blowing her focus all to hell. Still, she kept at it, and she finally managed to quiet her inner self. Concentrating on her breathing, she opened herself to the hill's magic, and the essence of life flowed all around and through her once again.

Regan visualized the town house in Howth and willed herself there. No whoosh or rush of air moved past her. Shifting her position, she tried again, with the same disappointing results. She kept trying, and after what seemed like hours, she had to admit defeat.

Desperate, she resorted to sending out a mental plea to any ghosts who might be hanging out nearby. After all the years she'd helped the dead, couldn't at least one of them return the favor? If a ghost did agree to help, how would they find her sisters? She groaned and buried her face in her hands.

What was she thinking, looking to the spirit world for help? Even if an accommodating spirit responded to her summons, she couldn't pin her hopes on a dead person. Most likely he or she would fail, and the disappointment would kill her. *Oh, wait.* She was going to die here anyway. Three or four days tops. How long had she been here already? Without the sunrise and sunset, she had no way of judging the passage of time.

Regan brought her pack around to the front of her and grabbed the bottle of water. She swallowed a third of the contents, and her stomach rumbled in a hungry protest. She should be taking prenatal vitamins and eating for two in the comfort of her condo in Tennessee, ten or twenty minutes away from her parents, grandparents and sisters.

"Shit." Regan curled into a ball on the hard ground and tried to sleep. Once she was rested, she'd try to transport herself again. "Not giving up, just recharging." Sleep wouldn't come, and she stared into the darkness, her mind circling around everything that had happened. What was Fáelán doing right now? Had he taken her advice and stayed away from his third-century lover? Did it matter anymore? He was lost to her, and she'd be dead soon anyway.

All the things she'd never get to do, the people she loved and missed, crowded her thoughts and brought a lump to her throat. Succumbing to self-pity, she shed a few more tears and closed her eyes. *Time to bargain.*

"Dear Universe, God, Goddess . . . whoever is in charge," she said into the darkness, "if you help me get out of this alive, I swear I'll keep ghost-whispering if that's what you want me to do. I'll never complain about my giftedness again either. Amen."

A subtle change in the atmosphere brought her back to full alertness, and she sucked in a breath. Regan sat up just as the faint scent of rain filled her senses. She didn't know whether to be immensely relieved or terrified. "Boann?" she whispered, praying Morrigan wasn't about to make an appearance. Again, no answer.

Her hands trembling, she fished her phone out of her bag and searched for the flashlight app again. The smell of rain grew stronger, and the air around her became charged. Regan hit the app, and light filled the cavern.

A portion of the rock wall directly across from her shimmered, and she could see hints of green grass, trees and sky beyond. "Thank you!" Boann was helping her, or her prayer had been answered. Either way, relief poured through her. OK, so she'd be a ghost whisperer for the rest of her life. Small price to pay.

Regan shot up so fast, it made her dizzy. The portal didn't lead to her town house, but she didn't care. Freedom anywhere from this black hole suited her just fine. Third century? Fifth? Who cared? Regan would dive through the opening to wherever the portal might lead, so long as it took her out of her underground hell.

She lunged across the cavern and leaped for the shimmering passageway. "Ooof." She slammed into solid rock and bounced off the wall, falling to the floor on her back. Her head thunked painfully against the ground.

Groaning, she touched her face, checking for injuries. Her nose dripped sticky blood, and so did a nasty gash at the center of her forehead. Every bit of her hurt, and flashes of gold dots danced before her eyes. An instant before everything turned to black, cruel laughter echoed off the walls of Regan's dark, dank tomb.

Chapter Thirteen

Still bleary from lack of a good night's sleep, Fáelán leaned over the trough set by the well within the timber walls of Fionn's stronghold and thrust his head into the icy water. He straightened, shook himself and swiped the water from his face. "Brr." Shivering and awake now, he washed quickly and dressed. Then he headed back to Fionn's hall to break his fast.

Dawn broke upon the eastern horizon, revealing a menacing gray sky. The scent of peat smoke, salty sea air, cattle and humanity permeated the air. Stinging sleet pelted Fáelán before he reached the keep, deepening his dour mood. "Too much worry and too little sleep," he muttered. He jogged the rest of the way and strode inside, rubbing his hands together for warmth.

"Fáelán!" Fionn's voice boomed from the high table. "Come, laddie. Break your fast." He pushed out the chair across from him with his foot.

Fáelán wended his way through the numerous tables filled with Fenians. All the Fianna rotated through duties and territories, and the warriors present were fortunate enough to have guard duty here in Fionn's keep for the winter. Along the way, Fáelán clasped forearms and exchanged greetings with those he knew well—those he'd fought beside or traveled with. He took the seat opposite his commander, and a servant filled his cup with ale. "Good morn to ye, my lord." Fáelán hoisted the cup and took a long draught.

"And to you." Fionn slapped Fáelán's back. "Eat. As soon as ye've filled your belly, we must be off."

"Where are we to go?"

"The answer came to me as I slept, and I have since communed with my fae relatives regarding your situation. We are off to King Lir's court as soon as may be. At my kin's behest, the king has agreed to an audience with ye." He waved his arm over the table. "Eat, laddie. The sooner we're off, the sooner ye'll be free of Morrigan's machinations."

"To the fae realm?" The thought of entering the void, no matter how pleasant the fae made it, twisted him into a knot. Aversion left a sour taste in his mouth. All night long he'd been awakened by strange, vivid dreams, visions of places and things he'd never seen, or at least he could not recall having seen them.

One thread ran throughout all the disturbing dreams, a constant—glimpses of a woman always out of reach. No matter how many times he called to her, she'd refused to turn her face to him. He longed to see her. He'd sensed she needed him, and he yearned to hold and protect her. That too made no sense.

What if Regan had spoken the truth, and they truly had been together in the future? Could it be Regan who wove in and out of his dreams? When she'd come to warn him, he'd cast her off and sent her away. Had he been wrong to do so? What a tangle—a tangle that kept circling back to the fecking fae.

"Could we not meet here? Is there no other way to reach King Lir? There must be a way that does not require—"

"Nay. If we wish to gain Lir's aid, we must go to him." Fionn gave Fáelán a shake. "Ye've gone pale, laddie. There's naught to fear. I'll not forsake ye whilst we are within his kingdom. Besides, the situation is not entirely unknown to the King Beneath the Sea. He will have sensed his daughter's mischief. What better way to end this than to appeal to her father, who is also her sovereign?"

"What shall I say to him?" Fáelán scrubbed his hands over his face. "I've no proof 'twas Morrigan who pursued me on my way here. I've no memory of being cursed, and I don't recall being held captive in the void." Even the word *void* set off a host of emotions within him. Rage being the uppermost—frustration coming in a close second.

Regan. My miracle, mo a míorúilt lómhar. Once again, the familiar words slid through his mind, and his breath caught. She was no stranger, yet he could not remember a thing about her. "How can I plead for help, when all I have is hearsay told to me by a woman from the twenty-first century?"

"Mmm. I see. Without knowing what ye suffered, your plea will be less than convincing. Especially since Morrigan has done naught but attempt to lure ye to her since Regan warned ye away from your lover's cottage." Fionn's expression turned pensive. "I believe I might have a solution, but 'twill mean delaying our journey for a day. Remain here. I'll be back for ye anon." He rose from the table and scrutinized Fáelán intensely for a long moment. "I see ye've lost your appetite. Eat anyway. 'Tis a command. Ye'll need your strength, laddie."

With that, his captain left him, and Fáelán exhaled the breath he hadn't realized he'd been holding. The thought of appearing before King Lir turned his stomach, but he could think of no way 'round it if he wished to get out from under the threat of being cursed, or from being perpetually pursued by Morrigan.

A shiver racked him, remembering the fae princess's attempts to draw him to her, her seductive siren's voice wrapping tendrils of magic throughout his mind and heart. More than once, he'd come to the point where he'd hovered between surrender and resistance. If it hadn't been for Regan's warning, and Fragarach . . . He shook his head and focused on his surroundings.

Fáelán took the knife from his belt and cut off a slice of the cheese laid out upon the table. He tore off a chunk of the bread and reached for the platter piled with smoked fish. He'd been commanded to eat, and so he would.

What could Fionn possibly have in mind that might help him? His insides quaked at what was to come. Surely the king's loyalty would lean in favor of his daughter. If he somehow came through his troubles alive and intact, Fáelán would marry. Aye, and he'd cleave only to his wife forever after. He'd learned his lesson. No more dallying with lasses he knew not at all, no matter how they tried to entice him into their beds.

By the time Fáelán had finished his meal, Fionn appeared in the corridor leading to the private chambers in his dwelling. His captain gestured for Fáelán to join him, and his nerves stretched as tight as a bowstring. He pushed away from the table and made his way to his captain, his feet dragging. When had his feet grown so heavy?

"Follow me," Fionn ordered, turning down the dark corridor. He opened a door, glanced back at Fáelán and stepped aside. "In ye go, laddie, and cease looking as if ye walk to your doom."

"Am I not?" he muttered under his breath. Fáelán had been in this room before, and the familiarity calmed him. This was where Fionn gathered his men to strategize, and where he listened to their reports concerning the various kingdoms they guarded. A heavy table of oak, surrounded by a dozen chairs, took up the center. Several oil lamps burned, lighting the interior against the darkness of the day. A single brazier glowed red with burning coal, and thick hides covered both windows to keep out the cold and the sleet.

Maps painted on the finest velum were laid out upon the surface of the table, and shelves held more scrolls of vellum and parchment. A steaming bowl of something had been set in front of one of the chairs. The food in Fáelán's stomach turned to a lump of clay in his gut. "Am I to drink this?" He moved closer to take a look.

"Aye. 'Tis my hope—nay, 'tis my belief—the spirits of the ingredients making up this concoction will help ye remember everything that has transpired with Morrigan and the woman who came to ye from the future."

"The spirits?" Fáelán lifted the bowl and sniffed at the contents. It smelled of herbs and something else, something earthy. "Ye speak as if herbs and such have conscious thoughts."

Fionn chuckled. "Think ye they do not?"

"Mmph." He studied the unappetizing brownish chunks floating in the potion. "If ye don't mind me asking, what are the brown bits?"

"A particular kind of mushroom that grows in the grassy places near the bogs."

"And the flecks of black?"

"'Tis a wee bit of ergot, the purplish blight that mimics grains of rye."

Should he be consuming a blight? "And the rest?"

"Herbs and a few berries ground together and mixed with . . . other ingredients. 'Tis best if ye not know all." Fionn seated himself across from Fáelán. "Go on, laddie. 'Twill go down easier if ye drink it all at once."

"Have ye ever partaken of this . . . mixture?" What should he call it? The word *poison* leaped to his mind.

"I have." Fionn arched his brow and cast him a look of such intensity, Fáelán was sure his captain saw to his very soul. Fionn grunted. "I take this when seeking answers to the gravest questions facing me, our king and our people," Fionn said, crossing his arms over his chest.

"What will it do to me?" Fáelán stared into the bowl, trying to determine what the other ingredients might be. *Blood? Eye of newt? Stag's hair?* His gut tightened, already rejecting what was to come.

"This potion will strip away any illusions clouding your vision and your mind. The spirits of the ingredients therein"—he tipped his head toward the wooden bowl—"will reveal the truth. Not the truth ye hope for, but the truth ye need. There's a difference, aye? Ye must be willing, humble and open for the spirits to speak, and even then, I cannot guarantee they will come. Are ye man enough, laddie? Drink up." Fionn jutted his chin, a challenging glint in his eyes.

Feck. Fáelán's heart climbed to his throat, and he swallowed a few times to force it back where it belonged. He brought the bowl to his mouth, his insides already rebelling. Still, he tipped the bowl and swallowed the foul, bitter brew. A few moments later, shudders racked him and nausea roiled through him like an ocean swell.

He gagged and fought to keep the contents of his stomach down. Saliva filled his mouth over and over, even as he swallowed it back, and his eyes watered. "By all that is holy . . . that was disgusting." He shook himself. "Uck."

Fionn laughed. "Aye, but do your best not to cast it up."

Could he? Of course he could. Had he not passed all the tests set afore him to be ordained as one of Fionn's elite warriors? He buried his face in his hands and propped his elbows upon the table. "I feel naught but a sickening in my gut. How will this help me again?"

"Give it time."

After a spell, the nausea retreated, only to be replaced by a strangeness overtaking him. His insides clawed to be out, whilst his outsides burrowed to be in. Fáelán groaned. "I like this not at all, my lord."

"What do ye seek from the spirits, my fine Fiann?" his captain asked, his tone low and soothing. "What do ye wish to remember? Think upon what ye wish to know whilst the spirits come to ye."

"Being cursed. I want to remember what befell me at Morrigan's hand, and I . . . I want to remember . . . my miracle," he whispered.

"Your miracle, eh?" Fionn chuckled. "Who or what might that be?"

Fáelán took his head from his hands and peered at Fionn. His captain's image blurred and distorted, and Fáelán blinked, trying to bring him back into sharp focus. "Regan."

"Ye remember all, laddie." Fionn leaned across the table and tapped Fáelán's forehead. "Ye just need help bringing the memories to the fore."

Fionn's tap reverberated through Fáelán from his forehead to the soles of his feet. He blinked even more and gazed around him in astonishment. Everything in the room began to move, taking on life. The table reached toward the tapestries upon the wall, and the tapestries melted into the floor, which had turned into a lake, undulating with waves that lapped at the walls. The flames of the oil lamps leaped and danced, and the red glow of the brazier expanded and contracted as if breathing. "Gods." He closed his eyes. "Everything has turned to melted tallow or beeswax. Everything is moving . . . merging."

"Why do ye think that is?" Fionn's voice took on a magical quality, filling every corner of Fáelán's mind.

"Beyond my ken," he murmured. Fáelán could no longer sit upright. His bones had melted as well, and he slid from his chair to the floor. Stretching out his arms and legs, he spread out on the solid floor that seemed to have turned into a lake. "It is all the same. We are all the same." *Nay.* That wasn't it exactly, but he couldn't find the words he meant to say. The floor's waves rocked him, and he suffered a fresh wave of nausea—and panic. The world around him was unrecognizable, and everything was out of his control.

"What do ye here? Why have ye summoned us?"

Fáelán sucked in a breath. A voice like stone grinding upon stone filled the room. Or was it only in his head? Was this one of the spirits Fionn spoke of? "I seek only what rightfully belongs to me," he rasped out. Anger surged. Though he should know the source, he didn't, and it only made him angrier. "'Twas . . . stolen from me. So much . . . taken."

"By what right do ye ask this of us?"

"I have no right, but I beg ye nonetheless. Memories of my time in the future . . . I want to remember. I need to remember being cursed."

"Are ye certain? Mayhap ye'd be better off not recalling what befell ye."

"Nay. For good or for ill, please . . . I must remember."

"So be it."

More strange sensations came over him, a tingling from head to foot and a powerful pressure inside his skull. Images flooded his mind. Sweet, innocent Nóra, the air being choked from her lungs, gripped by Morrigan's paralyzing magic. The tugging, whooshing sensation as he was dragged away to the void, helpless to do anything to save her. He cried out.

He'd been lost in an endless, horrifying grayish-green mist, because he continued to defy Morrigan's efforts to seduce him into becoming her consort. The dreams he'd had of this hell, they weren't dreams at all, but memories. Each word of Morrigan's curse pounded and throbbed painfully through his head. Like so much flotsam, he crashed against the sharp rocks of all that had happened, breaking apart, only to be caught up in another current of anguish.

The senselessness of it all pinned him to the floor where he lay. He covered his face with his hands and wept. Memories of his island prison, a place he loathed with every fiber of his being, came back to him in a rush. The endless loneliness had carved his heart from his chest and eroded his soul. How many times had he railed against the persecution? And all along he'd never known why Morrigan had imprisoned him. Now he knew. Regan had told him, hadn't she? He and Morrigan had a daughter, whom she'd hidden from him, stealing from him the right of fatherhood.

"Ahhhh, 'tis not right. *Morrigan* did this to me," he cried. "She deceived me from the start, murdered an innocent woman and kept me a prisoner for centuries. That fae bitch stole my life and punished me for defying her. She hid my daughter from me. I don't know my daughter," he sobbed.

As each recollection was restored to him, fresh grief raked talons through his soul. His family, clan . . . all dead and gone, over and over, loss upon loss. Through all of his imprisonment, Morrigan had taunted him and reveled in his pain. The weight of self-recrimination squatted upon his chest, and he could scarce draw a breath. All of it could be laid at his feet, because he'd been weak and led by lust.

Finally, Regan appeared, and bittersweet memories of their weeks together flooded his awareness. *Regan.* Even thinking her name cooled the fiery rage scorching his soul. Believing him to be a ghost, she'd done her best to goad him toward the light, whilst he'd insisted he was cursed, not dead. *Newgrange.* Their safe word. He smiled through his tears, remembering everything.

The morning he'd been freed from the void, they'd made love. 'Twas like nothing he'd ever known afore. She'd stolen his heart from the first moment he'd watched her at Brú Na Bóinne. Again he keened, awash in misery. Every conversation they'd had, the way she moved, smelled, felt . . . her generous, brave heart. Hardest of all were the memories of the night he'd been ripped from her. The night they'd declared their love, and he'd told her he'd rather remain imprisoned than put her in harm's way.

The sensations caused by the concoction gradually receded, leaving Fáelán bereft and as weak as a newborn. He stared at the ceiling as tears ran freely from the corners of his eyes. "Regan risked all for me, and I denied her," he said, his voice hoarse and breaking. "I remember everything."

With his memories came fresh fear. He pushed himself up to sitting and sought Fionn, finding him at the table, with scrolls of vellum from the shelves spread afore him. "Regan's coming to warn me, her preventing the curse and leaving Fragarach behind will have drawn Morrigan's wrath even more than when the curse ended. Regan thwarted the fae princess more than once, and Morrigan will want to punish her. No matter what I do, things go from bad to worse."

Stricken and shaky, he forced himself up from the floor and staggered to a chair, propping himself against the back. The table, chairs and tapestries no longer moved. Fáelán was exhausted, and his head ached. He blinked against the grittiness of his eyes. "King Lir is my only hope to set things aright. I see that now."

"Aye." Fionn lifted a pitcher and poured something into a goblet. He handed it to him.

Fáelán eyed the offering with suspicion. He took it and peered at the contents, and then brought the goblet to his mouth and gulped it down. Pure, cold water cooled his parched throat. "I owe ye a great debt of gratitude, Fionn. Though I never wish to experience the like again." He sank into the chair he'd been leaning against.

"*All* has come back to ye?" Fionn asked.

"It has."

"Tell me."

Haltingly, he related everything that had transpired between himself and the fae princess. Fionn nodded now and then, grunted a few times and listened intently. Fáelán ended the tale and sighed. "How long has it been since I drank the foul potion? I'm starving."

"'Tis nightfall, and you took the draught early this morn." Fionn rose, moved to the door and called for food to be brought to them.

His heart lurched. "Fionn, I need to get to Regan. Morrigan killed Nóra when she caught me in bed with her, and she'll do far worse to Regan. Morrigan will want her to suffer first, for she accomplished what the fae princess could not." He thunked his head against the table's hard surface, gratified by the punishing pain. "What have I done?"

He drew in a long, shaky breath and let it out slowly. "When I realized Regan could see me in the void, I thought only of gaining my freedom without giving the consequences to her a single fecking thought. How many must suffer because of my witless selfishness?"

He'd been caught up in his own inflated sense of importance as a Fiann, taking advantage of his status and the way the lassies swooned over him. "Selfish, immature and heedless," he muttered. "I do not deserve to be a Fiann."

"'Tis a heady temptation, all the attention bestowed upon ye as one of the Fianna. Few could resist, or would, for that matter. Besides, how could ye have known Morrigan's true identity?" Fionn shook his head. "Ye've suffered enough, Fáelán, there's no cause to blame yourself for what Morrigan has done."

"But—"

"We shall fill our bellies, and after a good night's rest, I'll take ye to King Lir Beneath the Sea."

"That's a metaphor, aye?" Trepidation spiked, and his pulse raced again. Being trapped in the void had been bad enough. He couldn't bear the thought of being leagues beneath the sea.

"A metaphor?" Fionn frowned. "I'm not familiar with the term."

Fáelán rubbed his throbbing temples, realizing how much from the future had been restored to him. "Are we actually to travel to a place beneath the sea?"

"Ah." Fionn snorted. "Nay. We'll enter Summerland and go to Lir's stronghold. He only *rules* the oceans, laddie. He does not live beneath them."

"Thank the gods, both—"

"Old and new?" Fionn said, a wry grin suffusing his features.

Their food arrived, and while they ate, Fáelán's sense of urgency grew. His knees bounced under the table, and 'twas all he could do to stay put. Regan needed him. If aught happened to her, he'd not survive the loss, nor would he want to.

"Eager to be off, are ye?" Fionn pinned him with a look. "Cease with your twitching."

Fáelán rubbed the achy spot over his heart. "Worry for Regan consumes me, my lord. I have Fragarach and my skills as a warrior to protect me, but Regan is defenseless. Can we not depart this very moment?"

"Nay. What ye experienced this day takes a heavy toll. Ye'll not do your woman any good if ye appear afore King Lir exhausted and strung as tight as ye are right now. I'll not take ye to Summerland until ye've rested, and if ye need a potion for that as well, I'll make one."

"No more potions." His stomach lurched.

"Aye, no more potions," Fionn grunted. "I've been thinking, laddie. Ye've served me faithfully and well for nigh on eight winters now. I owe you a great debt for blocking the arrow that would have taken my life whilst we fought the raiders from the Northland. Ye know I'll help in any way I can. After this trouble with Morrigan has passed, what do ye wish to do with the rest of your life? Do ye wish to continue on as a Fiann?"

"'Tis the truth, I'm torn in two. I've sworn an oath to ye, my king and country. Have I not? Yet Regan holds my heart, and she is with child. To break my vow to you and King MacArt would be grievous, yet to abandon the woman I love, and our unborn child, is also wrong. Morrigan denied me the opportunity to be a father to Boann. I'm not certain I can walk away from the second chance I've been granted."

"Think ye Regan would be willing to live in this time?"

Hadn't he already caused enough havoc due to selfishness? "Mayhap she would, but I would not ask it of her. Being a Fiann means we'd be apart far more than we'd be together. 'Twould be unfair to expect her to give up all she knows, only to see me for a se'nnight here and there. She has sisters she's close to and her own kin. In this century she'd have only me."

"Ye have kin. Would she not live with them? I know your ma and da would welcome her, would they not?"

"'Tis certain they would, but 'twould not be the same. Even though my da is chieftain to our clan, many would view Regan with suspicion and fear. What if my clan shunned her? I could not bear her unhappiness."

"No need to think on it overmuch. For truth, 'tis not our decision to make. King Lir will have the final say, and he might not be willing to allow ye to return to the twenty-first century."

Fáelán nodded, desolation rising to choke him. He knew Morrigan too well. Whatever he decided mattered not, for he might already be too late to save Regan.

***

Regan moaned, and even that soft sound sent shards of pain piercing through her throbbing head. She blinked her gritty eyes, and swallowed against the dryness of her mouth and throat. Blood crusted her face, and she reeked. So did her prison, because she'd been forced to turn a small corner into a latrine. Not pleasant, but what choice did she have?

Dim light filled the space, coming from what she had hoped was a portal out of the cavern. She touched the gash on her forehead, which had swollen and was undoubtedly black and blue. Turned out, the portal was more like a webcam screen, showing her the world beyond Tara, reminding her how trapped she truly was.

Regan turned her head, only to cry out in surprise. A tray had been left for her. Boann's doing, or did Morrigan plan to imprison her for eons, like she had Fáelán? Pushing herself up to sitting, her world spun, and she hurt all over. "Ohhh." She held her poor throbbing head between her palms, remaining still until the cavern ceased its sickening whirl.

Suspicion warred with her overwhelming thirst and hunger. Fáelán believed Morrigan had slipped him the Elixir of Life through the food he'd been given. She had no desire to live forever in a fae prison, but she did want to live.

The instinct to survive won the battle, and she crawled on her hands and knees toward the tray. The first thing she took was one of the two goblets filled with clear water. She gulped it down, no longer caring if it made her immortal or not. Survival first—deal with the fallout later. Never before had anything felt or tasted as good as the water soothing her parched throat. She swallowed the last drop and set the goblet down.

Bread, cheese and slices of some kind of roasted fowl were next, and she tore into the food like a starving person. Regan choked and coughed. *Oh, right.* She *was* a starving person. After being hungry for so long, it didn't take much before she felt full and uncomfortable.

Leaving the rest of the food for later, she rose slowly to her feet and inched her way to the portal, keeping a hand on the wall for support. The view had changed, and she recognized the unusual hue of the sky and the utter perfection of the landscape. She peered through the window into Summerland, the home of the Tuatha Dé Danann. Why this view?

"Oh." Her heart thumped. Three men came into view. Two of them were strangers, but she'd know the third man's swagger anywhere. "Fáelán," she shouted. "Here! I'm here!" She pounded against the stone wall until her palms were raw and stinging.

Hadn't she broken his curse? Why was he in the fae realm? She shouted again and again, knowing full well he'd never hear her. Regan shook her aching hands and moved away. Morrigan wanted her to see this, which could only mean she meant to make her suffer.

She paced around the cavern in an effort to keep from looking through the window. It didn't work, and she returned. The scene had changed again, and the three men now stood before one of the Tuatha Dé Danann. The faerie sat upon a throne of wood encrusted with mother-of-pearl. He wore a crown of polished coral, and he held a trident in his hand. He had to be King Lir.

Fáelán was speaking, his passion for the subject obvious. He gesticulated and strode around the ring of people who listened and watched; then he returned to stand before the king. His two companions stood to the side of the king's throne. Lir frowned and seemed intently interested in what Fáelán had to say. He gestured and spoke, and a woman appeared out of thin air to kneel before the king. *Morrigan?*

Regan couldn't take her eyes from the scene, but then the portal flickered and disappeared. "Dammit." She pressed her fists against the wall, frustration banding her chest. Without the portal, the cavern was pitch-dark. The scent of ozone filled the chamber.

Morrigan was coming for her; she just knew it. Regan turned and pressed her back against the wall. She held her breath, terrified to confront the creature who had caused so much misery. The air around her crackled with energy, and for all she was worth, she tried to whoosh herself anywhere else but here. Boann had said her magic might respond to her need, hadn't she? It didn't work this time either, and she remained pressed against stone and earth, still trapped.

An orb glowing with a silvery light appeared, and behind it the silhouette of a woman in a long, flowing gown. "Regan?"

"Boann," Regan whispered back. All the breath left her in a rush, and she sank to the floor in a puddle and sobbed with relief.

"Forgive me." Boann hurried to her and crouched down. "I could not get to you until now."

"All this time you knew I was trapped here?"

"Nay, but I knew something had gone awry with our plan, because Mother put me under a binding spell the moment I sent you through time. Yet another transgression," she muttered. "When King Lir summoned Mother to his court in the third century, that strand of time altered, and the spell she cast in this century broke. Then I was able to locate you."

"I think I saw that happen, the part where King Lir summoned Morrigan. What's happening now . . . or then?" Sweat streaked down her caked and filthy cheeks. "There was a . . . a window there," she said, pointing to the wall where the portal had been. "I saw Fáelán and two other men. He was speaking to King Lir."

"Aye. Fionn, the leader of the Fianna, arranged for the meeting with King Lir. Though you prevented my father's curse, my mother has continued to pursue him, and Fáelán hopes King Lir will put a stop to her harassment." Boann took her by the arm. "It is being discussed in the past as we speak. Rather than taking the time to find out, I thought it best to free you. Come. We must hurry." She tugged at Regan. "I must get you away from here whilst I still can."

"Wait." Regan stood on wobbly legs and raked a shaky hand through her matted hair. "Does this mean Fáelán has remembered his time in the future? Does he remember me?" Her voice hitched.

Boann faced the wall and did her runes-in-the-air thing. "I don't know any more than what I have already shared." A portion of the wall shimmered and waved. "Go. This will take you to Howth."

"You're not coming with me?"

"I cannot. To do so would only draw more trouble to you." Boann gave her a little push. "I'll come to you when I can."

"My pack. I dropped it somewhere." She searched the floor in the silvery light, finding her bag near where she'd fallen. "How long have I been here?"

"Regan," Boann snapped. "I've been trapped since the day I sent you through time to warn my sire, which was five days ago. Taking away the time you spent in the third century, I'm guessing you've been here for three mortal days, and if you do not leave now—"

"Sorry," she huffed. Had Boann just snapped at her? After the hell she'd been through, Boann's tone got on her last nerve. "I'm disoriented and probably a little dehydrated. Forgive me if I'm not as quick on the draw as I usually am." She grabbed her pack from the floor. "And by the way, the last time I aimed for one of these damned passages, I slammed into solid granite. I'm pretty sure I'm concussed."

"I can see that, and I beg your forgiveness," Boann said, still sounding impatient. "Off with you, before it's too late and you suffer far worse."

The fae princess shoved Regan none too gently into the portal, and she was caught up in the sickening rush. "Please let me land inside the town house and not in a messy heap on the sidewalk outside," she prayed. She came to a sudden ungraceful halt, flat on her already bruised face against a carpeted floor. "Ouch."

Screaming voices, familiar and beloved voices, filled her ears. Despite how miserable she was, relief flooded through her.

"Oh, my God! Is she alive?" Grayce screeched.

Regan groaned and rolled to her back. "Just barely." She inhaled the delicious aromas of something yummy. *Waffles and bacon?* Her mouth watered. "Something smells good."

Meredith helped her up to sitting. "What happened? My God, you look like you were beaten with a two-by-four. Who did this to you?"

"Regan, where the hell have you been, and how did you just appear out of thin air like that?" Grayce crouched down beside her. "If Fáelán beat you, he's a dead man."

"He didn't do this. The fae princess who cursed him is responsible." Her gut wrenched. Would she ever see Fáelán again? He had a sworn duty to his king, Fionn and Ireland. Like he said, he belonged in his own time, and he had no intention of leaving. "I have a lot to tell you, but first—"

"We need to get you to a hospital." Meredith took Regan's head between her palms, tilted her face and studied her wounds.

"It's too late for stitches, even if I might have needed them." Regan gestured toward the gash on her forehead. "I got this two days ago, and it's already started healing. A bath and clean clothes is what I need."

Grayce tugged at Regan's third-century gown. "What are you wearing?"

"It's a long story, and I've had a rough few days." After bathing, more food and a nap, maybe she'd be ready to talk. "What day is it anyway?"

"It's Tuesday morning, the twenty-seventh of June," Grayce said, sending Meredith a look of concern. "Come on. Let's get you cleaned up."

Everything that had happened the past couple of days swamped her, and she burst into tears. "I was trapped in a cavern under the Hill of Tara, with no way out, and . . . I . . . I didn't have any food, and I'm *pregnant*," she sobbed. "That couldn't have been good for my baby." Two sets of arms encircled her. "I've lost him," Regan wailed. "I b-broke Fáelán's curse, and then everything went to hell."

Her sisters made soothing sounds and helped her upstairs and into her room. They made her sit on the bed while Grayce gathered clean clothes and Meredith filled the tub. Regan was exhausted right down to her leptons and quarks, dammit, and her heartbreak went even deeper. A massive lump clogged her throat, and her chest hurt. All of her hurt, inside and out.

"I never sensed a thing." Meredith's brow creased. "I wonder why?"

"Fae magic or something about the Hill of Tara's energy maybe." Regan shook her head. "I don't know."

"Hmm. Do you need help getting out of your clothes?" Meredith asked, her expression filled with sympathy.

Regan managed a small smile. "No. I can manage. I'll come downstairs once I'm dressed."

Meredith nodded. "If you need us, you'll call?"

"I will. Make tea, please, and save me some of whatever it is you made for breakfast." Once the twins left, Regan stood up, still a little light-headed, and shuffled to the bathroom. Stiff and achy, she felt as if she were ninety-five and not still in her twenties. She caught a glimpse of herself in the mirror and grimaced. Both of her eyes were swollen, black and blue, as was the bridge of her nose. The cut on her forehead was an angry slash in a mound of purple and pale green. Her hair was matted with dirt and dried blood, and so was her face. She blinked against the tears filling her eyes and turned away. Physical aches and pains couldn't hold a candle to the emotional toll to her heart.

She undressed and stepped into the tub, and for several glorious minutes, she did nothing but soak, letting the hot water soothe her aching bones. Then she washed, and the water turned a rusty brown. "Yuck."

She drained the tub, stood up and washed again under the shower. Lord, but it felt good to be clean. Yawning, she dried herself and put on fresh, sweet-smelling clothes. Opening a bathroom drawer, she grabbed a couple of Band-Aids and applied them to the gash on her forehead, doing her best to bring the edges of her torn skin together. The cut on her nose wasn't bad, so she left it alone. At least both wounds were clean.

Regan gathered her dirty laundry from the floor and stuffed everything into the hamper. Then she grabbed a hairbrush from the dresser and sat on her bed to work the tangles out of her hair. A mistake, because that led to lying down and pressing her face into Fáelán's pillow. His scent still lingered. Had it been only a handful of days since he'd been taken from her? She curled herself into a ball, hugged Fáelán's pillow to her chest and fell into a deep sleep.

Chapter Fourteen

Fáelán paced and gesticulated before the fae king. Lir's throne was positioned at one end of a grand courtyard surrounded by cloisters and crowded with curious courtiers. Avid interest pulsed from the Tuatha Dé Danann nobles, becoming a palpable force pressing in around him. Fionn stood nearby, and so did his captain's fae relation, lending Fáelán courage.

He couldn't help but get caught up in the retelling of all that had befallen him at Morrigan's hand. He poured all the emotional turmoil he'd suffered into his words. "I was deceived, tormented and held captive for nigh on two millennia by one of your own," he called out, meeting the eyes of several of the spectators. "My mate risked her life, coming back through the ages to warn me. Because of Regan's bravery, I evaded Morrigan's curse this time 'round, but still the fae princess continues to hound my every step."

He turned back to the king. "I am beside myself with worry for Regan, Your Majesty. Your daughter choked the life from poor, innocent Nóra the night I was cursed. I've no doubt Morrigan means to—"

"Think you I do not know my own daughter?" Lir pointed at the fae sword at Fáelán's waist. "How come you by the Tuatha weapon?"

The fae king's unnatural gaze lasered through Fáelán, and he lowered his eyes to Fragarach. "'Twas loaned to Regan, so that when she came through time to warn me of Morrigan's curse—and Nóra's impending murder—I'd believe her. How she came by it, I cannot say, Your Majesty. When we parted, Regan was upset, and she left the sword behind." He placed his palm over the hilt. "I don't believe she meant to leave it, but 'tis glad I am that she did."

Lir's frown deepened. "Mananán," he shouted, "explain."

The fae prince stepped forward and bowed. "Your future granddaughter Boann brought Fáelán's mate to me in the mortal's twenty-first century, Father. They shared with me the tale you just heard and asked for my help. 'Twas I who suggested Regan travel back to this point in time to prevent the curse from ever happening. Doing so seemed the most expedient way to set things aright." He shrugged. "Boann asked for one of my swords as a token of proof, and 'twas she who guaranteed its return." He strode toward Fáelán. "I'll have it back now." He held out his hand.

"Not so fast," Lir boomed. "Did you know of Morrigan's curse when first she laid it upon this mortal?"

"Aye, Father, and I—"

"Why did you not come to me with all of this from the start?"

"I tried to talk Morrigan into freeing him many times, but she refused." Mananán dropped his hand. "I didn't wish to trouble you with an altercation involving a mere mortal. When Boann brought Regan to me, I offered the perfect solution, and bringing it to your attention didn't seem necessary. I dismissed the entire affair from my mind. I did not anticipate my sister's obstinate persistence in her pursuit of this mortal." He cut Fáelán a scathing look. "Nor did I anticipate the Fiann's appearance before you, bearing *my* sword and pleading for your intercession."

"In other words, you did not wish to implicate yourself in your sister's crimes." Lir sighed heavily.

"I had naught to do with her crimes." Mananán gazed around at the courtiers, who listened with rapt attention. "I did try to reason with her many times, sire, but she refused to heed my advice."

"Morrigan," Lir shouted, tracing a rune in the air with his hand. "I summon thee to my court. Now."

Morrigan appeared out of thin air before Lir's dais. She went down on bended knee and bowed her head, her hands folded gracefully in front of her. Fáelán's stomach curdled at the sight of her.

"Father," she said, her head still bowed. "What is your wish?"

"Upon one strand in the weft of time's tapestry, you will have murdered a human, given the Elixir of Life to a mortal without sanction and kept him unlawfully for nearly two thousand of their years. You also reneged on your oath to set him free once he'd met the conditions you yourself set forth. And let us not forget your deception when you came to him at the very first." His scowl deepened. "What have you to say for yourself, daughter?"

"She cannot lie to her father," Fionn whispered beside Fáelán. "He'll know if she tries, and then 'twill go worse for her."

Fáelán nodded slightly, his attention fixed upon the scene playing out in front of him.

"Everything this mortal told you is the truth." She lifted her head to meet her father's gaze, her expression pleading. "But, Father, I have conceived a child with him," Morrigan cried, turning her wrath toward Fáelán for an instant. "I am bound to him, and I . . . I only wished to make him my consort, so that we could raise our child together. He *refused* me," she said, her tone that of a spoiled child.

The familiar rage and frustration unfurled within Fáelán. Not only had the fae princess cursed him, but she'd kept any knowledge of his daughter's existence a secret. Regan had been the one to tell him, and he'd accused her of lying. Had his daughter longed for a father's love and guidance as she grew up? Did Boann hate him for what must seem to her like abandonment on his part? Morrigan had also kept his daughter from his family, and they would have showered her with love and kindness. His jaw tightened to the point of pain.

"The mortal declined your offer, daughter, which is within his rights." Lir's tone hardened. "Having kept your true identity from him from the start, you could not have expected the outcome to be any different. Punishing him for not wanting you, subjecting him to a curse he did naught to deserve, is unacceptable. From this moment forward, you will leave this man in peace."

"But, Father, I—"

"There is no excuse for your behavior. Bonded or not, you know the law. Be grateful Fáelán's mate had the bravery to undo the worst of your crimes upon this place in time, else your penance would be far greater." He rose from his throne. "Do not make things worse with petty excuses. You have shamed me. You have shamed the goddess."

Lir stepped down from the dais and stood before his daughter. "You are sentenced to reside here with me under supervision for the span of this mortal's life, so that I can be sure he remains unmolested."

King Lir pounded the end of his trident against the floor, and a wave of power surged through the hall, nearly knocking Fáelán off his feet. "And do not think for an instant I will not know if you coerce others to do your bidding against him. I will assign a companion to you, someone I trust who will remain by your side every moment, until all of Fáelán's days are spent. Do you understand?"

Morrigan nodded, her expression closer to cunning than contrition.

"As for you." Lir turned to Fáelán. "Your life is restored to you as it was before my daughter's interference. You no longer need concern yourself with the Tuatha. Go in peace."

Where was the relief he should be feeling? Instead, sorrow engulfed him. Not only had he been denied the chance to know his daughter; now he was to lose the only woman he would ever love, and he'd never know his child—his second child. Fáelán knew what he wanted. More than anything, he longed to be with Regan. Morrigan had stolen so much from him. After eons of deprivation, he refused to give up his one chance at happiness.

He glanced at Fionn, not even attempting to hide the misery stealing his breath. "My lord . . . I . . ." He cleared his throat. "Please release me from my vows to the Fianna. I need to be with Regan. I cannot forsake her or my unborn child."

Fionn studied him in that deep way he had and nodded slightly, his expression grave. "I release ye, my friend, and I wish ye naught but contentment and peace all the rest of your days. Ye've earned them, aye?"

Warmth seeped through him, and gratitude. "I am proud to have served ye, and I am grateful for everything ye've done for me." Drawing in a long breath, Fáelán stepped forward. "King Lir, I beg your indulgence for a moment longer."

"Aye?" The fae king cast him a look of annoyance. "What is it now?"

"I wish to be sent back to my life in the twenty-first century. I want to be with my mate. She carries my child, and I want to be a good husband to her and a father to our babe." And any other children they might be blessed with in the future. "I never knew my daughter, Boann. Do not force me to forsake another. After all I have suffered, am I not owed this one favor?" He glanced at Morrigan with all the loathing he held for her. "If not from you, then from her?"

"Hmph." Lir's brow lowered. "*Owed* a favor? You came asking me to settle the matter betwixt the two of you. Did I not do as you asked? Was that not favor enough?"

"Ye did, and 'tis grateful I am, but—"

"You were born in this place and time, and here is where you were meant to live out your short life. If I were to grant you another *favor*, 'twould alter the fate of many in what your kind call the third century." The king climbed the stairs of his dais. "Favor denied. Return to the earthly realm." Lir glanced at Fáelán, his eyes glowing an unnatural bright blue. "'Tis where you belong."

His heart pounding, and a cold sweat breaking out over his entire body, Fáelán squared his shoulders and lifted his chin. "I've been told that what has already occurred in the past, present or the future cannot be erased." He waved a hand in the air. "I know naught of strands or the weaving of time, but Morrigan has already altered time's tapestry. Has she not? If I am not sent back to my life in the twenty-first century, will that not affect the fate for many as well, including my progeny? That is unacceptable to me. What I am asking is reasonable and just." Fáelán swallowed convulsively, praying the demigod would not squash him like a bug where he stood.

"Who told you nothing can be erased?" King Lir's gaze settled upon his son Mananán.

The prince stepped forward again. "Boann shared that with Regan, whilst trying to convince the mortal woman to aid her sire. Regan feared if she undid Fáelán's curse, she'd lose her unborn child, and Boann wished only to put her mind at ease."

Warmth spread through Fáelán. His daughter had wanted to help him, and that gave him hope. Mayhap she didn't hate him after all. "Regan told the same to me when she came to the past. Changes have already been wrought, and it matters not whether I remain in the third century or return to the twenty-first." He'd grieved the loss of his third-century family eons ago.

"Your Majesty, I long to be where my heart resides, which is in the future with Regan and our child." In a last-ditch effort, he added, "Do you and I not share a bond of kinship through my daughter, Boann? Upon that tie, I beg ye, grant me this request."

Lir sat upon his throne, canted his head and scratched at his beard. "You are brave, Fiann . . . and foolish. Still . . ." He leaned back and rapped his fingers against the armrests. "Long have I been intrigued with the Fianna." He shot Fionn a challenging look. "Have you not claimed over and over the skill of your warriors is peerless, even greater than that of a Tuatha warrior?"

"I have, Your Majesty, and this lad is one of my finest." Fionn rested his hand upon Fáelán's shoulder.

"Hmmm." The king scrutinized Fáelán.

The thumping of his heart echoed inside his head, and Fáelán gripped Fragarach's hilt so tightly, his palm would surely carry the imprint of its runes for the remainder of his life.

Lir leaned forward. "I propose a tournament. This Fiann"—he pointed his trident at Fáelán—"against a champion of my choosing. Since the fae sword still hangs at your waist, I'll grant you Fragarach's use for this contest," Lir said, his tone mocking. "If my champion draws first blood, you remain in the century of your birth. If you draw first blood, then I shall consider your request. What say you?"

The king would *consider* his request? "Ah, feck," Fáelán muttered under his breath, and Fionn's grasp upon his shoulder tightened.

Fáelán caught movement from the corner of his eye. He bowed his head as if in thought and cast a sideways glance. Morrigan slipped away through the crowd.

"Well?" King Lir's voice boomed. "What is it to be?"

Fáelán knew Morrigan well enough to suspect the worst and to be on guard. Yet no matter what she schemed, what choice did he have but to accept? Though his innards had turned to watery porridge, he thrust out his chest and widened his stance. "Your Majesty, once I've drawn first blood, the battle will cease, aye?"

"Aye, Fiann." King Lir laughed. "You have my word as a direct descendant of the goddess Danu, my champion will not use fae magic to defeat you. Múiros, come forth," he called.

One of the guards standing along the wall sauntered forward, smirking as he met Fáelán's gaze. The fae warrior carried a shield and a lance, along with the sword at his back.

"This must be a fair fight," Fionn said, moving to stand in front of Fáelán. "Either grant my Fiann a lance and a shield, or have your champion set his aside."

"Agreed." Lir nodded to Múiros, and another guard came forward to take the lance and shield from him.

Fáelán rolled his shoulders before removing the scabbard and belt from his waist. The sword had always been his favorite weapon, and he excelled at the skill. He drew Fragarach from its scabbard, tossed the belt aside and held the flat of the blade to his forehead. He sent a prayer to whatever helpful spirits or gods might be listening. "For Regan, our child, my daughter, Boann, my clan and kin," he muttered under his breath. "Lend me strength, speed and the wits needed to defeat my foe."

***

"Regan," one of her sisters said, jostling her by the shoulder. "Wake up, sweetie, or you won't be able to sleep tonight."

"I doubt that. I'm pretty sure I could sleep for a week." Regan rolled to her back and stretched, taking inventory of all her aches and pains. "How long have I been out?"

"All morning," Meredith said, peering down at her. "We've made lunch. Grayce and I want to know what's been going on since we got your text telling us you might not be here when we arrived."

"OK. I'm hungry anyway." She swung her legs over the edge of the bed and stood up. "I look like hell, don't I?"

"Yes. Two black eyes, a nasty lump and cut on your forehead, and a swollen nose. You look like you might've been in a car accident." Meredith studied her. "How do you feel?"

"Beat up. Sad." She headed for the bathroom. "I'll be right down."

"I'll wait, in case you're unsteady on your feet."

Regan nodded and closed the bathroom door behind her. She avoided looking in the mirror. At least she was clean and had access to a bathroom. Quickly taking care of her needs, she then washed her hands and her face, brushed her teeth and headed downstairs, with her sister standing close by. Meredith and Grayce had already set the table. Regan's stomach gurgled with hunger. "Smells like chicken noodle soup."

"Yep, homemade, and we have currant scones from the bakery in the village," Grayce said, setting two steaming bowls on the table.

Meredith brought the third bowl, along with a plate holding the scones. Regan's mouth watered. "Yesterday I was convinced I was going to die in a cavern beneath the Hill of Tara. Today I get to feast on scones and homemade soup." She smiled, even though it hurt to do so.

"Are you ready to talk about what happened, Rae?" Grayce asked, taking a seat and placing a scone on her bread plate.

"I managed to end Fáelán's curse by traveling back through time to the third century, and then—"

"Hold up." Meredith's eyes saucered. "You what?"

"I'd better start at the beginning." Regan leaned back in her chair and sighed. "It's . . . the entire story is bizarre, and has been since I first met Fáelán at Newgrange." Regan launched into her story while they ate, and it took until the dishes were done before she finished.

"Let's move to the living room," Meredith said, her brow creased. "I have questions."

Regan huffed out a breath and raked her fingers through her hair. She never had gotten around to brushing out the tangles. "I can imagine." The teakettle whistled on the stove, and she fixed a pot of tea while Meredith took three mugs to the coffee table.

"OK." Meredith took a seat on the same chair where Boann had been a few days ago. "Here's what I don't get. If you prevented Fáelán from being cursed, then you would've also prevented the two of you from ever meeting. So . . . how is it you *think* you're pregnant?"

"I don't think I am; I know I am. Boann and her uncle explained it all to me. They said we don't understand how time works, and—"

"Think about it, Meredith," Grayce interjected. "I have visions about the future. The. Future. I'm not the only one. There are volumes of documented cases where someone foretold an event or a disaster. I see things that haven't happened yet—things that either will or will not occur, depending upon the choices made by every single person involved. If time is a single moment we call the present, and the future hasn't already happened, then visions and premonitions wouldn't be possible. Right?"

"I see your point, but like you say, things change according to the choices made by the individuals involved. Regan changed the past, so that has to have affected the future."

"Affect, yes but . . ." Grayce's brow furrowed. "Because of what I've experienced with my visions, I've often wondered if the future, the present and the past aren't all"—she whirled a hand in the air— "going on at the same time. I've read stuff, like the possibility of a multiverse, string theory, parallel universes where we live different lives. Did you know physicists at the University of Queensland in Australia have proven time travel is possible by sending light particles to the past?"

"No, I didn't, but leave it to you to look for the most outlandish explanation." Meredith snorted. "I don't think—"

"What I did in the past *did* alter the present." Regan sighed. "Because I went back to the third century and prevented the curse, Fáelán is no longer here. But that doesn't change the fact that he *was* with me a week ago. He and I *were* together. You've seen the pictures, and I have my memories. I know it's confusing, and I don't pretend to understand any of it either, but there's proof." She placed her hand over her abdomen for a second. "Speaking of visions, Grayce, have you had any concerning Fáelán? The last glimpse I had of him, he was at King Lir's court, and I'm assuming he was there because, even though he avoided being cursed, Morrigan still wants to own him."

Grayce shook her head. "You know how it is, Rae. I've tried, but I don't have any control over what comes to me. In fact, I haven't had any visions about anything for several weeks. I think I'm in remission."

"Remission?" Meredith's brow rose. "Having visions isn't a disease, Grayce."

"If you say so." Grayce shrugged. "Then I'm on a vision sabbatical. For whatever reason, nothing has come to me, and I'm glad. I hope they're gone for good."

"Grayce . . ." Meredith's expression filled with sympathy. "You—"

"Oh!" A tugging sensation hit Regan, and she sucked in a breath. It happened again, only stronger this time, and her mouth went dry.

"What is it, Rae?" Meredith asked, and both sisters stared at her, their expressions questioning.

"Something is . . . I feel like I'm being pulled." She looked from one twin to the other as the pull grew stronger. She gripped the armrest of the couch. "Oh no. I—"

The next thing Regan knew, the world was rushing past, and she was flying through space. And time? She landed on her hands and knees by the shore of a lake with water so clear, she could see the colors of the smooth pebbles at the bottom. A wooden bridge spanned the shore to an island, where a columned palace stood. The air had a familiar rarity to it, and the sky an unearthly hue of blue and pink. She'd been taken to Summerland, and she had no doubt who was responsible. Regan rose slowly from the ground, apprehension knotting her insides.

"We meet at last," an ethereal, feminine voice said from behind her.

Goose bumps prickled at the back of her neck and along her forearms. Terrified, Regan whipped around to face the fae princess. Defenseless, with nowhere to run, she was the rabbit cornered by the coyote. Morrigan was incredibly beautiful, but malice had hardened her features into a mask of twisted cruelty. "Morrigan."

The fae princess sneered. "Regan."

"Why have you brought me here?" Not sure she really wanted to hear the answer, Regan swiped her sweaty palms against her jeans. If only she could get air into her lungs, she might be able to think well enough to muster some kind of defense.

"Why, to watch Fáelán die, of course." Morrigan waved a hand, and a faint rune appeared in midair and then dissipated just as quickly.

"No!" Regan was propelled toward the bridge, whether she wanted to go there or not, and *not* was uppermost on her list of choices. Trying like hell to stop didn't change a thing. "Isn't murdering mortals against your laws? You . . . you're going to kill him?"

"Oh no. Not me." Morrigan walked beside Regan, her expression arctic. "You see, my father has forbidden me from molesting Fáelán in any manner. Because of you, I have been sentenced to remain under my father's thumb for the span of Fáelán's earthly life. I intend to make that a very short sentence." The faerie turned her hate-filled gaze toward Regan. "You, however, were not mentioned—an unfortunate oversight on my father's part."

"King Lir will know you're up to no good again."

Morrigan shrugged. "For the moment he's distracted with the ridiculous tournament he's arranged between Fáelán and our most renowned warrior. 'Twas to be a fight lasting only until one or the other drew blood, but fae warriors can be enchanted or bribed. Fáelán doesn't know it, but 'twill be a fight to *his* death. Your job will be to distract him, making it easier for my champion to fell him. You see, in the heat of a fight, accidents happen, and mortal blows occur whether intended or not."

"Oh, God." Regan's heart clawed its way up to her throat. A fine sheen of sweat beaded her forehead. "But . . . the fae have the means to heal mortal wounds. Won't your—"

"Healing humans only works if it's a wound caused by a mortal weapon. Unfortunately for you and Fáelán, a wound inflicted to a mortal with a Tuatha Dé Danann blade cannot be healed."

Regan's soul bled at the thought of Fáelán's death. Had he been right after all? Would they have been better off if he'd remained cursed? They could've been together, though worlds apart. How long would this creature beside her have allowed them to continue on that way before she put an end to their relationship? Regan's eyes filled, and a fist-size lump clogged her throat. She and her boasty Fiann never really had a ghost of a chance of happily-ever-after after all.

They'd reached the island, and Regan was forced to climb a short flight of stairs and enter the palace through double doors thrown wide. Morrigan compelled Regan through a large hall with walls covered in murals of life beneath the sea. The beauty of the scenes came into sharper focus, and the colors were so lifelike, Regan couldn't tear her eyes away.

She shook her head and forced herself to avert her gaze. She was walking to an execution, knowing full well hers would be next, and she was caught up in the aqua blue, coral and green of the murals? They must hold an enchantment.

They left the hall and entered a courtyard crowded with fae standing in a circle, watching something going on in the center. Regan lifted her gaze toward King Lir, who sat upon his throne. His attention was riveted to the spectacle in the center. Morrigan forced her to move through the masses toward the front.

Regan lost her breath, and her heart pounded so hard she feared it might rupture. Fáelán and a fae warrior were circling each other, swords drawn. Sweat dripped from Fáelán, and he was breathing hard, while his opponent didn't show any sign of tiring.

Morrigan shoved Regan forward. She stumbled and fell to her hands and knees on the ground a few feet from the two combatants stalking each other. The spectators cried out as Fáelán's gaze met and held hers. His adversary's sword arced through the air, aiming straight for Fáelán's exposed neck. "Look out," she shouted, knowing it was too late. Her heart shattering, Regan shut her eyes. She couldn't watch, couldn't bear seeing the man she loved lose his life because of her.

Chapter Fifteen

The sight of Regan, her face battered and bruised, cut Fáelán more sharply than any blade ever could, and in a flash, Morrigan's scheme became clear. Sweating, his lungs straining for air, Fáelán acted reflexively. He dropped and rolled. The blow meant to sever his head from his neck met naught but air, and the momentum unbalanced Múiros. Fáelán sprang up from the ground in a flurry of offensive strikes and blows, forcing Múiros to retreat.

This was no contest of skill; he was in a fight for his life. How had Morrigan gotten to the fae warrior without King Lir's knowledge? The princess knew him not at all if she believed using Regan to distract him would make him an easy target. Seeing her only renewed his determination, and resolve surged through his veins. Fáelán's need to get to Regan, his instincts to protect, lent him strength. "King Lir," he shouted. "Look to your daughter."

The clash of steel against steel reverberated through him, and Fáelán's focus sharpened. He couldn't afford to think of aught but surviving, no matter how badly he wanted to hold Regan—no matter how desperately he wanted to tell her he loved her. If the fae king paid heed to his shout, he had no way of knowing, and he had no choice but to trust Fionn to look after Regan. He closed his mind to all but the task at hand.

Striking high, then low, he feinted and parried, advanced and retreated. The shrill ring of his blade against the fae's filled the air. He fixed his attention upon Múiros's eyes, seeking the tell—a slight tilt of his head, a glance to the left or right. Where the head willed, the body followed. His lungs burned now, and sweat trickled down his back and chest. His muscles quivered with fatigue, while Múiros seemed not to tire at all. Gods, he had to end this soon, or all would be lost.

"What did the princess promise ye?" Fáelán taunted. "A night between her royal thighs? While ye lie with Morrigan, think on this . . . *I*, a mere mortal, was there first." Fáelán thrust his hips a few times, mimicking the sex act. He laughed as if he hadn't a care in the world. Sweat dripped into his eyes, blurring his vision, and he blinked. "Trust me, laddie, the whore is not worth the price she'll extract from your hide." He shrugged. "Besides, I've had better—far better, and much sweeter."

"How dare you speak of our princess in that manner. *She* is a direct descendant of the goddess. Compared to her, *you* are an insect." Múiros roared, raised his sword and came at Fáelán in a mindless fury, exactly as he'd hoped. Fáelán didn't flinch, nor did he retreat. He watched. His enemy's eyes darted to the left, and his knee turned slightly.

Fáelán pivoted and crouched a fraction of a second too late for Múiros to change tactics. Múiros's swing continued on its arc, even as he attempted to change its trajectory. Fáelán spun away, slicing through his enemy's sleeve to the skin beneath. He knocked Múiros's sword arm down and away with the same swing, and the point of the warrior's sword hit the ground. Múiros hissed with pain and glanced at his wound.

Fáelán jogged out of reach. Blood dripping from his wound, Múiros came at him again, his eyes blazing with a murderous glint.

"Shite. 'Tis over. Stop him, King Lir," Fáelán shouted, backing away. "Your champion is bespelled."

Múiros continued his charge, his sword raised and his expression glazed and predatory. Keeping his eyes upon the crazed warrior, Fáelán continued to back away. What was taking King Lir so long? *Feck.* Knowing the fae, Lir was probably enjoying the spectacle.

Fáelán tripped on something behind him, nay—*someone* tripped him. He went down and caught a glimpse of Morrigan's evil glee as she sidled away. The spectators gasped and cried out, but not one of them bothered to intervene.

Múiros was upon him then, and it was all Fáelán could do to divert the blows raining down on his head. Múiros kicked him in the ribs over and over, and pain exploded, hazing Fáelán's vision. The fae warrior straddled him, making it impossible to roll away. "Lir, stop your man!" he shouted. "Can't trust the bloody, fecking fae," Fáelán rasped out. He reached up and grabbed the bespelled fae by the balls, squeezing for all he was worth.

Múiros cried out and tried to pry himself loose. Fáelán kept a firm grip on the man's most vulnerable assets and scrambled to his feet. He crowded Múiros, rendering all but the hilts of their swords useless. Continuing to exert excruciating pressure, Fáelán slammed his forehead into the man's face. Triumph flared at the satisfying crunch of cartilage and bone. Then he brought Fragarach's hilt down, slamming it into the wrist of his opponent's sword arm.

Fáelán shoved Múiros hard and once more moved out of his reach. Múiros staggered back, blood dripping from his nose and arm. Groaning, he dropped his sword, leaned over and covered his balls with both hands.

The objective of any battle was to survive, and given the circumstances, Fáelán saw no reason to fight fair. He went in for the kill, Fragarach's point aimed for the warrior's throat. The sword but a finger's width from its mark, Fáelán's muscles seized, and he was frozen in place. Gods, he hated fae magic. Completely vulnerable to attack, panic flared, but then he realized Múiros couldn't move either.

King Lir approached, a blaze of color against the fog of bloodlust clouding Fáelán's vision. A thunderous expression suffused the king's features, and the blue of his eyes swirled and glowed with a light of their own. Gods, he hated that about the fae too.

Lir touched Múiros with his trident, and the warrior dropped to his knees and bowed his head. "Tell me," the king commanded his defeated champion.

The magic holding Fáelán dissipated at the same time. He wiped the sweat from his eyes with his sleeve and took a deep breath. His heart still pounded, and his limbs had the consistency of seaweed, barely able to keep him upright. Still, not only had he lived through a fight with one of the Tuatha; he'd defeated his adversary. A frisson of anticipation raced through him. He couldn't wait to bask in Regan's admiration, and of course, she'd hold him in her arms while she sang his praises. After all, he'd done it for her.

"Morrigan promised to take me as her consort if I agreed to kill this mortal, sire," Múiros told the king. "I refused, and she placed a compulsion spell upon me. 'Tis still upon me. I beg you, sire . . . command her to set me free." The muscles along Múiros's jaw twitched, tension pulsed from him and he held one hand over his bleeding arm. "I swear by the goddess, I mean the Fiann no harm."

King Lir shouted his daughter's name, and she appeared. Lir glowered at his daughter. The very air carried the weight of his disappointment and anger. In that moment, Lir looked far less the fae king and more the weary father facing his impenitent offspring. "I am beyond incensed, Morrigan. Did I not tell you to cease molesting this mortal? And not a moment later, you plotted his murder and cast a spell upon my chosen combatant?"

Fáelán scanned the surrounding area for Regan and Fionn. Courtiers drew closer to witness the new drama unfolding between their princess and her father. He couldn't see through the crowd to the cloisters, and a band of anxiety tightened around his chest. A different kind of terror gripped him. Was Regan safe, or had Morrigan taken her life?

He still held Fragarach, and the fae princess, the source of all his troubles, stood but an arm span away. All she had done to him, all the years she'd tortured and taunted—his blood boiled and frothed into a white-hot rage. 'Twould be so easy to plunge the fae blade into her black heart. If he did, he'd ensure she didn't ruin anyone else's life the way she had his. But he'd won King Lir's challenge, and ending Morrigan's existence would also be the end of his. Thanks to Regan, he finally had reasons to live. His blood lust receded, and sanity prevailed.

Lir fixed his neon-blue gaze upon his daughter. "Remove the compulsion you placed upon my champion."

Morrigan sighed, muttered an incantation under her breath and gestured with one hand over Múiros's kneeling form.

"Thank the goddess," the warrior said, sagging forward.

"Daughter," King Lir said, his tone tinged with bitterness and anger. "I bind thee. Forthwith you are without magic." He touched her with the tines of his trident. "You are confined to your living quarters under my roof until you have proven yourself reformed. I suggest you spend your days reflecting upon how you might improve your character, and how you can be the best role model you can be to the daughter you carry. By the goddess, *you* are a direct descendant of Danu! You bear a responsibility to our people. 'Tis high time you took that responsibility seriously."

The king touched Fáelán with his trident, and a powerful current shot through him. "Mortal, I have placed a protection ward upon you. If Morrigan attempts any mischief against you or yours, the harm she intends will come back to her threefold."

Fáelán nearly dropped to the ground with relief, and Morrigan shot daggers at him with her glare. King Lir waved a hand in the air, and she disappeared. Now that the spectacle had come to an end, the fae courtiers began to wander away in groups, no doubt discussing the day's events.

Múiros sat on the ground and wiped at the blood from the lower half of his face with the hem of his tunic. "Fáelán, you bested me fairly, and I am spent. I apologize for—"

"No need." Fáelán offered him a hand up. "Spent ye say? Ye did not even break a sweat."

Múiros accepted his help and rose to stand beside him. "The Tuatha Dé Danann do *not* sweat." He said the words as if the mere thought of perspiring disgusted him.

"I am indebted to ye, Your Majesty. Will ye see Fragarach returned to Prince Man; along with my thanks for the help he gave to my mate?" Fáelán handed the fae sword, hilt first, to the king.

"I will." Lir gestured to a hovering servant, who took the sword from Fáelán. "You acquitted yourself well, Fiann, and with honor. As agreed, I will—"

"Forgive me, Your Majesty, but did you see what became of the woman Morrigan shoved to the ground during our fight?"

"I saw no woman. Morrigan must have cloaked her presence from me. At your warning shout, my attention turned to my daughter and then to Múiros. I sensed naught amiss." Lir frowned. "Despite what humans believe, we Tuatha are not omniscient."

"Well met, laddie, well met." Fionn slapped Fáelán on the back as he and Alpin reached him.

"Fionn," he began. "Where is—"

"What have you to say about my Fenians now, King Lir? Did I not speak the truth? I would pit any man of mine against one of yours any day, confident that mine would emerge victorious." He grinned. "My Fianna are far superior in strength, skill and wit."

"I commend you, Fionn. Your boasts were not without merit after all." King Lir nodded. "Even with my champion's compulsion, Fáelán prevailed." He pulled at his beard and the corners of his mouth quirked up. "That last move . . . the tenacious grip, and the head butting . . . Such . . . er . . . skills must have taken *weeks* to perfect." He flashed a wry grin.

Fionn barked out a laugh. "Aye, well, I did mention my Fenians possess *wit*, did I not?"

"Let us consider holding more tournaments in the future," Lir suggested. "'Tis clear my warriors need motivation to improve their skill. With no real enemies at present, I fear they've grown lax."

"Gladly, sire." Fionn's eyes lit with enthusiasm. "Send word when ye wish to hold the event, and we shall plan a variety of contests together. Hand-to-hand, lances, archery and swords, my men excel at all forms of combat," he boasted.

"King Lir." Fáelán could stand quietly by no longer. "I fear for my mate, Regan. Morrigan used her to distract me during our fight, and I need to know what became of her."

Lir waved his hand in the air, as if brushing Fáelán's worry aside. "'Tis likely once I bound Morrigan's magic, your mate was returned to her rightful place in time. Be at ease."

'Twas *likely*? Be at ease? How could he be when he didn't know for certain? He prayed Regan truly had been returned to twenty-first-century Howth, and the sooner he was there with her, the better. "I won the tournament, and ye promised to grant my wish to return to my life in the twenty-first century. I'm ready."

"Promised?" The fae king barked out a laugh. "I agreed to *consider* your request should you win, and so I shall. And whilst I consider the matter most carefully, we shall hold a feast to celebrate your victory."

Fáelán swallowed the groan rising in his throat. 'Twas well known fae feasts lasted for days on end, and the Tuatha Dé Danann had the ability to stretch and contract time to suit their whims. One of their days could last a second, a year or a century. Fáelán was about to protest, when Fionn caught his eye and shook his head ever so slightly.

"I am honored, Your Majesty." Fáelán bowed. The king and his champion left them. Fáelán turned to Fionn's fae cousin. "Alpin, is Regan still here, or has she been returned to her own time?"

Alpin frowned. "Your mate was here?"

"Aye. Regan was the woman Morrigan shoved to the ground but five paces from where Múiros and I fought."

"Hmm. We did not see her." Alpin placed his hand upon Fáelán's shoulder and steered him toward the doors leading to Lir's hall, and Fionn followed. "Morrigan likely hid her presence from all but you."

Fáelán rubbed his aching temples. "But . . . the fae who watched the tournament, they cried out when it happened."

"Aye, we all did. Ye turned from Múiros when his sword was but a hair's breadth away from your neck, laddie." Fionn grunted as he came to his side. "I feared for ye, I did."

"Feck." Exhaustion stole his ability to think clearly, and he didn't know what to do. Frustrated, impatient, his jaw tightened with the effort to refrain from shouting and stomping his feet. "If Morrigan was able to mask Regan's presence from her father, couldn't she also have hidden any harm she might have done to her?"

Alpin's gaze filled with sympathy. "'Tis unlikely, but who can say with Morrigan? She is powerful, and we all know her to be duplicitous and without honor."

What if Morrigan abandoned Regan to the mist? What if she'd taken Regan's life afore Lir bound her magic? When last he'd spoken to his love, he'd denied ever having laid eyes upon her afore. He'd treated her with suspicion, sending her on her way. How was she to know his memories had come back to him?

He'd hurt Regan and abandoned her when she needed him most. That he'd caused her grief weighed heavily upon his spirit. Worse, he couldn't bear the thought she might be gone from this world without ever knowing he loved her. "Find Regan and send me to her, Alpin. I beg you."

"I cannot." Alpin shook his head. "I will not incur the wrath of my king, and neither should you. Stay. Allow our king to celebrate your victory. 'Tis a great honor he bestows upon you, and he's more likely to grant your request if you do naught to anger him. What I will agree to do is to search for your mate's whereabouts and see that she is well."

"I'd be most grateful." How was it that, after all he'd been through, he was still a prisoner of the fae?

Alpin cast him a thoughtful look. "If King Lir does grant your wish, do you not wish to visit with your kin and clan before you depart?"

He'd been so consumed with worry for Regan, he hadn't given his family a thought. Now his need to get to Regan warred with his desire to see his family one last time. "Aye, if ye can assure me Regan is well, I shall visit with my kin afore taking my leave." He forced himself to unclench his jaw.

"My mam and sisters wept, and my da scolded me the day I returned home to tell them I'd been cursed." He glanced at Alpin. "'Twas ye who gifted my kin with the ability to see me in the void, so they could help me over the centuries. Do ye have any recollection?"

"Not at a conscious level. Though our paths crossed, I was not meant to share more than that brief instant with you, so I have forgotten." He shrugged. "If I wished to bring back the memories I could, but I see no need."

"What about ye, Fionn?" he asked, slanting his captain a curious look. "'Twas ye who came to my aid and summoned Alpin to help me. Do ye have any memory of that time?"

"Nay, and for the same reason. Our paths diverged. If ye wish, I can take the same potion I gave ye, and—"

"Ugh, don't remind me of that foul brew." He shuddered at the thought of the potion he'd consumed for the sake of his memories.

"I agree with Alpin. Should Lir be willing to send ye to the future, ye'll regret it if ye do not spend time with your kin," Fionn told him.

"I'll do my best to persuade King Lir on your behalf. All will work itself out for the best. Be at ease, Fáelán."

Twice now he'd been told to be at ease, and the words crimped his gut. He was at the mercy of King Lir, who might keep him in his realm for a feast lasting centuries. If that were the case, once he got free, he'd have no kin left. Be at ease? Not possible when he couldn't be certain the love of his life was safe, or that he'd ever see her again. Gods, he loathed the fae.

"I hope like hell I'm never jerked through time like that again," Regan said, finishing her tale. She tucked her legs under her at one end of the couch, glad to be with her sisters in twenty-first-century Howth again. Grayce sat at the other end, and Meredith stood in the kitchen, making coffee. Worn thin from stress and grief, Regan wanted sleep way more than she wanted caffeine, but she needed something to do with her hands. Holding a mug would have to do.

"Did you actually see Fáelán's head severed from his shoulders?" Grayce studied her.

Meredith set three steaming mugs on the coffee table before settling into the armchair. "That's not at all helpful, Grayce."

"I'm just trying to point out—"

"No," Regan said, her tone flat. "I closed my eyes, and a second later, I was whooshed back here. Do you think I wanted to see . . . to watch . . ." Her voice broke, and she shook her head. She was almost numb with grief. Almost.

"What I saw was the sharp edge of a sword inches from Fáelán's neck. Morrigan used me to distract him, and it worked. Instead of keeping his eyes on the man who was trying to kill him, Fáelán was looking at me. I don't see how he could've . . . how he might have prevented . . ." She bit her lip, unable to continue.

When their eyes had met, she'd had no idea whether or not Fáelán remembered her or not. But then, why would Morrigan have come for her if Fáelán still had no recollection of who she was and what they'd meant to each other? If Fáelán had regained his memories, that made being used against him all the more deplorable.

"I thought ending his curse was the right thing to do. I believed I was helping him, and instead . . . Oh, God. I'm the reason he died!" she sobbed.

"You didn't witness his death, so you don't know anything for certain." Grayce slid closer and put her arm around Regan's shoulders. "Seems like we'd know it if he had. We'd sense something. Once you two fell in love, he became family, right?" She turned to Meredith. "Are you picking up on anything?"

"No, but then *he's* in the third century, while *we're* in the twenty-first. I don't know that I'd get anything about him with that much time separating us. Honestly, I'm still having difficulty wrapping my head around the whole time-is-not-linear thing. I still don't see how—"

"Now who's not being helpful," Grayce griped, narrowing her eyes at Meredith.

Regan grabbed a tissue and wiped her eyes. "I want to go home." Her sisters exchanged a long look, one of those twin-silent-communication moments they often shared. "What?" Regan's gaze bounced from one to the other.

"Well . . ." Grayce gave Regan a quick hug. "Don't you think you ought to give things a few weeks before heading home?"

"What for?" A shaky sigh escaped. Regan picked up her coffee mug and wrapped both hands around the hot ceramic, needing to anchor herself to something solid and non-whooshing. "I've paid for this town house through the end of next May. You two are welcome to stay as long as you want, but . . ." She shook her head, struggling to breathe past the gaping hollowness in her chest. "Ireland has lost its appeal for me. Everywhere I look, I'll see Fáelán. Constantly being reminded that

I'll never see the father of my child again is not my idea of a good time. Maybe someday I'll return, but right now all I can think about is getting away. I just need to . . . to be somewhere else."

"What if Fáelán isn't dead?" Grayce persisted. "What if he comes to this century looking for you?"

"Why would he?" Regan blinked. "How could he? Even though he was able to move around while in the void, he couldn't travel through time. Otherwise he would've returned to the third century and prevented the curse himself."

She swiped at her cheeks again. "Besides, when I went to the third century, he believed I was a faerie trying to ensnare him or something." All the hurt she'd suffered at his rejection and wariness rose to engulf her. "He didn't remember me at all, and as he pointed out, he'd sworn an oath to serve and protect third-century Ireland. He had absolutely no desire to leave his time, and I don't blame him. He was living the life he loved."

"Still . . ." Grayce canted her head to peer at her. "I feel very strongly about this. You need to wait a few weeks before leaving. Don't ask me why, because I can't say. And no, I haven't had a vision. Maybe there's something you're supposed to do here yet."

Regan studied her sister for a moment, and then she turned to Meredith. "What do you think?"

"I agree with Grayce, and even if I didn't, staying won't hurt anything."

Regan considered their suggestion for a few moments, knowing better than to ignore either of their gut feelings. She frowned. Did she have something to accomplish before she left? *Oh, right.*

"When I was trapped under the Hill of Tara, I swore if I got out alive, I'd continue ghost-whispering, and I'd never complain about being gifted again. I met a spirit while at the archaeology museum. Maybe I'm supposed to help her cross before I leave."

Grayce nodded. "Could be."

Regan set her coffee on the table, leaned back and covered her face with her hands. "I'll think about staying. In the meantime, I'm going to bed. I know it's only six, but the past several days have worn me out." That and being so sad sucked the energy right out of her.

"OK. Grayce and I will watch over you."

"No. Don't do that." Regan dropped her hands from her face and rose from the couch. "Go be tourists. Take the rental car, head to the Temple Bar area in Dublin and visit a pub or two. Listen to some live Irish music. Just because I'm a mess doesn't mean you two have to sacrifice your vacation." She waved toward the front door. "Go. Have supper somewhere fun, and tomorrow we'll go tour a few sites together."

"But, Rae, how can we enjoy Ireland knowing you're hurting?" Meredith shot up from her chair and circled the coffee table to give Regan a hug.

"You two just graduated. This is supposed to be a celebratory trip. I'm going to be OK, and honestly, I need some alone time." She hugged her sister back. Memories of the morning she'd met Fáelán flooded her mind. He'd been so vulnerable and proud at the same time—a little desperate too. His masculinity, inner strength and charm had captured her completely, and she'd fallen for her brave Fiann. Her heart broke all over again.

"How about a compromise? I'll stay for a few weeks, if you two will promise not to let the fact that I'm mourning ruin your visit. Give me tonight to rest, and I'm sure I'll feel more like myself tomorrow." Not likely, but she'd put on a good show for her sisters.

"Deal." Meredith released her. "Try to eat something. There's food in the fridge."

"I'm not hungry right now, just dead tired." Regan headed for the stairs. "At some point, can we stop by the museum, so I can help the ghost I met cross over?"

"Of course," Meredith said, gathering her purse and the keys to the rental car.

"Tomorrow, we can tour Christ Church Cathedral or something." Regan tried like hell to muster a smidgeon of enthusiasm as she trudged toward the stairs and her waiting bed.

Her sisters called goodbye, and the front door shut behind them. Regan walked into her bedroom, confronted with Fáelán's things, which were right where he'd left them. The sight of his phone, keys and jacket stole her breath and split her heart wide-open. She crossed the room and fell facedown across the mattress.

When she'd first come to Ireland, she'd wanted to do an ancestry search and rid herself of the gift of sight. Finding a way to shut herself off from her abilities no longer drove her. After everything she'd seen and experienced in the past several weeks, her complaints seemed petty. Insignificant. She was who she was meant to be, and if it hadn't been for her giftedness, she never would have met Fáelán. No matter how much she hurt, she didn't regret a minute of her time with the only man who had loved and accepted her for who she truly was.

Regan curled into a ball on her side and placed her hands over the baby, the baby she already loved with a fierce protectiveness she didn't know she possessed. She'd been given a precious gift, and their baby would always be a link to the only man she would ever love completely.

Chapter Sixteen

It had taken Regan more than a day or two before she could pretend to feel more like herself. All she really wanted to do was sleep and grieve, with the occasional meal thrown in for good measure. She had two reasons to get out of the house: her sisters, and she'd sworn to continue helping ghosts. She had a particular ghost in mind, and there was where she meant to begin.

Sighing, Regan faced the imposing, columned entrance of the National Museum of Ireland. This time Grayce and Meredith flanked her. The museum would open in two minutes. Was it too much to hope they'd remain the only people visiting this morning? Yep. This was the last day of June, and a Friday morning at the height of the tourist season. The museum would likely be teeming with tourists by lunchtime. Hopefully she could push at least one ghosty into the light before the place was packed.

"OK, here's the plan." Regan turned to her sisters as the entrance doors were unlocked from the inside. "If the ghost I met appears, Meredith and I will pretend we're talking to each other while we're trying to convince her to cross over." She and Meredith had done this ghost-whispering thing together too many times to count, but never in a public place where everyone would see them. The last thing she wanted was to draw attention. "Grayce, you can kind of shield us, and keep a lookout for groups coming our way."

"All right. Let's do this thing." Grayce opened the door and held it for her and Meredith. "Ohhh, can we stop in the gift shop on the way out? I have two credit cards I haven't maxed out yet," she said, coming up beside them.

Regan huffed out a laugh. "Sure." Despite the constant ache of missing Fáelán, she did feel a little stronger today, and she had her sisters to thank. "I'm so glad you two are here." She glanced from Grayce to Meredith. "Follow me." Regan led them to the main floor exhibit hall and to the case holding Fáelán's armband.

"Oh, my God," Meredith muttered. "This place is packed with spirits."

"I know, but we aren't going to spend more than a few hours here. If we can help more than one ghost during that time frame, fine. If not, we cut them off."

"Fine by me." Grayce peered into the glass case. "Setting limits and taking care of yourself first is a good thing, Rae. Mom and Dad have a tendency to push too hard, especially with you two, because you see dead people. Lucky for me, visions can't be forced."

"I know better than to let anyone push me anymore." She was going to be a mother, and dammit, she would live a balanced life. From now on, what she did or did not do with her gift of sight was entirely up to her. "I've decided to help ghosts I randomly encounter, but I'm not going to get involved anymore with the living who want to commune with their dearly departed. Dealing with grief-stricken people only leads to dealing with *more* grief-stricken people, and that's what got to me. It's hard to say no to people who are in so much pain."

She had a much better understanding now of what that grief entailed: exhaustion, the numbness and detached feeling, the constant empty ache and the anger. Fáelán chose staying in the third century over her, dammit, and now he was gone. Really gone. Constantly being around others who grieved, the bereaved who were unwilling to let go, would not help her move on.

"Speaking of closure, how are you doing? Is there anything Grayce and I can do to help you cope with *your* loss?"

Regan's gaze caught on Fáelán's armband, and her breath hitched. She still sensed his energy as strongly as ever. How was that possible? "I've been thinking about how to say goodbye to him ever since I woke up this morning. When the time is right, I'm going to trespass onto Newgrange again. At first I didn't think I could bear being anywhere near the site, but saying my final farewell where Fáelán and I met feels . . . right. I'll hold my own service for him at sunrise."

Grayce ran her hand back and forth across Regan's shoulders. "We'll go with you."

"No." Regan shook her head and sighed. "I need to do this by myself. It's hard to explain, but letting him go will be the last intimate moment I'll ever have with Fáelán. I don't want to share that with anyone." A few tears trickled down her cheeks, and Meredith handed her a tissue. "Thanks. I'll always love him, you know?"

"Of course we know, and the three of us will do something special when you get home, something to mark the moment." Grayce patted Regan's back.

"I'd like that." She sniffed.

Meredith moved closer to the display. "Which one of these was his?"

"The wolf effigy with the garnet eyes." Goose bumps rose on Regan's arms and the back of her neck as the temperature took a sudden drop. "Take your places. We have company."

Grayce moved a short distance away to stand where she could watch the entrance to the *Ireland's Gold* exhibit. Regan turned to face the spirit, relieved to find the same lost and confused young woman she'd encountered before. Meredith took her place, so she faced Regan.

"Help me," the spirit's whispery voice implored. "I want to go home. I can't find my way, and I don't know where I am."

"We're here to help you," Regan told her.

"Can you tell us where you come from?" Meredith added. "What is the name of your village? If we knew, we could direct you there."

Another entry for her manual on ghost-whispering: say whatever it takes to help a confused spirit cross over. Regan stood in front of the case filled with gold artifacts, listening as the ghost described where she'd lived. "You aren't far from home," she lied. "Look." She pointed in no particular direction, knowing it would take a while yet to get through to a spirit who had lingered as long as this one had. "Do you see? There's the path leading to your village."

Grayce warned them tourists were on their way, and Meredith shifted, so it appeared as if the two of them were talking about what they saw in the exhibit in front of them.

"I miss my children and my husband," the young woman said, still stuck in the loop of her fear and confusion. "I don't know why I'm here. I want to go home."

"We understand," Meredith said, her tone compassionate. "Will you let us help you?"

The spirit truly looked at them then, and Regan smiled. "Please allow us to see you on your way home to your husband and children." It took a long time and a lot of persistent repetition before she and Meredith finally got through to the confused soul, but the young woman finally grasped the fact that they really could help her.

"I would be most grateful for your help. My husband is a rich and powerful man. He will reward you for your aid to me."

"We need no reward, my lady. Look behind you," Regan told her. At this point, it was crucial to keep the ghost's attention off the case holding the bracelets she'd attached herself to. "Do you see the road?" Regan glanced at Meredith, mentally handing her the baton in their tag-teaming effort.

"Do you see the way, my lady?" Meredith pointed away from the gold artifacts.

"I do! I see the path."

"Good. Your family will light the way for you now." Regan studied the apparition, gratified to see the woman's gaze fixed upon the direction Meredith had pointed. Once a spirit took on that faraway look, they were close to crossing over. "Do you see the light?"

A whispery gasp, and the ghost began moving. "I see my husband. He . . . he is beckoning to me."

Regan smiled at the happiness infusing the spirit's whispery voice. "That's wonderful. Go to him."

"Incoming," Grayce said, nodding toward the stairway leading to the exhibit.

The confused spirit now moved with purpose, her face lit with joy. The group of tourists entered the exhibit just as the ghost crossed over. The temperature returned to normal. "We're done here, and I'm starving." A deep satisfaction settled over her. She could do this; she could help spirits cross without losing sight of her own life.

Meredith surveyed the hall. "I'm sensing a lot of clamors for help."

"I know, Mere. Me too. There will always be a clamor for help, but we don't always have to answer. We deserve to have lives, and right now my life includes needing to eat."

"I guess you're eating for two now, huh?" Grayce teased as the three of them made their way out of the museum.

"Other than having to pee frequently, I don't really feel pregnant yet. It's still really early." She tried to imagine herself with a huge belly in front of her. "I guess that'll change quickly enough."

"I'm looking forward to being an auntie." Meredith smiled.

"Me too. Don't forget, I want to stop at the gift store," Grayce said, hurrying ahead of them. "I won't take long."

Meredith stood beside Regan at the edge of the gift store while Grayce shopped. "A lot has happened in the past several weeks, hasn't it?"

"It has. You were right when you said my mind would be blown. Everything I experienced has changed the way I look at the world." She glanced at her sister. "I'll be all right, you know. Eventually." She blew out a breath. "Wow. How am I going to explain all of this to Mom and Dad? It's hard to imagine; Mom and Dad are going to be grandparents, and you and Grayce are going to be aunts."

"I wonder what your little one's gifts will be."

"Me too." No matter what his or her gifts were, Regan would not push her child to do anything he or she didn't want to do.

Grayce joined them, holding out her wrist so they could admire her bracelet. "What do you think? It's made to look like the gold band around the Ardagh Chalice."

"Very Celtic. It's nice," Regan said as they headed toward the exit.

Meredith held the door open. "The National Gallery of Ireland is only a few blocks from here. I read they have a gourmet cafeteria. Do you want to eat there before we head to Christ Church?"

"Yes, and I love you two," Regan said, her eyes tearing again. She swiped at her cheeks. "Lord, this is annoying."

Grayce flashed her a sympathetic look. "Do you remember the story Mom told us about how she knew she was pregnant with me and Meredith?"

"Yeah, I do." Regan smiled through her tears. "She was reading the Disney version of *The Fox and the Hound* to me, and by the end of the story, she was bawling like a baby. That's how she knew."

Meredith directed them to turn the corner. "Grief and pregnancy hormones are going to make things doubly tough for you, Rae."

"I know." Regan studied the sidewalk, and a deep, dark chasm of sadness opened inside her. How easy it would be to step right in and let it close over her, but Fáelán wouldn't want that. And she had their baby to think about. She needed to find ways to cope, and saying goodbye would help. "The double whammy is another reason I want to go home."

Fáelán had bathed and dressed with care, even though he had naught but garments from the third century to don. As he left the village of his youth, his insides churned. He would never see his parents, sisters, nieces and nephews or his clan again, but at least they knew he was well. Not like the last time, when he came to them after being cursed. Then he'd broken their hearts.

Not only had he just said his final farewell to his family and his clan, but he was also leaving behind the daughter he'd never met. "Don't forget to tell Boann to find me in the future." He cast Fionn's fae cousin a sideways look.

"I won't forget." Alpin pointed down the trail. "I shall open the way to Howth for you when we reach the cover of the forest ahead."

"My thanks to ye." He hadn't remembered Regan when she came to the past for him, and a new worry surged. "Will Regan remember me, do ye think?"

"Aye. The two of you exist upon the same thread in the tapestry of time, for your life stories are shared. The thread in the twenty-first century intertwined with the thread from this time the moment Regan came to warn you about Morrigan."

"Hmm." Morrigan's curse had brought him and Regan together. He'd not considered that afore hearing Alpin talk about the threads of time. "I suppose I must be grateful to Morrigan for cursing me then."

Alpin laughed. "I would not go as far as that."

"I am greatly indebted to ye, Alpin. Not only did ye grant your aid when I was cursed, but ye sought Regan's whereabouts and reassured me she was well after Morrigan took her. And now ye are sending me home. How can I ever repay such a debt?"

"'Twas King Lir who asked me to see you back to the twenty-first century, and as far as the rest goes, think nothing of it. I have a blood tie to Fionn; he is like a brother to me. Know this, mortal. Not all of Danu's descendants are as selfishly cruel as Morrigan." Alpin shook his head. "She has brought great shame upon our people more than once. If she remains without magic and under her father's supervision for all eternity, 'twould be a good thing."

"My daughter also played a part in ending the curse. Knowing she has not grown to be like her mother gladdens my heart." Fáelán stopped next to the edge of the forest. "This will do, aye?"

"Aye." Alpin strode several paces into the forest.

His heart flopping around in his chest like a fish out of water, Fáelán followed. Anticipation mixed with a healthy dose of trepidation coursed through him. By God, if his woman was brave enough to step through time, he could do no less.

Alpin raised his hand and drew a rune in the air. The air began to shimmer and wave. "This will take you to Regan's door. I wish you well, Fáelán."

He shook his arms, rotated his head and neck, took a breath and blew it out. Why did he feel as if he were preparing for battle? "I can do this."

"Aye, with a wee bit of help." Alpin gave him a push, and the faerie's laughter followed Fáelán into the passage.

Time and the world rushed past Fáelán, and he landed upright in front of Regan's cheery red door. He took a moment to steady his nerves, stepped forward and knocked. Naught happened.

The eastern sky had just begun to lighten, and the fog of early morning hovered above the ground. 'Twas likely Regan was asleep, and she hadn't heard his knock. He tried again, harder this time. The scent of impending rain came to him, and he glanced at the sky. The setting moon and a few stars still shone. 'Twas partly clouded, but . . . The air around him charged with electric energy, and the temperature dropped.

He tensed, and his pulse raced. He'd been assured Morrigan could not escape, and he had King Lir's ward to protect him, but still . . . Morrigan was resourceful, devious and vindictive.

A woman appeared, her features illuminated from the light beside Regan's door. Fáelán stared in wonder. Regan had spoken the truth. His daughter had his nose, mouth and chin. She looked so much like his mam, the impact gut-punched him. Unlike him, she was garbed in jeans and a blouse from this era, and her long, curly hair hung down her back. "*Mo a iníon*, is it ye, Boann?"

"Aye. It is me, *mo a athair*," she said, her tone low. "Long have I waited . . ." Her voice faltered. "I have so longed to meet you, Father."

Fáelán opened his arms. "Since the day I learned of your existence I have longed to know you as well, *mo a cailín*." Boann walked into his embrace, and he gathered her up. "I'm more sorry than I can ever say that I was not there for ye as ye grew into the lovely young woman ye are today. I owe ye a great deal, and we need to talk." He released her and peered into her eyes. "But first, I must—"

"Her sisters are within, but I kept the sound of your knocking from them, so I could have a few moments with you. Regan is not here, Father."

Fáelán's heart dropped, and the worry he'd carried for her crashed over him. "*Cá bhfuill sí?*"

"All is well. She is at Brú Na Bóinne, saying goodbye to you." Boann stepped back. "She believes you died the day you fought Múiros, and she mourns your loss."

"I need to go to her." He glanced toward the curb. His car and Regan's were both gone. "Feck." He plowed his fingers through his hair. Regan must have had his MINI Cooper returned to his kin in Waterford. "I'll have to wait, then, won't I?"

"If you wish, I will send you to her."

"Aye, do so. But . . . will ye stay, Boann?" His throat tightened. "Promise me you'll be here when we return. I long to get to know ye."

A broad smile lit her face. "I promise." Boann lifted her hand and created a portal for him. "Go. Regan awaits."

On impulse, Fáelán kissed his daughter's forehead, and her shy look of pleasure filled him with gladness. "Introduce yourself to Regan's sisters whilst I fetch Regan. If I have aught to say about it, Grayce and Meredith will soon be kin to us." He stepped into the shimmering doorway through space, anticipation quickening his blood.

Fáelán landed on his feet at the crest of the hill in front of the passage tomb's entrance. Regan stood in the misty dim light, with her back to him, talking and gesturing to . . . no one that he could see. Her yoga mat was laid out on the ground beside her. Incense burned from a narrow wooden holder, and she'd set a bouquet of wildflowers upon the ground. The scent of the incense floated to him on the breeze, and the sight of Regan melted his heart. After all they'd been through, after all she'd done for him, at long last they'd be together. "What are ye about, *Álainn*?"

Regan whipped around and gaped, and then she burst into tears. "Oh, Fáelán, you're a ghost after all. I was afraid this would happen, and now I really do have to help you cross over."

"Nay." He frowned and stepped forward on shaky legs. "I'm no *scáil*, I'm—"

"Don't say it!" she cried. "Don't tell me that after everything I went through, you're cursed *again*. Dammit. How did this happen?" She covered her face with her hands and growled. "The cycle is starting all over, isn't it? So my sisters were right, and you didn't die the day I saw you fighting. You went back to that *other woman* . . . and now—"

"Jealous are ye, love?" He couldn't stop smiling or prevent his eyes from growing moist. His knees were weak. His mouth had gone dry, and his poor heart hammered against his ribs. More than anything, he longed to hold Regan close, make love to her and vow to be hers for all the rest of his days.

"Wait." She dropped her hands and frowned at him. "*Now* you remember me? Now, when it's too late?"

"How could I forget your constant wheedling about the light I'm to walk into?" He canted his head and flashed her a wry look. "Do ye think I've forgotten how ye defied my wishes, and put yourself in harm's way to see my curse ended?" He crossed the distance between them. "How could I forget holding ye in my arms and loving ye until the wee hours of the morn?"

He could scarce breathe, and he drank her in with his eyes. "I've missed ye, *mo a míorúilt lómhar*. By the gods both old and new, I've missed ye desperately, and I never wish to be parted from ye again as long as I live." He cradled her face between his hands and pressed his forehead against hers.

Regan placed her hands on his wrists, tears sliding down her cheeks. "I . . . I don't understand." She tilted her head back, and her gaze roamed over his face as her grip on his wrists tightened. "You . . . you're really here? But I saw . . . Before I closed my eyes, the blade of that sword was only—"

"Ah, but I didn't die that day. I was able to keep my head upon my shoulders, and I've been working hard to return to ye ever since." Studying the fading bruises marring her beloved face, Fáelán traced a finger along the cut on her brow. "Ye'll have a scar here," he whispered, kissing the wound. "'Tis a badge of courage to remind me of all ye've done for us."

"Y-you're really here?" she whispered, a dazed look upon her face.

"Aye. The curse is no more, and Morrigan can no longer hurt us."

"You killed her?" Regan's eyes widened. "I didn't mean to leave Mananán's magic sword behind, but now I'm glad I did." She lifted her chin, a look of satisfaction flickering over her features.

Fáelán laughed. "Nay, I did not kill her, my bloodthirsty bride-to-be. Her father bound her magic and imprisoned her. He also placed a ward of protection upon me and mine, preventing any further mischief should Morrigan somehow escape." Fáelán brushed his lips across hers, and his blood heated at the sudden intake of her breath. "Alas, I am no longer immortal. King Lir assured me I have been restored to my natural state."

"I'm glad." She studied him, her expression hopeful, vulnerable. "Your bride-to-be?"

His poor heart turned inside out. "Aye, if ye'll have me, my wee brave Fiann. Do ye still love me, Regan?"

"Of course I still love you." Her voice quavered. "I'm just . . . still having trouble believing you're really here. I thought I'd lost you."

He'd expire if he couldn't have her soon. They were alone in a sacred place, with the sun just beginning its ascent. "If 'tis proof ye are needin', that I can provide." Fáelán placed his hands upon her hips and drew her close. "I've something in mind, love—a new sun salutation of the sensuous sort." He pressed his erection against her, eliciting a husky laugh.

Fáelán covered her mouth with his and kissed her deeply, reveling in the way she tasted, the way her curves fitted against him so perfectly. He came up for air and tightened his arms around her, pressing her breasts against his chest. "'Twould be a shame to waste the yoga mat already laid out for us, aye?"

"You want to . . . uhm . . . *here*, where someone might see us?"

He nuzzled her temple. "Did ye not tell me the park doesn't open until nine, and . . ." He swallowed against the welling emotions overpowering him. "Ye aren't the only one who needs proof this is real, *mo a lómhar*. We're together at long last, and I'm so in love with ye. After all I've been through, the empty years spent in captivity, is it any wonder I can scarce believe I've been granted this chance at happiness? I need ye, Regan. I need your arms around me, and I need to feel our bodies and souls joined."

She encircled his waist, laid her head against his shoulder and melted into him. "Go on then," she told him. "All right. Prove to me this is real. Prove to me we're together in the same place and in the same century." She kissed his neck and then nipped and sucked at the same spot.

He hissed out a breath. His pulse quickened; heat surged, and he kissed her again, running his palms down her sides to the curve of her waist. Soon, very soon, she'd be large with their babe growing inside her, and knowing so filled him with pride and fanned his desire to a fever pitch.

"I love ye with all my heart, Regan MacCarthy," he rasped, scooping her into his arms and carrying her to the yoga mat. He lowered himself to the mat and placed her gently at the center. "Let me show ye how much."

Smiling, she nodded. He rose, took off his cloak and spread it over her. "Do ye recall how ye draped your cloak over me after tying me to the tree and forcing me to spend the night outside in the cold?"

"How could I forget your hostile glare, or your total lack of recognition?"

As he stripped out of his clothes, he told her, "I started having strange dreams after ye left, and ye were in them all. I'd call to ye, but ye would not turn toward me." Fáelán slid under the blanket he'd made of his cloak. "Then Fionn gave me this awful potion to drink, and all of my memories came back to me."

"Talk later. Proof now." Regan drew him to her for a kiss.

Chuckling low in his throat, Fáelán deepened the kiss and helped her out of her clothing, fondling and tasting her bare skin as he removed one garment at a time. "Ah, but I love the way ye feel." He caressed the curve of her hip and pressed against her. "And I love the way ye smell." He groaned, cupping one delectable breast whilst kissing the other. Regan gasped and arched into him, and he was lost in the delight of reacquainting himself with each of her curves and her velvety-soft skin so warm to his touch. He brought his hand between her thighs, opened her folds to touch the slick, welcoming heat of her core.

Regan explored his body as well, driving him mad. And when she stroked his erection, and then squeezed, all thought ceased and he nearly came.

"I want you, Fáelán." Regan sighed into his ear. She took the lobe between her teeth and nipped, while fondling his balls.

A shiver of pleasure racked through him, and he covered her. Settling himself between her thighs, he gazed at her. "I love ye, Regan. Ye alone own my heart, and from this day forward, everything I do will be for ye and our family."

He entered her, coming home at last. There was nothing between them, just he and Regan, skin to skin, heart to heart and soul to soul. He swore the strands of their lives intertwined then, beginning to weave the rich tapestry of their lives together. Their past, present and future converged, sealing the deep bond between them for all time.

Fáelán thrust into her heat, faster and harder. She moaned and writhed beneath him. Crying out his name, she came apart, pulsing around him, and he was filled with awe. A tender protectiveness washed through him as he followed her over the edge, mindless and shuddering with his release. He collapsed beside her and pulled her into his arms. *"Mo a choíche grá,"* he whispered into her ear. "My forever love, I am home at last."

"My forever love," she whispered back, running her hands up and down his back.

Content to the very marrow of his bones, he wrapped himself around the center of his world and kissed the tender spot behind her ear. "Ye've a crowded town house in Howth."

"Mmm."

"Boann is there, awaiting our return."

"Mmm?" She snuggled closer.

He grinned. "We should dress, love. We've things to do, aye?"

She let loose a long sigh. "I suppose."

He threw off his cloak and reached for his tunic. "Who were ye talking to when I arrived?"

"Two of your Fianna buddies, only they were definitely dead and not cursed. Both died in a battle near here."

Had they fought with Fionn the day his captain was slain? As they dressed and gathered Regan's things, he recalled all the good folk he'd left in the past, and those he would soon be reunited with in the present. Glancing at his woman, he thought about the new life she carried, and the family of his own he'd soon have to love and protect. "Ye never said, Regan."

"Said what?" She hoisted the strap of her tote bag over her shoulder.

He rolled up her yoga mat and tucked it under one arm. "Whether or not ye'd have me."

She laughed. "I'm pretty sure I just did, and I'm hoping I'll *have* you again tonight, only in a bed."

He reached out his hand, and she twined her fingers in with his. "Don't tease me, *mo a grá*. I need to know. Will ye be my wife?"

Love shone bright in her lovely gray eyes as she gazed at him. She squeezed his hand. "I will."

"Where shall we live, *mo a míorúilt lómhar*?"

"In the present." She leaned close and kissed his cheek. "Right here and now."

Epilogue

Three months later, County Waterford, Ireland

Regan sat at the vanity in the bride's room of the two hundred-year-old stone church. This church on the outskirts of Waterford had been attended by Fáelán's family for generations. She stared into the mirror while her mother placed her wedding veil upon her head. Turning her head left and right, she checked to see that it was straight. "Perfect, Mom. Thanks."

Her mother stepped back, her eyes growing overly bright. "Beautiful. You positively glow, Regan, with happiness and from pregnancy." She sniffed and dabbed at the corners of her eyes. "I can't believe you're going to live an ocean away. I'll hardly ever get the chance to see you, my new son-in-law or my first grandchild."

Regan's eyes misted too. "We'll visit often, and with the Ahearns moving into a cottage in town, we'll have room enough for you and the entire family to visit whenever you want. In fact, I expect all of you to visit when Baby O'Boyle arrives."

Jim and Kathryn's decision to buy a home of their own had come as a shock to Fáelán. Her poor Fiann had moped for days. Now that he was finally free to live his life, he had a need to surround himself with his family. Boann came and went as she pleased. All she had to do to fit in was to dress in modern clothing and dim the brilliance of her aqua eyes. Speaking of her soon-to-be stepdaughter . . . "What's taking Boann so long?" She'd sent her off to make sure everything was going smoothly, and that they'd begin on time. A frisson of excitement shot through her, and she glanced at her engagement ring, an emerald-cut diamond set on a band of gold etched with Celtic knots. Fáelán had placed it on her finger a week after his return.

"She only left a minute ago." Meredith met her eyes in the mirror. "I'm sure she'll be back with Dad in tow any minute. You look absolutely gorgeous, Rae."

Regan grinned. "So do you and Grayce." Meredith, Grayce and Boann were her attendants, while Fáelán had Jim and two other of his nephews to stand with him.

Grayce turned and primped in front of the full-length mirror. The attendants wore elegant navy-blue knee-length, off-the-shoulder silk crepe dresses, while Regan's wedding gown was similar in style and fabric, only full length. Her baby bump had just begun to show slightly. "Did I tell you Fáelán and I have leased a Georgian town house in Dublin? I'm turning one room into a yoga studio, and I'll teach prenatal yoga classes there while he works on his PhD in archaeology at UCD. We'll stay in Dublin during the week and in Waterford on the weekends and breaks."

"Uh . . . yes, like three times now." Grayce laughed.

"I was talking to Mom." She shot her sister a disgruntled look.

"That sounds wonderful," her mom said. "What about the important work we do? With your gifts, you need to make yourself available to—"

"No. I don't. I'm not advertising as a ghost whisperer, Mom. If I happen upon a confused spirit, I'll facilitate their crossing, but that's it."

"Oh." Her mom frowned.

"I intend to focus on *my* family and *my* life. You know how it can be. You let someone know, help them find closure, help their deceased to cross, and pretty soon, everyone is at your door, wanting you to get rid of the ghosts or other beings in their houses, or wanting to talk to their dearly departed. I can't do it anymore. I won't."

"But we were given these gifts so we could help those in need. We have a—"

"No, we weren't." Grayce snorted. "We have these abilities because one of our ancestors shacked up with a faerie and gave birth to a child who was half fae."

A soft knock on the door, and Boann walked in, followed by Regan's father. "It's time," Boann announced. Her smile lit up the room, and her bridesmaid's dress set off her extraordinary beauty.

"Are you ready?" her father asked.

Regan nodded. Her heart racing, she accepted her bouquet from Meredith and took her father's arm. Her mother stood in place on Regan's other side, and her attendants lined up behind her. The church's ancient pipe organ began playing music, signaling the wedding march would start as soon as she appeared at the entrance.

Her father patted her hand and leaned close. "Breathe, sweetheart. You don't want to faint halfway down the aisle, like someone else we know." He flashed a wry grin her mom's way.

"We've been married for thirty years, Gene." Her mother huffed out a breath and shot him a mock scowl. "How long will it take before you let me live that down?"

"If we're lucky, another thirty years or so."

Her parents exchanged a look so full of love, a lump rose to Regan's throat. She had that with Fáelán—the kind of love that would last a lifetime, and she couldn't wait to say "I do." She and her family made their way down the short hallway to take their places. Regan once again lost the ability to draw air into her lungs as she caught sight of the man she loved enough to brave faeries and traveling back through time.

He was so very handsome and distinguished in his tux, with his hair neatly pulled back. Was she really marrying a man who had lived for nearly two thousand years—a man who had been born in the third century? She smiled and blinked against the tears of joy filling her eyes.

The wedding march began, and she started down the aisle. Their gazes met and locked, and he winked. Happiness and certainty bubbled up, even as her knees went weak. Why, yes, she was marrying a man from the distant past, and she knew without a doubt they'd live happily ever after in the present.

Dear Readers

There are many perspectives and theories about the space-time continuum. Since Einstein identified time as the fourth dimension, the science community has argued that there are anywhere from ten to twenty-six dimensions. All agree, however, that time is not flat, linear or one-directional. In fact, physicists at the University of Queensland, Australia, were able to send light particles into the past, proving that time travel is possible.

For the purposes of this book, I went with a simplified version of the multiverse theory. The simplest explanation for this theory came to me through a documentary on public television. Physicists explain there are a finite number of elements in the universe, and these elements combine in different ways to make up all matter. Think of these elements as a deck of cards, and start dealing poker hands over and over with that same deck. If you keep dealing, you're going to get duplicate hands.

Scientists posit the same occurs with the finite number of elements. As the elements continue to be "dealt," duplicates are inevitable. Duplicate universes must therefore exist. Duplicate planets able to sustain life must exist. And as DNA is also continually dealt, duplicates of ourselves must also exist.

The Tuatha Dé Danann in my fantasy world understand time and how it works, and they know about alternate realities. So when King Lir tells Morrigan, "Upon one weft in the tapestry of time," what he's saying is: in another reality you did *X*, *Y* and *Z*. Even though another's actions may have created a new thread in the weave of time, the old one still exists and continues.

For the purposes of this story, nothing that happens anywhere upon the time continuum can be erased; it can only be forgotten. Neuropsychologists have proven we don't lose our memories; we simply lose the ability to retrieve them. This worked for my imaginary world. So, yes, somewhere in time, our duplicate hero still struggles, and that's OK, because he too will eventually find his miracle.

Acknowledgments

They say it takes a village to raise a child, and the same can be said for raising a "child of the mind"—a story. I've worked with the same incredible critique partners for over a decade, and a big thank-you goes to Tamara Hughes and Wyndemere Coffey for your insightfulness and friendship! I want to also thank the Montlake Romance crew for giving *Tangled in Time* a home, and a special shout-out to Melody Guy, my developmental editor, and to the thorough line and copy editors who have helped whip this story into shape! Finally, I want to thank my readers, because you all make this writing journey a joy.

Glossary

Fionn MacCumhaill (FEE-on Mac-Koo-uhl)—Legendary descendant of the fae king Nuada of the Silver Hand. As a youth, Fionn caught and ate "the salmon of knowledge" and became enlightened. He went on to become a great leader of men, and he commanded the Fianna, an elite army formed to protect Ireland from foreign invaders during the third century.

Fiann (FEE-un)—a single soldier in Fionn's army

Fianna (Fee-AH-nuh)—plural term referring to Fionn's army as a whole

Fenian(s) (Fen-ee-un[s])—Another term for the Fianna, referring to their multiple campfires burning across the island during the summer months. The fires were said to resemble the stars in the night sky, and so the term *Fenians* refers to that phenomena.

Tuatha Dé Danann (Too-wuh Day Duh-NANN)—The children of the goddess Danu, mythical demigods who came to Ireland in a ship in the clouds, bringing with them several magical items.

Duma na nGiall (Doo-muh nuh nGill)—the Mound of the Hostages

WORDS AND PHRASES

Álainn (AW-lin)—beauty

An bhfuil Gaeilge agat? An dtuigeann tú? (Ahn weel Gae-Al-guh a-gat? An tee-gun too?)—Do you have the Irish? Do you understand?

Buíchas le dia. (Bwee-uh-has le dee-yuh)—Thank God.

Cá bhfuill sí? (Kaw weel shee)—Where is she?

Cén chaoi a bhfuil tú? (Ken heh uh weel too)—How are you?

Dia dhuit (Dzee-uh rit)—hello

Go raigh maith agat (Ga rah mah a-gat)—thank you

Mo a athair (Muh ayhar)—my father

Mo a cailín (Muh cah-LEEN)—my girl

Mo a choíche grá (Muh kee-keh graw)—my forever love

Mo a grá (Muh graw)—my love

Mo a iníon (Muh i-neen)—my daughter

Mo a míorúilt ansa (Muh meerroolt AN-sa)—my dearest miracle

Mo a míorúilt lómhar (Muh meerroolt low-war)—my precious miracle

Níl sí anseo, athair. (Neel shee awn-shah, ayhar)—She is not here, Father.

Scáil (Skawl)—ghost

Sidhe (Shee)—Originally, this word referred to the mounds under which the fae were banished to dwell, but over time it has come to mean anything referring to the fae.

Slán abhaile (Slahn a-way-yuh)—safe home

Slí Cheann Sleibhe (Shlee Ken Shlev)—Slea Head Drive

Tá an aimsir go hálainn! (Taw an AHM-sheer guh HAH-lin)—It's a beautiful day!

Tá me go han-mhaith. (Taw meh guh-han maht)—I am very well.

Tá tú go hálinn, maise. (Taw too guh HAW-lin muh-isha)—You are beautiful indeed.

Tá tú go hálinn, mo a grá. (Taw too guh HAW-lin, muh-a graw)—You are beautiful, my love.

About the Author

Photo © 2013 A Dannette

Barbara Longley is the award-winning author of the Novels of Loch Moigh. She moved frequently throughout her childhood and learned how to entertain herself with stories. As an adult, she has lived on an Appalachian commune, taught on an Indian reservation and traveled the country from coast to coast. After having children of her own, Barbara made Minnesota her home.

Barbara holds a master's degree in special education and taught for many years. She enjoys exploring all things mythical, paranormal and otherwise newsworthy, channeling what she learns into her stories.

Barbara loves to connect with readers via Twitter @barbaralongley, on Facebook at www.facebook.com/Barbara-Longley, or through her website, www.barbaralongley.com. Readers can learn all about her new releases through her Amazon Author Page, www.amazon.com/Barbara-Longley.